A BETTER HEART

CHUCK AUGELLO

Black Rose Writing | Texas

©2021 by Chuck Augello
All rights reserved. No part of this book may be reproduced, stored in a retrieval system or transmitted in any form or by any means without the prior written permission of the publishers, except by a reviewer who may quote brief passages in a review to be printed in a newspaper, magazine or journal.

The author grants the final approval for this literary material.

First printing

This is a work of fiction. Names, characters, businesses, places, events, and incidents are either the products of the author's imagination or used in a fictitious manner. Any resemblance to actual persons, living or dead, or actual events is purely coincidental.

ISBN: 978-1-68433-826-9
PUBLISHED BY BLACK ROSE WRITING
www.blackrosewriting.com

Printed in the United States of America
Suggested Retail Price (SRP) $18.95

A Better Heart is printed in Calluna

*As a planet-friendly publisher, Black Rose Writing does its best to eliminate unnecessary waste to reduce paper usage and energy costs, while never compromising the reading experience. As a result, the final word count vs. page count may not meet common expectations.

PRAISE FOR

A BETTER HEART

"Lively, engrossing, fast paced, and spot on when it comes to nailing what's wrong with animal abuse but in a realistic, not preachy way. A great read, a great beach novel, a great book to pass on."
–Ingrid Newkirk, founder, People for the Ethical Treatment of Animals

"Augello (*The Revolving Heart*) has crafted a sweet, funny character study centered around a fiery animal-rights polemic. The novel's great strength is that the philosophical points come from characters who feel like fully formed people rather than rhetorical devices—and that the dialogue is sharp. Madcap and accomplished, this comic novel boasts big surprises, heartfelt characters, and a passion for animal rights."
– Booklife

"Finally! A story about animal rights that informs and entertains rather than preaches. By the bottom of the first page, I'd already laughed several times...In a novel of family drama and adventure, Augello manages to successfully address the connection of humans and non-humans."
– Independent Book Review

"Between the intrigue and the moral and ethical conundrums...Augello creates a solid psychological and social examination of rights, choices, and their consequences. A wry dose of humor that excels in tongue-and-cheek observations, the result is a fun, literary story that offers many sweeping lessons about the road to a better heart that will linger in the reader's mind long after the story ends."–D. Donovan, Senior Reviewer
– Midwest Book Review

"A promising new literary voice."
– Kirkus Reviews

"Augello has a natural ability to balance heavy themes with humor."
–Jessica Purgett, *The Mark Literary Review*

For Dolores Augello, Margaret Burkat, and Hart the Cat,
who changed everything.

OTHER TITLES FROM CHUCK AUGELLO:

The Revolving Heart

A
BETTER
HEART

PART ONE – AUGUST 1999

-I-

Twenty-three candles, twenty-three incandescent wicks throwing shadows on the walls as Allison shuts her eyes and prepares to make a wish, the muscles around her lips afraid to let go and truly smile like her twenty-third birthday might deserve a good time. The candles are lit, her friends are gathered around the table eager to sing; the strawberry shortcake is fresh and perfectly frosted with the buttercream icing she craves, *Happy Birthday, Allie* written in red loops across the top, "Allie" spelled correctly this time, not like last year's cake, her name spelled "Alley" as if they were celebrating some dark city pathway between two tenements. Twenty-three candles poised for a birthday wish, and Jesus God, does she really need a wish right now, with Momma in the hospital and Marty in the County Lock-Up while his baby grows inside her (or maybe it's Kenny's baby) and all Allison knows is that she *really* needs a birthday wish to come true this year, and do those twenty-three candles know how important this is, what a shitstorm her life has become? Twenty-three and her world is slipping from crappy to full-blown terrible, and as she leans over the table to make her Hail Mary hope-for-a-better-life birthday wish, please-please-*please* let this one come true, she opens her eyes and ...oh shit, the candles have gone out again, her birthday cake is melting, and why didn't Beth remember that strawberries give her a rash?

"Cut!" I put down the camera and check out the cake. "Is it really that hard to keep twenty-three candles lit?"

"Sorry about that, Kevin."

"There's one of those candle lighter things in the kitchen."

"Are you sure this angle doesn't make my nose look big?"

"Are we breaking for lunch now? Is the pizza here?"

"Dave, will you please shut up? How can I stay in character if you keep disturbing my preparation?"

1

"The icing is starting to drip. I read that if you douse it with hairspray..."

"You're *not* using hairspray on that cake. I'm starving."

"Kevin, can we shoot it from *that* angle, from the left? I hate my nose."

"Kevin, where the hell is the pizza?"

Welcome to *Exit 23*. Perhaps one day this will be an amusing story on the commentary track for the Criterion Collection DVD, but right now it feels like another reason I should have gone to law school like my brother. No, I had to be a filmmaker instead, an *auteur,* and while somewhere in this giant boondoggle of a production is the seed of a quality low-budget film, that seed is shrinking by the hour, just like the available balance on the film's bank account is shrinking, and when the two pizzas I ordered to feed the crew finally arrive, it's likely I will pay for them with the nickels and pennies I've been saving since second grade, my cash on hand otherwise limited to a single dollar bill.

"Kevin, we need to talk," Jill, our lead actress, says. "It's about Allison. I'm not feeling her right now."

Film School Rule #2 – Always be available for your actors.

"Okay, guys, let's take a ten-minute break," I say, clapping hands. "The pizza should be here any second now."

On cue, the crew (or more accurately, the random group of friends I've cajoled into helping) loiters around the set (aka-my living room) as I kneel beside Jill and feign mastery and expertise. By now I shouldn't have to fake it. We've been shooting for weeks. It's my script, and the character of Allison Pinckney, the twenty-three-year-old small-town girl battling abandonment and a broken heart while clinging to her dreams is just a female, better-looking version of me. I know precisely what's in Allison Pinckney's heart, the passion and the energy and the yearning for beauty, the need to break free. Things may seem bleak, but my film *will* be finished on time for its premier at the Garden State Film Fest 1999, and it *will* land a distribution deal and win the $50K festival grand prize. Screw Y2K and all those end-of-the-century fears about the world falling apart; for me the year 1999 is far from over. Maybe the computers will crap out and planes will drop from the sky; maybe the world *will* fall apart, but for now, the bigger problem is how can I make the marginally talented Jill Willoughby transform into Allison Pinckney? And how can I find the missing element to elevate the script from melodrama to art? Does *Exit 23* need social relevancy, a hero's journey, or a rare disease? It's out there, I know it, the elusive "it" that will bring everything together and make my film important to someone other than me. I just need to find it.

"I know the focus should be on her interior life, on being pregnant and everything, and Marty being in jail," Jill whispers, leaning in so the others can't hear her, "but I can't stop thinking about my nose."

"Your nose is beautiful," I say, kissing its elongated tip. Film School Rule #7 – Lie when necessary. "It's the perfect nose. It's Gwyneth Paltrow's nose. When people see this film, they'll wonder how I got Gwyneth Paltrow's nose to work for scale."

"I hate Gwyneth Paltrow's nose. It's hideous. Is that really what you think?"

"Trust me, Jill: your nose is the perfect nose for this film. Remember, it's not *your* nose that people will be watching. It's Allison's nose."

She takes a second to process.

"Right, Allison's nose," she nods, and I sense her gears spinning, conjuring the ghosts of old acting teachers and their lessons on inhabiting a character. "Are you sure it won't detract from the scene? Maybe we could try it from a different angle?"

The crew is growing restless, and if we're going to catch the remaining natural light, we need to start shooting *now*.

"How about we try it again, only this time I want you to focus on *Allison* worrying about what Jake might think of her nose. Her anxiety is really about Marty and the baby—"

"—and Momma in the hospital."

"—and Momma in the hospital, absolutely, but she's distracting herself by thinking about her nose."

"Okay, I can play that." With a deep, measured breath, she folds her hands into prayer pose and touches her heart. "Fuck it. Let's *do* this."

"Okay, everyone, places. Scene 27B."

I hear a few grumbles and a hushed "where's the goddamn pizza" but it's a solid crew and everyone is ready within minutes, and yes, it's kind of a cliché but there's an undeniable rush of pleasure at the sound of the word *Action!* All twenty-three candles are lit, Jill is once again Allison Pinckney, and as the other actors start singing "Happy Birthday," I begin to relax. My

3

cast and crew are so hard-working and supportive that I'm flat-out in love with each one of them, and as I watch the scene play out, I'm no longer in the dining room of my childhood home on 23 Davenport Drive. I'm inside Allison Pinckney's childhood home with her best friend and brother and her secret love Jake as they celebrate her birthday. Maybe what's missing is already here and I'm too distracted to see it. Everything is exactly as it should be and then—

The front door opens and a 70-year-old man in a yellow raincoat enters the scene carrying a capuchin monkey.

"Birthday? Today's not my birthday," my father says, "but let's celebrate anyway."

The monkey buries his face in the raincoat.

"Cut!"

Behind me, our sound guy whispers, "He forgot the goddamn pizza."

$$\cdot \quad \cdot \quad \cdot \quad \cdot \quad \cdot$$

An hour later the cast and crew are gone, except for Veronica, who handles make-up, costumes, hair, props, continuity, and nearly everything else, and who sometimes sleeps over; and my father, who technically owns the house, his name on the deed and all that, and who, since his arrival, hasn't budged from the couch, where he snores and farts in deep slumber, the capuchin nestled beside him, the monkey clutching the banana we gave him but refusing to eat.

It's been four years since I've seen him. (My father, not the monkey: I've never seen the monkey before.) My father: Edward Stacey, stage name Brian Edwards, Guinness World Record Holder for most appearances in a motion picture with over 623 credits to his name, excluding his multiple roles in Mexican horror flicks under the name "George Gringo." Years back he carried his resume in a three-prong portfolio, each role carefully typed out, along with the film name, production date, and director. Among the highlights were his roles as Dead Body #7 in Alfred Hitchcock's *The Birds* and Man with Napkin in *Some Like it Hot.* Name a film and my father was probably in it, though only for a second, his face and body somewhere in the background, in the crowd, in the forgotten patches of the screen where the audience never looks. That's him, the ubiquitous Extra, specializing in corpses, enemy soldiers destined for the bayonet, and working stiffs stuck standing at the bar while the main characters banter and shine.

Only once did he land a speaking role. In the 1964 gangster flick *The Guns of Philadelphia*, directed by Nigel Band, my father assumed the role of Concerned Neighbor, who, at the 7 minutes and 43 seconds mark, enters the scene and says, "Hurry! Call a doctor, now!" His voice is deep and mellifluous, his face a masterpiece of neighborly concern, the camera pausing on him for 2.5 seconds (60 frames in film math) before cutting to a reaction shot of the actor Guy Madison as Johnny Bones, the film's protagonist, Concerned Neighbor's narrative arc extinguished in a single cut. My father always described it as a time of great hope as he waited for casting directors throughout Hollywood to recall his bravura line reading ("Hurry! Call a doctor, now!") and insist that Brian Edwards be cast in their next project. And while his next role, in *Attack of the Swamp Bats* (1964- directed by Herman Orange) did include dialogue, ("I knew that swamp was evil. Yes, Yes, evil!") Dad's scene was cut for length, and in short time he was back to portraying silent, usually dead characters like Stampede Victim #4 in *All across the Prairie* and Man on Bus in *Paradise Fever*.

My favorite moment of my father's career: 1974's *Soylent Green*. In the final scene, moments before Charlton Heston belts out his classic warning about the main ingredient in the film's eponymous food, (spoiler alert: it's not vegan), there's my father as one of four men carrying Heston to his doom.

"Look, there's Daddy's shoulder!" Mom said the first time I saw it, late at night, on the USA Network. I was six years old, and that shoulder sealed my fate: I was going to be a filmmaker.

• • •

I'm in the kitchen finishing up the stir fry when Veronica enters and drinks the rest of my Snapple.

"He's still sleeping," she says, handing me the paprika as if she'd read my mind. We've been friends since our undergraduate days at the state university, and lately we've been more than friends, though we've never defined what any of it means. In a better world she'd be the film critic for *The New York Times*. Her Master's thesis on spatial anomie in *Ferris*

Bueller's Day Off is brilliant, but the world isn't fair, so instead she writes freelance for *Cineaste* and the local newspaper and adjuncts at two County Colleges teaching Intro to Film Studies when she's not helping out on *Exit 23* and every other film I've ever made (or failed to make.)

"How can he sleep in that raincoat?" she says. "I shook his shoulder and offered him the bed, but he insisted he wasn't tired and fell back to sleep."

She grabs a stray carrot and takes a bite. Veronica is short, dark-haired and pretty, with pale skin and a touch of rosacea, which I like. She's graceful and sarcastic like an actress in a 1940's film noir. The first time I saw her, in the college bookstore, we argued over *Raiders of the Lost Ark*, which we both disliked but for different reasons.

"At least the monkey seems nice.," she says.

"How can you tell?"

"He hasn't shit on the couch or started masturbating."

"That *is* nice."

"Has your father always loved animals?"

"Humans are animals and he's always loved himself."

I douse the veggies with cayenne pepper and shake the pan.

"I can't believe he just showed up in the middle of the shoot. I wonder what he wants."

"You *are* his only family. Why assume he wants something?"

"Everybody wants something," I say, without much conviction.

"Maybe he just wants to come home. It must be hard being old in Hollywood. It's tough being old anywhere."

Among Veronica's part-time gigs is cutting hair at a nursing home. (Her mother owns a hair salon and taught her to cut and style. Veronica grew up in the salon watching movies on cable in one of those chairs with a giant hair dryer over her head.) The old ladies at the home love her like a granddaughter as she snips and fluffs their thinning locks. Veronica's own hair is a lush dark garden of curls, perfect for fingers to twirl and stroke. The camera loves her, but she refuses to be in my films.

"The last time we spoke he was doing *The Sunshine Boys* at a community theater in Kansas. I sent him a Christmas card, but it came back address unknown."

"Well, he's in the next room. Go ask him. Or ask the monkey. He seems pretty sharp."

I lower the flame, add some soy sauce, and let the stir fry simmer as we head for the living room. On the couch Dad slumps into the cushions, snoring softly, his right hand resting on his lap, the other in the pocket of the raincoat. I notice the wedding band; my mother's been dead for thirteen years, but he still wears the ring. Would he wake if I yanked it from his finger and shoved it down his throat? The monkey perks up, his left eye shifting between Veronica and me. His right eye is cloudy and listless, as if blind, the banana stashed behind him like a guarded treasure.

I touch Dad's shoulder, hoping to stir him; the monkey, sensing harm, climbs onto his lap and moves his lips, his diaphragm contracting, but there's no sound, only the slightest wheezing, and my father pushes him away, his head turning. "Not now, Henry ...go to sleep."

The monkey (Henry?) grabs Dad's shoulder and boosts himself to the arm of the couch, his tail tucked and curled as he peers out with his one good eye. Beyond my childhood love for *Planet of the Apes* and its tacky sequels, I know nothing about monkeys, but this one is small, no bigger than a housecat. His scalp is topped by a cap of dark fur, his hairless face a light peach complexion, the rest of his fur a creamy white, except for his lower legs and arms, which are black-haired like his crown. A disposable diaper covers his bottom, the diaper slit so his tail can escape.

My father pivots his head, and I shake his knee.

"Dad, wake up!"

"Henry, leave me alone."

The monkey rests his chin on my father's head, his tiny paws playing with Dad's hair.

"Aw, that's so cute," Veronica says.

"Will you help me?"

"Well, it *is* cute. Maybe we should let him sleep."

There's one foolproof way to get an actor's attention, even a career extra like my father. "Places!" I call in my best director's voice, and as expected, Dad snaps alert. Even the monkey seems ready for the scene; tail twitching, he lifts his head and scans the room as if searching for his mark.

"Okay, okay," Dad says, wide-eyed now, his arms stretching as he shifts in his seat, the monkey jumping onto his lap. Noticing the yellow slicker, my father checks the ceiling.

"Why am I wearing a raincoat inside? Is there a leak in the roof? I said you could live here, not neglect the place."

In his prime my father was a handsome man, that strange Hollywood obsession with looks requiring that extras, even the dead bodies, be attractive. At 70 he's held up pretty well; he needs a trim, but his hair is a full, distinguished grey, and as he slowly awakens, the slack muscles of his face tighten; his eyes focus and his posture turns ramrod straight, the virile septuagenarian ready for the shoot. I can see why he's been on screen 623 times, over 700 if you count his Mexican days as George Gringo.

"There's nothing wrong with the roof. You showed up in that raincoat and fell asleep."

"That's nonsense," he says, unfastening the snaps and shaking his head. "My own son, trafficking in scuttlebutt!" He sees Veronica and smiles. "Hello, my dear; Brian Edwards, at your command. And you are...?"

"Veronica Merrin."

He wastes not a second as his voice drops to an evil growl, his face like an angry hawk with a headache. "Merrin!" he shouts.

The frightened monkey jumps from his lap and scoots across the couch, shrinking into the corner while Veronica, who gets the reference, who gets *every* reference, smiles unflustered. Father Merrin, played by Max Von Sydow, was the wise old priest in Willian Friedkin's *The Exorcist.*

"Veronica, such a lovely name," Dad says, his voice turned cultured and smooth. "I was on set with the legendary Veronica Lake in 1970 for an underwhelming little film named *Flesh Feast.* I'm sure you've never seen it. It was her last role, bless her heart. Alcohol had taken its revenge, but she remained a beautiful woman, and her performance as Dr. Elaine Frederick was the finest interpretation of a female mad scientist trying to resurrect Adolf Hitler that the cinema has ever seen."

He gazes beyond us, as if the misty wonders of Old Hollywood had materialized outside the living room window. "Miss Veronica Lake, such a marvelous woman, an absolute treasure."

It's the perfect Brian Edwards line reading, a heartfelt buck of ham.

"It's nice to meet you, sir," Veronica says.

"Please, I'm neither Gielgud nor Olivier, just a poor working actor making his way in the land of dreams. Call me Brian."

"Your name is Edward," I remind him.

"And yours is insolence." He turns to Veronica, pleading his case. "I grant him permanent use of the family domicile and he repays me with a smart mouth. I'm wounded, sincerely!"

It's true—he could have sold the house years ago, and I've been lucky to have a home rent-free since I left film school. My brother has paid the property taxes for the last four years, allowing me a comfortable home base from which to pursue my career, and I'm grateful, (sincerely, as Dad might say) for the help I've been given.

But what he doesn't mention, or rather *who* he doesn't mention, is my mother, who actually paid the mortgage on the house for so many years when he was too broke to pay it himself. When his acting career failed to take off, he convinced her to return to her family in New Jersey, and for years she worked as a legal secretary near Princeton while "Brian Edwards" stayed in California, building his resume of non-speaking roles. He'd come home once a month to charm her and drain her bank account, then return to Hollywood, or sometimes Mexico, where he once fell in love with and married a 19-year-old would-be Mexican starlet, living as a bigamist until the starlet dumped him for a stuntman. Why Mom never divorced him I have no idea. The only thing that makes sense is that she loved him and thought that living 3,000 miles away was better than not being with him at all. When Mom was killed in a car crash during my freshman year in high school, my 19-year-old brother became my guardian, my father staying in California for the sake of his "career." Mom's life insurance paid off the mortgage, and the house, upon her death, became his property alone.

"Would you like something to eat?" Veronica says. "Kevin has made a stir-fry. Your son is an excellent cook, and I'm sure we can find something for your friend."

The monkey, Henry, hops from the cushions and jumps into Dad's arms, nestling his face in the open folds of the raincoat.

"You're his safe place; that's so sweet," Veronica says. "How long has he been with you?"

"Henry? Not long. He is, as they say, a recent addition. His story is quite remarkable, but that matter can wait. I'm utterly famished. Lead me to the table, my dear, though of course I know the way, it being, after all, *my* house."

The last two words are meant for me as he takes Veronica's arm and rises from the couch, his unsteady legs proof of his seventy years. I'm still clueless as to why he's here, but my resentment softens as he shuffles across the hardwood floor, Dad's face brightening at the proximity of a pretty young woman, Henry's tale swinging like a pendulum marking each step.

In the kitchen I divide the stir-fry over three plates and pour glasses of iced tea, and when I finish setting the table, Veronica hands me the raincoat and suggests I hang it in the guest room, which is the master bedroom, *my* room still being my childhood bedroom. I've lived alone in this house for almost five years, but I keep certain rooms vacant, as if waiting for past occupants to return.

There's a hook on the back of the bedroom door. As I hang the raincoat, I see a bulge in the inside pocket, most likely a bag of treats for the monkey, but when my hand brushes the interior fabric, I feel a hard, familiar shape, an object I've handled as a prop, but never for real.

Reaching into the pocket, I remove a black snub-nosed .38, perfect for any B-movie cop or private eye.

Whether it's real or a prop I can't tell, but what *is* real is the stack of ten, twenty, and fifty-dollar bills bundled in a rubber band next to the gun. A quick thumb-count shows that it's more than two thousand bucks, the bills crisp and flat, as if straight from the inside of a bank teller's tray.

I shouldn't be surprised. My father always did bear gifts on those rare occasions when he came home from a shoot.

•　•　•　•　•

It's 10:00 PM. Veronica is back at her apartment, Dad and Henry are asleep in the master bedroom, and my brother and I stand in the driveway dodging gnats beneath the full August moon.

"Don't jump to any conclusions," Mike says. My brother the lawyer, always on the lookout for a plausible defense. He reaches into a bag of McDonald's French fries and shoves a fistful into his mouth. "It's possible he has a permit."

"For the monkey or the gun?"

"I'm not in the mood, okay?"

Lately my affable brother has grown short-tempered.

"Go upstairs and get the gun," he says. "I know a cop who owes me a favor. He'll find out if it's registered or stolen, and if it's stolen, he can make it disappear."

"You know a cop who owes you a favor? That's so film noir. Do you also know a beautiful dame who's tough but can't be trusted?"

"No, but I have a brother who's a pain in the ass."

"Hey, me too!"

"Will you get the goddamn gun?"

I'm one step ahead of him. I pull the .38 from the back of my jeans like Belmondo in *Breathless* and hand it to Mike, who examines it, feels its weight with each hand, flipping the barrel to see if it's loaded. There's a single bullet in the chamber. "Seems like the real deal."

He pops the trunk of his car, wraps the gun in a towel, and stashes it beneath the spare tire.

"What do I say if he asks about it?"

"He won't."

"But what if he does?"

"I'm sure you'll think of a suitable line."

"Improv is dangerous. Maybe I'll write something, just in case."

I swat a mosquito and duck a swarm of gnats flying sorties in front of my face as Mike unwraps a cheeseburger and tears into the bun. My brother is five years older, smarter, better looking, but lately he's added weight and acquired a permanent fatigue around the eyes. Cheeseburgers at 10:00 PM—it's not a good sign.

"I've got some Crisco in the kitchen if you need extra fat."

He flips me the finger, which in New Jersey sign language could be interpreted twenty-seven ways, but this time its meaning is clear.

"Melanie has me on a special diet. Wheatgrass, macadamia nuts..." He holds up the burger before finishing it off. "This is the closest I'll get to cheating on her."

"A McDonald's cheeseburger: that's a pretty sad affair."

"We're trying to conceive. Until we do, I'm a sperm delivery system."

I know more about it than he thinks, but I don't let on. He grabs the last handful of fries and savors the final bites. The salty scent is familiar as during high school I worked at Mickey D's, the burger-flipping minimum wage financing my first short films. Mike crushes the carton and tosses it through his car's open window. "Don't tell my wife."

"I'll swear I saw you with an apple and a handful of almonds."

I look back at the house, keeping my voice low in case Dad can hear us through the open window.

"What do you think he wants?"

"The house," Mike says. "It's the only asset he has. Within a week he'll mention selling it."

"He can't sell it. He gave it to me."

"He said you could live here, that's all. It's his house, and any court will see it that way."

"What if we prove that he's mentally incompetent? Is that a thing?"

"Yes, it's a thing, but the judge will see an unemployed filmmaker living rent-free trying to steal a 70-year-old man's house."

"I'm not unemployed. *Exit 23* is in production. I won third prize at the—"

"—Long Island Film Festival three years ago for a seven-minute short. I know, but a judge won't care. Put Brian Edwards in a courtroom and you'll have no chance."

"Maybe we can buy him out."

"We?"

"Well, you, and I'll pay you back when I get a distribution deal. Do you know how much Kevin Smith made from *Clerks*?"

"Do you know how much a junior associate lawyer earns?"

"A ton."

"Only compared to unemployed filmmakers." He looks sadly at the empty McDonald's bag. "I've got my own problems. I'm not buying the house for you."

Suddenly it feels like every bug in the state is circling my face. I *can't* lose the house. It's my film set, my office, my base of operations; it's where my mother's ghost still looks out for me, which I've never told anyone, not Mike, not even Veronica. I've seen my mother's ghost. We had tea together last Mother's Day. This house, which I should have left years ago, (who in his right mind tries to build a film career in New Jersey?) is keeping my mother's spirit alive, and should it be sold to some smiling young couple with two kids and another on the way, her ghost will pack up and go wherever the dead wind up when they're done with this world and leave me forever.

"Let's not jump to any conclusions," Mike says. "All we know for sure is the money, the monkey, and the gun. First thing tomorrow I'll call my friend and find out about the gun. We can deal with the monkey later."

"His name is Henry."

"The gun and the money I can understand, but the monkey...Jesus."

"I think he might be blind in one eye. Veronica noticed some scars on the back of his scalp."

"A damaged monkey, great; let's hope Dad's not financially responsible."

"Did you ever see that photo of a monkey with his scalp cut off and his brain exposed? I think it was at some lab in Texas."

"I don't really have time for that," Mike says. "I concern myself with people."

"We had to write about it in a philosophy class freshman year. The professor expected us to be pro-monkey but most of the class didn't care as long the experiment made sense."

"I doubt Brian Edwards is experimenting on monkeys."

"Not unless it's a speaking role."

"Maybe that's how we play it," Mike says. "Cast him in your movie."

"There's no part for a 70-year-old man."

"Write one. What does Brian Edwards love more than anything? Himself, on a movie screen; give him some dialogue and tell him the house is part of the production. He'll be all yours."

It's a solid idea, certain to work. Immediately I start thinking of a new character, creating backstory and motivation and a dynamite scene in which the character arrives at the hospital as his daughter is dying. Allison will explode over this grandfather figure she barely knows, and the grandfather, guilt-stricken but self-righteous (and maybe addicted to opioids) will strike back, raising his hand to smack her across the face, but at the last second, he'll stop and break down in tears, and as Allison's fury dissipates, she'll place her hand on his shoulder, the camera holding the moment an extra beat as she kisses his forehead.

Sentimental and melodramatic, perhaps, but if we can get it right, the audience will love it. Is this the missing element? Is Brian Edwards that special something that every film needs to make it stick in a viewer's mind?

The full moon throws its light across the lawn, and in the upstairs window we see our father looking out between the curtains, Henry sitting on his shoulder pawing at the sash.

For so many years Mike and I played in the front yard without a father to toss us a ball, teach us to ride a bike, or just look after us so we wouldn't stray into traffic. If we needed a father, our only option was watching TV and hoping to catch him in the background. Does he see us now, his two boys as grown men, standing in the driveway wondering if he plans to remain the eternal Extra, glimpsed for a moment before the camera turns elsewhere, or if this time he's come for a leading role, the story's inspiring protagonist, or perhaps its villain?

"I assumed we'd never hear from him again," Mike says. "I thought he'd die in some Hollywood flophouse."

"I knew he'd come home."

"You *wanted* him to come home. There's a difference."

I look toward the house, wondering if he'll wave or offer to join us, a father reunited with his sons, but he's gone from the window. In the dim light the curtains hang still, parted just enough for the monkey, perched on the sill, to gaze out at the moon.

It's 8:00 AM. Dad is still sleeping, but the monkey and I are awake.

I'm at the kitchen table, drinking coffee, trying to write a scene for the new character my father might play, an alcoholic ex-truck driver who's come home to mend fences before he dies. A lit cigarette smolders on the table. I don't smoke, but my mother did, and the smell of Salem Lights is comforting. I average a pack a week, sometimes more during times of high stress, a bad habit that will probably doom me, second-hand smoke and all that, but which I've no intention of kicking, it being one of the few remaining connections to Mom.

Across the table Henry sits on a folded bath towel and stares at me, a paper plate filled with peanuts, walnuts, and orange slices set out before him as breakfast. So far, he's sucked two orange segments and spit them out, eaten four peanuts, and pegged me in the face with two walnuts, his aim surprisingly sharp. Clearly, he's not impressed with my role as auteur. Still, I resist the urge to fling the walnuts back, my tenuous sense of dignity averse to going tit-for-tat with a capuchin. Veronica was right about the scars on his scalp. He's got more stitches than a baseball, a lattice of dark scabs in a three-inch circle beneath a patch of peach-fuzz fur.

The creak of the bedroom door is as jolting as a scream, and Brian Edwards-Edward Stacey-my father, whoever he is, comes downstairs, dragging toward the table in baggy striped boxers and a dingy white undershirt, his uncombed hair patted down with Vitalis. Henry perks up the moment he sees him, dropping a walnut shell and swishing his tail as Dad grabs the cigarette and takes a long drag before snuffing it out.

"You shouldn't smoke," he says.

"I don't. It's Mom's cigarette."

"She shouldn't smoke either." He pats Henry's head and yawns. "It's customary to offer a guest a cup of coffee."

"If it's your house, then I'm the guest, not you. Maybe you should serve *me* coffee."

The smart-ass comment is needlessly antagonistic, but I'm pissed at him for extinguishing Mom's smoke.

"Very well," he says. "How many sugars? I assume you take it black?"

He pauses, his timing perfect, giving me ample chance to regret my tone as Henry nails me on the chin with an orange slice.

"No, I'll get it. Sorry for the attitude. I'm working on a tense scene and that energy must have slipped out."

I *am* sorry—I was raised to be respectful toward my elders. "Two sugars?"

"And a touch of cream if you have it. If not, a teaspoon of milk. My tolerance for the bitter brew has waned over the years."

As I step from the table, he glances at my notebook, squinting to decipher my scratch.

"Rewrites for your current production?"

I call out from the kitchen as I pour his coffee and add the cream. "I may need to delete a character. It's a small but important part, and I hate to cut him—"

"Him?"

At film school we practiced it. You wind up in an elevator with (fill in name of BIG STAR) and you have the perfect role for him/her in your low-budget flick. How do you convince BIG STAR to take the part?

"He's an older male, the main character's grandfather. There's an intense hospital scene between the two of them, but I haven't been able to cast it. We don't have the budget to go beyond SAG indie rates, and I can't find anyone who's right for the role."

"An intense hospital scene?"

"It's a cathartic moment. I might be able to repurpose some of the dialogue, but..."

"So, it's a speaking role..."

I don't fish, never have, but this must be the feeling when the trout is circling the bait.

"He's got the second-best speech in the script. But without the right actor, it doesn't work."

"And you've auditioned how many?"

"At least thirty. I even contacted a friend who works for a casting agency in Manhattan. I can go as high as $600 a day for a three-day shoot, but we keep striking out."

I hand him the coffee while Henry pushes the peanuts around the plate.

"Perhaps I could see the pages?" he asks.

"Of course." (Left unsaid—as soon as I write them.) "I'd welcome your input on how to salvage that great speech."

"Why salvage it when it can still be performed?"

"Do you know someone?"

He checks his teeth in the shine of the coffee mug and straightens his posture. "Kevin, my darling son, I was born to play this role."

Film School Rule #14 – The key to selling someone is making him believe it was his idea from the start.

"That would be great, Dad, but you're retired. You should be relaxing, enjoying life with your monkey."

"An actor never retires!" he says, his voice straining for the back row of the theater, Henry jumping on the table, applauding.

"Wow, I don't know what to say. We'd be lucky to have someone with your experience on the set, but I can't ask you..."

"You're not. I'm asking you. I want to read for the part."

Though I've never acted, I've spent hundreds of hours watching others act, and I know enough to let a moment breathe. I count the beats in my head.

"This is...amazing. Thank you."

Though his boxers and undershirt reveal certain bulges best left hidden, I step forward and embrace him, whether as director or son I can't be sure. He's a head taller than me, and my nose bumps against his shoulder as I breathe his Aqua-Velva. And while my instinct as his son is to pull away, fast, the director orders me to hold the moment for all it's worth. I'm caught in his arms as his hands clasp behind my back, and is it the actor or the father who hugs me with such raw physicality and emotion?

Over the years his presence in my life as "father" has been less influential than his left shoulder was in *Soylent Green* when I was six. My father has always been an image on a screen, a dead body, a face in the crowd, at best a late-night pitchman in a commercial for cheap life insurance, the jovial stranger showing up at holidays with plastic trinkets for Mike and me, always disappearing within days. That father I know how to deal with. But this flesh and blood figure whose breath warms my neck as he hugs me is as unfamiliar as the capuchin monkey watching from his seat on the table. Dad's heavy hand pats my back, and suddenly Henry joins the embrace, leaping to the shelf of Dad's shoulder, one monkey arm wrapped around my father's neck, the other around mine.

We stay huddled by the table until Dad releases me, Henry hanging onto him as my father eases into a chair and sips his coffee. If the moment requires dialogue, I have none. Dad finishes his coffee and then heads upstairs to shower and prep for his audition, his monkey close behind, hopping the stairs two at a time.

I call cast and crew and reschedule the day's shoot so I can write the new scene, but first I have a status meeting with Monica and Bob, my primary investors. Keeping them happy supersedes every Film School rule ever written.

When the phone rings I'm almost out the door, but something tells me to grab it. It's Mike, calling from the courthouse. He's due before the judge in ten minutes, but his cop friend already has the skinny.

"It's unregistered," my brother says. "Probably stolen, but he can't be sure. There's a defect with the serial number, a scratched-out digit; it looks intentional."

"Shit."

"It gets worse."

So much for warm family hugs. "Is it the cash?"

"No, the monkey," Mike says. "He's wanted by the F.B.I."

-2-

Because Monica Lafferty was my mother's best friend, and because she and her husband Bob have put up a major chunk of *Exit 23*'s budget, I ignore the naked corpse twenty feet away.

"This is outrageous," Monica says, holding her pen like an icepick ready to strike. "He has no right to be in that house. None whatsoever!"

"His name is on the deed."

"What name is that? George Gringo? I should drive there right now and boot him in the ass. The way he treated your poor mother!" She touches my shoulder, the steadfast family friend commiserating. "She needed a husband, not some wanna-be movie star who abandoned his family for three-seconds of screen time in *Teenage Cave Man* or some other crap. That bastard!"

Her energy is so intense I'm surprised the dead body doesn't rise and shout "bastard" too. We're in the basement workroom of the Lafferty Funeral Home, the business Monica and her husband Bob have run for nearly thirty years. At the far side of the room Bob works on their newest corpse, a gaunt older woman, the emaciated frame and ashen skin-tone screaming cancer. I look away as he dabs make-up on the poor woman's sunken nose. It's a ghastly profession, but Bob and Monica do it well, Bob handling the bodies while Monica manages the business. They own three funeral homes, drive high-end BMWs, and when I graduated from film school, Monica handed me a check for $52,000 and told me to make a movie.

"You're not responsible for what happened. Remember that," she said, a statement that, by its mere existence, suggested just the opposite.

Since then there have been other checks, and I hope one day to pay her back with the profits from the film. Whether she believes in me or just pities me is an open question. Another question: does she blame me for my mother's death?

She and Mom were best friends since third grade, and after Mom died, Monica began looking after me like a hawk guarding her young. Since Mike was already in college, a distracted guardian at best, I became her pet project, her way of doing right by her departed friend. Every time I see her, she still slips me fifty bucks for "pocket money." Someday I hope not to need it.

I told her about my father because she'd be hurt if I didn't but kept quiet about the gun and the stolen monkey. Mike, with little time to talk, was sketchy on the details, and with Monica irate over Dad's return, spilling the news about potential larceny charges feels akin to piling on.

"If he gives you any trouble," she says, pointing toward Bob and the corpse, "we'll get him on the table and start embalming him. It'll be the last time George Gringo plays dead."

Bob, scraping dried skin cells from the corpse's chin, adjusts his face mask and signals thumbs-up.

"Seriously, we're here for you," Monica says. Her perfume, an elegant mist of lavender and roses, distracts from the formaldehyde hovering over the room. When the phone rings Monica steps toward the desk and grabs the receiver. "Just a sec, hon..." she says, and then "Lafferty Funeral Homes, this is Monica Lafferty, how can I help you?"

On the desk is a photo of Monica and Mom from before I was born, the two of them on the deck of a cruise ship holding margaritas and flirting with the camera. My mother is younger than the age I am now, her eyes sparkling and pretty. Sometimes I visit the funeral home just to look at that photo.

"Of course we can help you," Monica says, exiting the room for privacy, leaving me with Bob and the dead body. In film school we had a required workshop on horror movie make-up; for three weeks we played with severed heads, floating eyeballs, and a plethora of creative amputations. In lieu of finishing my assignment on exposed intestines, I took an Incomplete.

"So how's that flick of yours coming along?" Bob asks, teasing the woman's frail hair with a pick and spraying it with a gel that smells like Elmer's Glue. He's a short guy in his mid-fifties, his greying hair buzzed like a Marine, his face as bland as a paper towel, the opposite of Monica, who is always polished and prepped and vibrantly attractive. I've heard that widowers will hit on her while arranging to bury their wives, proving that people, overall, often suck. At least she and Bob seem a happy couple. Years back they would visit my parents during the rare times when my father was home, Bob and Monica sitting on the couch holding hands, my mother alone on the love seat smiling adoringly at my father, who stood center stage regaling them with tales of Kim Novak, Vincent Price, and Steve McQueen, stories I realize now were 100% crap. Curious about this "father" person who seemed more real as a face on TV than as an actual person, I'd watch, fascinated, from the second-floor landing, our living room like the set of *The Mike Douglas Show*.

Bob grabs a tweezers and pulls a stray hair sticking out from the dead woman's mole.

"I'm expecting big things," he says, dropping the plucked hair into a plastic baggie. "We saw that *Blair Witch Project* last week. Everybody involved is raking in the dough, I hear. That jittery camera gave me a headache, but those last five minutes...wow. That kid standing in the corner in the final scene...he's dead, right?"

"It's ambiguous."

"I think he's dead. Scary as hell," Bob says, plucking another hair. "I needed a shot of Drambuie to get to sleep that night. Is it too late to add a witch to that movie of yours?"

"Well, it's not that type of film."

"I know, but people like horror flicks. A witch, a zombie, a guy in a hockey mask ... *The English Patient* would have been more entertaining with a witch instead of that Dafoe guy."

Bob and Monica are credited as Executive Producers for *Exit 23*—the credit of choice for those who write checks—so no matter how ludicrous the suggestion, a thoughtful nod and a respectful "Great idea! I'll think about that!" is the best response. *The Blair Witch Project* has been out for almost a month and its runaway success has filmmakers everywhere dreaming large, even me, though *Exit 23* is not that type of film, and I'm not that type of filmmaker, though perhaps I am. My first film, at age fourteen, was a total horror.

In the basement of our house there's a VHS cassette of the first scene I ever directed: my mother backing her Ford Escort out of our driveway, adjusting her necklace and applying lipstick as she checks the rear-view mirror. Because I botched the zoom the first three attempts, she backed out of the driveway a fourth time, perhaps bored and not paying attention, not bothering with a seatbelt since it obscured her pretty neck. (She'd once been an actress, briefly, and had met my father on the set of *The House That Wept Blood*.) A Chevy pick-up driving the speed limit crashed into her Escort the moment it left the driveway. It should have been nothing, some dents a good body-shop could pound out in an hour, but the velocity of both vehicles was enough to propel my mother's head straight into the dashboard, just enough to snap her neck, just enough to kill her.

I captured it all with my camcorder, my first car crash reel, something every aspiring director should have. Had any of the first three takes not been muffed, my mother would still be alive.

For a year I didn't watch a single film, but since it was the only way to see my father, (he declined to come back from Hollywood to raise me, though I did get a monthly check averaging twelve bucks; life insurance, and Monica and Bob, kept me afloat) I eventually started watching again, studying them closely for their secrets, and when forced to select an undergraduate major, I picked Film Production over the equally impractical Philosophy, and most days making movies is what I live for. Or what I tell myself I live for.

Monica sweeps back into the room, making notes on a pad, mumbling, "...with you in a minute, hon..." while Bob brushes rouge across the dead woman's face. I stare at the floor, keeping my mind blank, until Monica pulls out a chair and tells me to sit.

"Okay, let's hear all about that film of ours," she says, the choice of pronoun intentional, their investment granting them half-ownership in the final product. (Film School Rule #17 – In the course of production, expect subtle reminders of who's in control.) But the thing is: I'm up to the task. I give them updates and anecdotes and estimated completion dates, praise Jill's performance as "transcendent," offer to preview the raw footage, and name drop an associate of Martin Scorsese with interest in a distribution deal, the last tidbit mostly bullshit but not a complete fabrication, the person in question being someone I know who has never expressed any *disinterest* in distribution, and if the name Scorsese is good enough to get Bob to look up from the corpse and smile, it all comes under the rubric of keeping the investors happy. Maybe I *am* on the right path. I'm the son of George Gringo—one can't expect the truth *all* the time.

"I'm so proud of you," Monica says, pecking my forehead with a motherly kiss. She slides the $50 into my shirt pocket, and Bob calls out encouragement: "Give that witch idea some thought, kiddo!" and with that I'm off to the library to write a new scene for my father and save my house. Though these updates could be replaced with a five-minute phone call, I keep returning for a face to face, and to see that photograph of my mother, young and happy on a Norwegian cruise ship, years from her fatal car crash as her son watches closely through a lens.

·   ·   ·

"You need a mobile phone," Melanie says, sitting on a hotel bed wearing nothing but red socks and a hotel robe. In the hierarchy of bad ideas, this one's near the top: my sister-in-law wants me to impregnate her.

The air conditioner hums white noise, spitting out vanilla-scented air. We're on the sixth floor, facing the parking lot, the beep-beep-beep warning of a delivery truck backing toward a loading dock audible through the curtains and glass.

"I can't be tracking you down every time I need you. It's almost the year 2000. Who *doesn't* have a cell?"

It's not the first time she's harangued me about it. According to Melanie, within ten years a person's mobile phone will be the hub of his or her life, not just a phone but a computer, a social connector, even a video camera capable of shooting a feature film. The last one seems far-fetched, but Melanie, who works for AT&T in some vague role in "product development," insists it's already in the works. Everyone will be a filmmaker, shooting mini features with their phone and uploading them to the internet for the world to see. My career hasn't even started yet, but already the field is crowding, a thousand little Spielbergs chasing art with their phones.

At least my sperm is still in demand, the reason I'm in a hotel with my almost-naked sister-in-law about to cuckold my older brother for the sake of his marital harmony. For two years they've been trying to conceive with no luck. About this I know more than I should: ovulation schedules, homeopathic supplements, the optimal positions for fertilization. (I've seen the illustrations—Melanie likes to draw.) The problem is Mike's low sperm production, and six months of treatment with an acupuncturist, a Navajo medicine man, and a Vietnamese herbalist have yet to raise the count. Melanie is thirty-four, three years older than Mike; in their kitchen there's a calendar on which she X's off each day on which she fails to conceive, her equivalent of the Doomsday Clock in Times Square. She's the middle child in a traditional family of three sisters, her two sisters having already spawned five offspring combined. To call Melanie competitive would be an understatement. She burns to prove her eggs equal to her sisters'.

That's where I come in, my DNA close enough to Mike's that no one would suspect. She's still trying with Mike, but if she tries with me too, the odds increase.

"I hate the idea as much as you do," she told me, "but would you rather I fuck a stranger?"

One morning she showed up at the house unannounced, dressed for work in her skirt and blazer. It was strange seeing her without my brother, and I braced for a quick berating for my having taken so much of their money, but instead she talked about *Exit 23* as if she really cared, downing a full cup of coffee before making the ask.

"You owe this to your brother," she said. Did she mean morally or financially, payback for all those $500 "investments" he'd given me? "He keeps a brave face, but his sperm count is killing him, and it's hard for me not to resent him. We've started fighting all the time. Seriously—if you love your brother, Kevin, you'll have sex with me, and we'll keep doing it until I'm pregnant."

We were in the basement, Melanie standing behind me, my editing deck set up on a card table, a close-up of Allison Pinckney frozen on the screen. "She's pretty," Melanie said, her hand resting on my shoulder as she leaned toward the monitor for a closer look. "So, this is how you edit film...I expected something fancier."

Her reflection superimposed over Allison's so that both faces appeared on screen. For the first time I noticed the similarity between them, the wavy blonde hair, the light complexion, the dark red curve of their lips.

"Mike's done a lot to help you," she said. "Isn't it time you helped him?"

l never agreed, but l never refused either, which Melanie took as a "yes." Since l've been sworn to secrecy, l haven't discussed it with Veronica, who would hate the idea on so many different levels, the whole "female desperate to conceive" a plot point too 1950's to consider, the reduction of a female character to her ovaries, the ham-fisted screwball comedy of the coitus scene itself. And how would she feel about me being with another woman? We're not a couple, exactly, but nor do we see other people. Maybe one day she'll write an essay on the films of Eric Rohmer to share her thoughts on infidelity and commitment.

The painting over the hotel bed is a Georgia O'Keefe style rip-off, a vagina masquerading as a rose, some hotel manager's idea of a joke.

"l know we were scheduled to do this on Thursday, but l made some recalculations and today is the optimal time. l'm due back at the office for a 2:00 PM meeting, so let's not dilly-dally," Melanie says, the robe slipping down her shoulders as she hands me a *Playboy*. "Go in the bathroom and get ready."

l check out the cover. Albert Brooks is the interview—he was great in *Broadcast News*.

"Don't *read* it. Go in the bathroom and get yourself hard."

"What?"

"We're not doing any foreplay or 'getting in the mood'. Get yourself ready and l'll do the same."

She lies back on the blue comforter and starts touching herself under the robe. l don't exactly watch, but l don't look away. Realizing l haven't left, she cinches the robe and sits up.

"Don't look at *me,* you pervert. That's what the magazine is for."

"You want me to ...?"

"Jesus, you *have* done this before, haven't you?"

"Looked at *Playboy*?"

"Been with a woman? You sleep with Veronica, right? l assume your father gave you 'the talk'."

Having been in the family for six years, she should know better. There was no "talk" because there was no father. l learned about sex from *The Readers Digest Condensed Guide to Human Sexuality*, the paperback edition left in my room one night by Mike. Though l wasn't a big reader, l worked through the pages dutifully, wondering what had been condensed and if the missing parts were something I might need.

The first time I saw a naked woman, I was watching Brian DePalma's *Dressed to Kill* on HBO, Angie Dickinson (or her body double, as I later learned) caressing herself in the shower before her fantasy lover begins strangling her. In my twenty-seven years I've seen four naked women in real life, and probably five hundred on the screen. Veronica loves to unpack this, what it means to be stimulated predominantly by illusion, so many of those naked on-screen women meeting a violent end. She knows about three of the women, herself being one of them, but my first encounter with a nude female body remains unspoken, an incident kept secret even from Mike.

For my 16th birthday my father invited me to California, where he was doing industrial training films between his gigs as a corpse, the offer so unexpected, and so uncharacteristic, that it seemed like a dream. He was forty-three when I was born, almost sixty during that one and only visit with him in L.A. On one of our rare phone calls I'd mentioned how much I'd admired Tim Burton's *Beetlejuice*, and when I arrived at LAX my father greeted me at the gate dressed in the same black and white striped suit and disheveled shock wig Michael Keaton wore in the film, the first time Dad had made an effort at something related to me. At sixteen I was too old for dress-up games, but it didn't matter. Walking through the airport with Beetlejuice carrying my suitcase, his left arm lovingly around my shoulder, people smiling and giving us the thumbs-up as we passed, was the first time since my mother had died that I considered the possibility of being happy. But I should have remembered the movie—Beetlejuice was a trickster.

Later that day my father left the hotel room he had booked for us, telling me he was going out to get my present. That we weren't staying in his apartment was a warning sign I should have noticed, but I was sixteen and stupid, and who wouldn't rather stay in a Hollywood hotel? He'd promised I could order room service, anything I wanted, even wine or a scotch and soda. I sat on the bed flipping channels, wondering if I'd see my actress crush du jour, Rosanna Arquette, sunning at the hotel pool, thinking how great it would be to stay with my father forever.

He'd been gone five minutes when a woman entered the room. High heels, a platinum blonde wig, enough make-up to cover a billboard; gold hot pants two sizes too small for her mottled hips and thighs, her ample cleavage hanging out like twin Nerf balls waiting to be fumbled. I'd never seen a prostitute in real life, but I'd seen hundreds on the screen, and I knew where the scene was headed the moment she walked through the door.

"Happy birthday, honey pie," she squealed in a fake Southern accent, her lips forming a cavernous smile as she scratched her neck and scanned the room, the harshness of her eyes betraying her smile. On TV, a commercial for the movie *Child's Play* aired, the evil Chucky doll chasing a screaming teenager down a hallway with a knife. "Your Daddy wants you to have the best birthday ever, sweetie, and Rhonda Sue is here to make it true."

She blew me a kiss, the bags beneath her eyes jiggling as she laughed. When you're sixteen, everyone over a certain age falls into a bucket marked "old." Probably she was fifty. That my father had solicited a prostitute for my birthday present felt right out of a *Porky's* sequel, (a film in which he had appeared as a barroom extra,) a dubious act but perhaps well-intentioned; that he'd solicited an aging bargain-basement prostitute added another level of insult. Where was Rebecca DeMornay from *Risky Business* or any of the other pretty young hookers I'd grown up watching? Rhonda Sue undressed with the seductive charm of someone waiting for a pelvic exam. She handed me a baby wipe and told me to clean my wick, which sent me straight for the bathroom, where I stood fully dressed behind the shower curtain until I heard my father return.

"We're all done, yes indeed," Rhonda Sue said, perhaps worried Dad wouldn't pay if he knew I'd locked myself in the john rather than do the deed. When I finally emerged, he slapped my shoulder and congratulated me on becoming a man. Then we sat on the bed and watched the horrible Mr. T movie *D.C. Cab*, waiting for the three seconds in which my father appeared in the background eating scrambled eggs in a run-down diner.

"Will you hurry up?" Melanie says, waving me toward the bathroom. "I told you. I've got a two o'clock."

My sister-in-law is attractive, nothing like the ghoulish Rhonda Sue, and the idea of sleeping with her, excluding the betrayal and the taboo, is enticing. I love my brother, and I'd like to help. Melanie's plan is a good one. If she does conceive, we'll never know who the father is. Mike and I have the same blood type, the same color eyes; we're both 5′10, right-handed, our facial features best described as "pleasant." The biggest difference is what we've done with our lives. He's graduated law school, passed the bar, joined a firm with a good reputation, and is happily married to a strong, successful woman. I've killed my mother, won third prize for a seven-minute short at a minor film festival, and am financing my current project mostly through the pity of my dead mother's best friend. Flash forward thirty years and the child's paternity will be obvious. If he or she is confident and successful, we'll know Mike's sperm made it through. If the poor kid is floundering, spending his or her days watching bad movies on HBO, point the finger at Uncle Kevin.

Melanie taps her fingers against the bedpost and checks the clock, her face turned toward the window. A grim determination settles in her eyes as she yanks the *Playboy* from my tenuous grip and tosses it on the bed. She checks her watch, that two o'clock meeting getting closer every second, then stands and opens her robe. So now I've seen *five* naked women, and the question of etiquette is tough. Arousal being the sole purpose of her reveal, to look away seems rude, but this *is* Mike's wife, and to stare at her breasts or the wisps of pubic hair between her legs feels piggish and violating. Melanie is right—if I had a mobile phone, I could call Veronica and ask for guidance, some scholarly references on the hazards of the male gaze.

"You're allowed to look," Melanie says, and so I do. The robe drops to the floor, like robes always do in adulterous hotel room scenes, and I consider the moment as if it were a sequence of shots from *Exit 23*. Where exactly do I place the camera as Melanie unbuckles my belt and snaps open my jeans? And what about each character's motivation? Melanie's is clear enough, but my own is a slip-slide of levels: an altruistic desire to help them conceive, the natural physical desire for sexual release, and perhaps a third, more troubling motive to outdo my brother in this one aspect of life.

"Missionary is best," Melanie says, smoothing a towel over the comforter before leaning back and spreading her legs. "Gravity helps."

She looks me over to make sure that I'm hard, and I wonder if it's too late to hide in the bathtub like I did with Rhonda Sue. Will family gatherings ever be the same now that my sister-in-law has seen my penis? How can I ever again say "Pass a turkey leg, please" at Thanksgiving dinner without visualizing the lovely planes of Melanie's thighs? Not for the first time I consider myself more child than man, and I need to do something about that, but I'm not sure what it is, so like a good boy eager to please, I do what my sister-in-law asks.

I want Melanie to enjoy it, too, so I forget the Readers Digest version and use everything I know, yet except for an occasional "thank you," she is unresponsive, glancing at the bedside clock and tapping my shoulder, whispering, "We need to finish, please." And so I do, my body shuddering with release, and though I expect her to be dressed and out the door before my pulse returns to normal, she holds me inside her when I try to pull out, eager for every last drop.

"Cross your fingers," she says, "and keep tomorrow night free. The seven o'clock hour is supposed to be the most fertile."

"I have plans with Veronica tomorrow night."

"Bring her along. The extra female energy can help with conception." She reads my face and smirks.

"That's a joke. Don't bring her. But be ready for 7:00 PM."

•   •   •

In film school they warned us that everyone we meet will offer suggestions on how to improve our scripts. Family members, hair stylists, the technicians at Jiffy Lube, the high school kid behind the counter at the pharmacy; the moment someone hears that you're working on a screenplay, an idea will be offered, unsolicited advice given.

This rule, I now learn, also applies to monkeys.

Henry's notes are simple. When I step into the kitchen for something to eat, he grabs the first few pages of the new scene and rips them from top to bottom. A turkey sandwich in hand, I return to find a half day's work scattered like yellow confetti on the floor, Henry happily chewing on page three.

"Stupid monkey," I yell, waving my fist, and Henry cowers as if I've struck him with a whip. His cry is a soft, pitiful *meek-meek*, and as he runs off to hide in the nook between the cabinet and the wall, I see the bald spot on the back of his skull, a patchwork of scabs dotting his skin.

"Hey, I'm sorry," I tell him, scooping up the remnants of the torn-up scene. "But that was a lot of work, and I didn't make a copy. You can't just rip up someone's script."

He curls fetal-like, covering his eyes with his tiny palms. My father isn't home, so it's just the two of us. I grab some popcorn from the cupboard and offer him some, but he won't look up, won't stop trembling in a ball against the wall, a stream of urine leaking from his diaper, pooling at his feet.

According to Mike's cop friend, seven capuchin monkeys disappeared from a lab in Utah three months ago. It was a big story out west but never made it to the New York market. I hadn't heard of it, though if I had, I would have paid no attention, relying on Veronica for current events or simply ignoring everything except *Exit 23*. The shaved scalp and scars suggest Henry is one of the missing seven; for confirmation we'd need to check the roof of his mouth, where Mike says labs tattoo serial numbers to identify their property. I've yet to do this and doubt I ever will. Henry is one of the seven—I can feel it. The question is: how did he wind up with my father, and what are we going to do about it?

Henry hides his face with both hands as his tail twitches, his legs drawn up against his stomach. "Really, it's okay, the scene needed work anyway," I tell him, keeping my voice low. To comfort a dog, you pet him or her, but what do you do with a monkey? I wipe up the urine, then sit on the floor beside him, holding out my hand for him to sniff, but he ignores me, turning his head, hoping I'll disappear if he refuses to look. There's an indentation on both sides of his forehead, actual bolt-sized dents.

"Jesus, what did they do to you?"

Henry drops his hands and suddenly jumps into the crook of my lap, his nose rubbing my chest. It's unexpected, and I start to push him away, but his tiny hands grab my thumb, not letting go. I pat his head, unsure of what else to do, and he seems to like it.

Growing up, we never had animals. Mom didn't like them, and my father was never around. Henry's body is warm, his fur soft and faintly ticklish as I stroke the back of his neck. Each time I stop, his tail thumps my knee, so I keep petting him, which is calming for me, too. When my foot turns pins and needles, I stand up, Henry still clinging as I bring him to the couch. One by one I peel off his fingers and set him down against the cushion. His good eye looks up as if to thank me before he burrows behind a throw pillow, his head peeking out just enough to keep watch.

Outside a car pulls into the driveway, the scrape of metal against pavement jarring as always, the engine idling high. I check the window, figuring it's my father back from his errands.

Instead, it's a police car.

I freeze under a rush of thoughts—hide the money, hide Henry, hide myself. The only one that sticks is my default strategy for everything since age fourteen: call Mike.

Three rings, four rings...it's too late for him to still be in court, but what if he and Melanie are going at it? Peeking through the curtains, I see my father in the back seat, his image feint behind the tinted window, the front door opening as a uniformed patrolman unfolds his long body from inside the cruiser.

Finally, Mike's voice snaps over the line. "I'm busy. Call me back—"

"There's a cop in the driveway with Dad. You'd better come. He's getting out of the back...he's not in handcuffs but the cop is holding his arm. What do I do? Do I hide Henry?"

"Calm down," Mike says. "Don't do anything. Let it play out and don't get involved."

"What if they take him away?"

"Then the problem is solved. He can't sell the house if he's in prison."

"I meant the monkey."

"Who cares? I hope they do take him away."

"He has dents in his head. I think he's been through hell."

"He's a monkey," Mike says. "He'll get over it. Just don't get involved. Call me back when you know for sure what's happening. I'll talk to you later. I need to make a kale smoothie. Melanie has me on a schedule."

When the doorbell rings Henry runs upstairs, a smart move, and I wait until he's gone before opening the door. If only there was time to write some dialogue, tense banter between a cop and the suspect's son, Gene Hackman as the gruff cop, Johnny Depp as the sensitive son.

My father stands on the porch, his face slack, a three-inch bandage over his right eyebrow. There are scratches on his skin, a bruise to the left of his nose. The cop, who's about my age, holds him by the upper arm.

"There was an incident," the cop says. "Your father...this *is* your father, right?"

I spare him the minutia of our family history.

"He passed out while driving and rammed a telephone pole. The airbag deployed or it might have been worse. The car is totaled, but your father's okay."

"A minor mishap," Dad says.

"It's not a minor incident, sir," the cop says. "Instead of a telephone pole, what if you'd rammed a school bus?"

The cop stays on the porch as Dad wobbles into the house.

"We took him to the Emergency Room, and he checked out fine." He calls after my father. "You're a lucky man, sir."

"Ha! Paul Newman is a lucky man. I'm a struggling actor."

"The car is at the impound lot. You've got 48 hours to pick it up; after that the garage fees start adding up. Fifty bucks a day, so I suggest you get the car."

Dad scans the living room, looking for Henry but playing it cool.

"We issued him a summons and took his license. He'll get a 90-day suspension automatically, and a doctor's sign-off is required if he applies for reinstatement."

"It was nothing. A bad chicken wrap for lunch. Mountains out of molehills," my father says, heading for the couch.

"Sir, this was a serious incident." The matter-of-fact tone tells me he knows nothing about Henry or the stolen gun. "There are strict penalties for driving with a suspended license, including a potential jail sentence."

"I'm no stranger to hard time," Dad says, meaning his four seconds on screen in Buzz Kulik's 1969 film *Riot*.

"We'll fetch the car first thing in the morning," I say. "Thank you for driving him home."

"Of course," he nods. "Hey, did he really know Alfred Hitchcock?"

"He was in *The Birds*, at the nine-minute mark. Don't blink."

"*The Birds*...I've heard of that. I'll check it out at Blockbuster this weekend." He turns, but then pauses, as if there's something more. "Your father told me you're making a film. He said you won some festival award."

"That's true," I say, shocked that Dad knows about the festival or anything else about me.

"Hey, if you ever need someone to play a police officer," the cop says, handing me his card. He drops his hand to his holster and sneers Clint-like, "Go ahead punk, make my day!" His smile is huge, child-like. "Pretty good, huh?"

He calls out to my father as he steps from the porch.

"Be careful, sir. Remember, no driving."

"Thanks again, Officer."

My pulse eases back to normal as the cruiser pulls away.

"Please, no lectures," Dad says once I join him in the living room. "It's no big deal."

"You totaled your car."

"It was a thirteen-year-old Taurus with three hundred thousand miles. Consider it a mercy killing."

"You could have hurt someone, hurt yourself."

"Are you disappointed that I didn't? How poetic to have both parents killed in a wreck." He avoids my eyes. "Where's Henry?"

"Upstairs. He bolted when the doorbell rang."

"Good boy."

"Do you need water? We might have some Excedrin."

"I need a time machine," he says. "Any chance you can make me young again?"

"The right lighting can subtract ten years."

"I'll take it." He presses his palm against the bandage. "What did you do with the gun?"

"What gun?"

"Save it. You gave it to your brother, right? At least you left the cash."

"He says the gun is stolen."

"I'm sure it is," Dad says, "though I didn't steal it. Did he say anything about Henry?"

"Something about a lab in Utah ..."

"True again, though it wasn't me who stole him."

"Who did?"

"That's not a good thing for you to know," he says, "and honestly, I'm not certain myself." He rotates his neck, slowly, as if the wrong move would cause his head to eject. "Don't worry, I won't be here long. Allow me a few days rest and I'll be on my way. Have your brother write up whatever papers are necessary, and I'll sign them before I leave. This house is yours. It could've been mine, but as we both know, I was elsewhere."

There's a weary sincerity to his voice that makes it hard not to believe him. He was never that good an actor.

"If you must know, and you probably should, I have a condition," he says. "Nothing fatal, nothing *imminently* fatal; this won't be one of those dying father scenes. But I've passed out before and been lucky. Today, the luck ran dry."

He peels the bandage from his forehead, an ugly red gash underneath. There's a bruise at his left temple, the same spot as Henry's dent.

"My heart ...there's a problem with the valves; something like that. I stopped listening once the doctor said 'myocardial.' I'll be alive until I'm dead, and when I'm dead, it won't matter. I've played so many corpses it should be a cinch." He breathes deeply, his chest wheezing. "I really should get some rest."

His legs buckle as he stands, and he drops back to the couch, grabbing the sofa arm to break his fall. I reach out to help, but he waves me away.

"Give me twenty minutes and I'll be my old self again. Go work on your film."

"I can stay—"

"I'm not an invalid. It's just a valve problem. Like a car. Cars have valves, don't they?"

He kicks off his shoes and stretches his legs across the couch.

"Watching an old man take a nap is boring cinema. Not even Brando could make it play. Please, cut to a better shot."

His forehead is beaded with sweat, so I check the thermostat and raise the AC two degrees. Some comforting action seems required, aspirin or a blanket, even a glass of water, but he shakes me off, and all I can think to do is to go upstairs and get Henry.

Soon Dad and his monkey are asleep on the couch, the capuchin curled on my father's chest, his head resting over the weakened heart; a sliver of yellow paper from my torn-to-pieces scene still wedged between Henry's left toes. Dad's right—a movie needs action, movement for the eyes to follow—but it's something I've never seen, my father holding Henry as if he were his son, a paternal tenderness previously unknown, and if a camera was near, I'd film every second of their peaceful sleep.

• • • •

After dinner with Veronica, I park outside the local multiplex and start writing a new scene on a yellow legal pad, proximity to a movie screen often an effective muse, but not tonight. A giant poster for *The Blair Witch Project* covers the brick wall next to the theater entrance, and I feel dwarfed by its presence, the poster so big I could fit inside the lead actress's dripping nostril. I try writing Dad's scene as if it were meant for another actor, Richard Farnsworth or perhaps Wilford Brimley, but the dialogue in my head is all Brian Edwards, the word "myocardial" worming its way into every line, and I give up and drive home as the 10:00 PM showing of *Blair Witch* lets out, swarms of happy filmgoers stumbling bleary-eyed toward their cars.

When I reach home, the house is dark except for the TV, Dad and Henry no longer on the couch, Craig Kilborn and *The Late Late Show* with a guest I don't recognize filling the screen. Exhausted, I kill the TV and head upstairs.

In my room I light a cigarette, place the ashtray on the windowsill, and fall into bed. As a child I had frequent nightmares about snakes and chainsaw maniacs and weird stuff like drowning in melted ice cream; I once woke up screaming after dreaming about the word "skullduggery." I'd shout out to my mother, who'd rush into my room and sit at the foot of the mattress smoking a Salem Light until I fell back to sleep. My mother dressed for bed as if preparing to shoot a love scene, her nightgowns short, silk, usually a dark red, her toenails always painted, her skin redolent of the strawberry lotion she applied every night. Perhaps she thought Dad might come home unexpectedly and she wanted to be ready to please him.

Eventually we developed a routine. Superstitious, my mother believed in good luck charms and special pendants able to ward off evil spirits, her favorite a four-leaf-clover she'd found in Killarney during a childhood trip to Ireland. She wore it in a locket around her neck, the one piece of jewelry she was never without, the four-leaf-clover preserved in laminate, and one night, when I woke up screaming from another dreadful dream, she unclasped the locket, removed it from her neck, and set it on my pillow.

"As long as it's near, nothing bad can ever happen to you, sweetie," she said, kissing my forehead, the smooth silk of her nightie brushing my cheek. I soon fell back into a dreamless sleep, and the next night, as she kissed me goodnight, she placed the locket on my pillow and touched my hair, an unspoken ritual forged. From that night forward I slept with her four-leaf-clover beside me.

When I turned twelve, I began to wonder if I was too old, her nightie a source of confusion, but I never asked her to stop. A four-leaf-clover rested on my pillow each night until she died. But for her, at least, its luck ran out, the locket hanging from her neck as she backed out of the driveway for the fourth and final take. When the police pulled her from the wreck, the locket was gone, and though we searched long—*I* searched long—it was never found. The video I'd shot that day, when finally viewed months later, proved that she'd been wearing it when she got into the car, but at the moment of impact, when she'd needed its luck the most, the four-leaf-clover had failed her.

I lay in bed, the harsh smolder of the dying cigarette filling the room. I hate the smell, but I light it every night, the smoke a comforting scent, also a carcinogen.

Maybe I drift off, the cigarette extinguished when I check the ashtray, but suddenly I hear noises coming from the master bedroom, what sounds like heavy breathing and the squeal of a 20-year-old box spring. Is this it: my father's heart attack, the massive myocardial event that will make his absence permanent?

I rush toward his room, the gasping breaths louder now, uncontrolled, and I push open the door. The lamp is off, but two candles burn atop the bureau, and in the glow of the flame I see Dad lying in bed, one hand on his bare chest, the other on the naked ass of the young woman riding him. A red nightie lies on the floor beside a pair of striped boxer shorts.

The woman peeks over her shoulder, her cowgirl gyrations not missing a beat as her arms cover her breasts.

Dad, seeing his son gaping in the doorway, slaps her on the ass and says, "That's a wrap."

-3-

It should be easy: a simple tracking shot of Jill-as-Allison walking across a bridge, five seconds of screen time as a transition between scenes, the kind of grunt work relegated to the assistant director on a Hollywood set. Chances are it won't even make the final cut, but we still need the footage, and Jill, Veronica, Dave, and I have driven three hours to a little town in Hunterdon County in pursuit of the perfect bridge. The clouds have cleared, providing ample natural light, and though we're filming without a permit, there's no one around to bollix the scene, except for me, who can't seem to focus on anything other than my 70-year-old father and his 23-year-old wife.

"Give Dave the camera and let him shoot it," Veronica says, standing at my shoulder while I pan along the shore of the Musconetcong River tracking a discarded Molson bottle floating downstream. The sun reflects off the green glass like a halo, and it seems the perfect image, simultaneously crass and holy, like America itself, a comment I should use one day for the press junket at Cannes.

"This is exactly what I want," I tell her, "the juxtaposition of beauty and trash."

"Then how about those Big Mac cartons trapped in the rocks over there? Maybe McDonald's will kick in some bucks for product placement."

"He's been married for nine months," I say.

"So? You wanted to be the ring bearer, is that it? Dress up in a little tuxedo and watch Daddy tie the knot?" Her hand finds my shoulder in support, but I can tell she's impatient and cranky. "Put things in perspective, Kevin. You're both grown men. There are bigger things to worry about."

"The house—she'll definitely want the house."

"I was referring to Henry."

"Is he married, too?"

Twenty yards away, Jill stands on the bridge's outer walkway, slapping the back of her thighs. "Goddammit. That's the third bite!"

She wears cut-offs and a white T-shirt, hiking boots and a baseball hat, her ponytail threaded through the back of the cap. In the film, Allison has just stormed out of Jake's apartment after confronting him about spending the night with Wendy, a scene we've yet to shoot. The bridge is perfect, a two-lane wooden crossway built in the 1930's with New Deal money, a guardrail separating the path from the road. Jill bends and pivots, checking her skin for bite marks.

"Shit! Veronica, I need some touch-up here."

"Don't worry, the camera won't pick it up," Dave says. "It's a long, tracking shot."

"Trust me, if these legs are on screen, people will be watching. Veronica!"

"Can you add a shot in which she's covered in peanut butter and attacked by ants?" Veronica says, quiet enough so that Jill won't hear.

"How about slathered in honey and chased by bees?" Dave adds.

"Give her a break," I say. "It's her face and body on screen. That's a vulnerable feeling."

"Then why don't you do the touch-up?" Veronica offers me the make-up bag, her eyes squinting against the sun. "All she needs is a few dabs of concealer."

"I'll do it," Dave says.

"You'd never stop," Veronica says. "We'd be here all day while you touched up every inch of her."

"That's true," Dave says.

"Veronica! Will you hurry up? My legs are being ruined!"

"Coming, dear!"

Jill bends in an elaborate twist, searching her legs for imperfections. "All these bugs...Kevin, how can I stay in character under these abysmal conditions? I'm starting to swell."

"Maybe she's allergic," Dave says.

"She's a Jersey girl. If she was allergic to mosquito bites, she'd have died ten years ago."

Veronica flips me her migraine face. "Once her legs achieve the desired state of perfection, can we get the shot and go the hell home?"

"Yeah, I'm due at work at..." Dave says, checking his watch. "...shit. I'm going to be late."

In film school Dave aspired toward cinematography, but his father's video store went belly-up when a Blockbuster opened across the street, forcing Dave to drop out when the next tuition bill came due. He works part-time at UPS; I pay him fifty bucks a day whenever he helps on set.

Veronica trudges off, digging through the make-up bag as Jill hectors her to hurry, Veronica's legs, in jeans, as equally fetching as Jill's.

"Is she pissed at me?"

"I don't think so," Dave says. "She probably should be."

"Did I say something?"

"Look at it this way, man; how many times have you gone to the library to help with the research for one of her essays?"

"It's different. Film is a collaborative art. Cinema Studies is an individual pursuit. I'd help her if she asked."

"Directors...you guys think the world revolves around you. And you're right, on set. But the whole world isn't a set."

He hands over the camera and I zoom in on Veronica touching up Jill's bug bites with a Q-Tip and concealer.

"My father is married to a twenty-three-year-old."

"You told us in the car."

"It's freaking me out."

"Sounds like a decent set-up for a porno. I hear those films pay pretty sweet. Not that we'd use your father, but if we found the right couple, we could make some real cash."

My disdain must be evident.

"Hey, it's still filmmaking," Dave says. "We focus on the craft. Is it that much different from what we're doing? We both know this transition shot is really about Jill's ass catching eyes on the preview reel. It sells. If we could make a few extra bucks doing skin flicks, why not? Didn't you love *Boogie Nights*?"

In film school I had a few offers but the guys involved seemed mobbed-up, and I kept imagining my mother's ghost watching me direct a blow job.

"We're not doing porn, Dave."

"Hey, easy for you to say ...you're not hauling boxes at UPS. What about weddings? Bar mitzvahs? Hell, porn might be easier. No hyper parents or bitchy brides."

Veronica returns, scratching her neck at her own mosquito bite. She wears a floppy white hat to protect her face from the sun. "Okay, Mr. DeMille, she's ready for her close-up."

Her back turned, she leans against the guardrail, staring at the river as she kicks a pebble into the water. It feels like that pebble is me. I hand Dave the camera.

"See if you can get the shot," I say, and join Veronica by the rail.

An empty bag of Lay's Potato Chips rides the current downstream, a mallard duck gliding on the surface behind it. Everything beautiful is eventually ruined by people.

"I was reading Peter Singer last night," Veronica says.

The name is unfamiliar, though maybe he's the critic for *The Boston Globe*, some hack without an ounce of Veronica's analytical pizazz. A stupid review from a prominent voice can throw her off for days.

"Your stuff is so much better than his."

"That makes no sense. Peter Singer, the philosopher...*Animal Liberation*...we read it sophomore year."

"Right, *that* Peter Singer."

"You never read it, did you?"

"I remember that class. I mentioned it to Mike the other night. I got a B."

"You copied my notes and I rewrote your paper."

"That's ethically dubious. See? I paid attention in Philosophy."

"I can't stop thinking about it," she says. "He writes about these experiments in which monkeys are subjected to thousands of electro-shocks and exposed to chemical weapons while forced to keep a flight simulator in balance." Her hands grip the railing, her knuckles bulging. "It's impossible to read without crying. Day after day these primates— sentient beings, like us, like Henry—experience these horrendous levels of stress and fear and pain. They vomit all over themselves, bang their heads against wire grates...they curl in their cages alone screaming for hours. It's just sick."

I shouldn't be surprised by her mood. During that class her reaction had been visceral, leaving her in a funk for days. At the other end of the bridge Jill rehearses her walk, variations on the country girl strut, Dave prepping the shot, searching for the best vantage point.

"In one experiment, they separated baby monkeys from their mothers at birth and put them in wire cages in total isolation for an entire year. They had no contact with other monkeys, or humans, or anything. Complete deprivation with the stated intent of producing psychological damage so they could measure the fear responses. Educated professionals were paid to do this. Some asshole got a grant."

"People suck."

"They gave these poor baby monkeys a stuffed toy as a surrogate mother. They were so desperate for nurturing they would hug the stuffed toy and not let go. And get this—these bastard scientists rigged the stuffed toys with wires that gave off these painful electric shocks. They wanted to see what would happen if the surrogate mother suddenly became a source of pain. And the baby monkeys were so desperate for a mother they wouldn't let go even when they were shocked. They suffered the pain again and again just to feel a mother's touch. Can you imagine?"

Of course I could—I would have suffered them gladly to have Mom back after the accident.

"I was up all night," Veronica says. "That level of rational, pre-meditated cruelty...someone wrote protocols ...it makes me want to jump off this bridge. I keep thinking of Henry...what he must have been through at that lab. Do you know how much pain can result from even a single electro-shock?"

Dave and Jill are both out of range, though Veronica's voice, rising with her ire, might carry along the river. They know about my father's monkey, but not Henry's status as a wanted ape.

"Those scars on his scalp indicate some type of implant. They stimulate different parts of the brain to register the response. It's extremely painful, so they put their heads in a vice so they can't move. Otherwise they would thrash around, trying to escape the pain. Imagine it...your head's in a vice, you can't move, there's a wire inserted in your brain, and these shocks keep coming and coming. It's like the pain of a migraine multiplied by thirty, a scalding needle jammed into your brain."

Those indentations above his tiny ears, permanent dents.

"They separate the mothers and the babies at birth...raise them in total isolation." She turns, furious and beautiful. "Your father deserves a medal."

"He had nothing to do with getting Henry out of the lab. Dad's never risked his neck for anyone other than himself."

"How do you know? I get that he was an absent father, but that doesn't dictate every aspect of his character. Other than those three-second glimpses of him on TV, how much do you really know?"

"Whose fault is that?"

"Does it matter?"

"Yes."

Crouched like a baseball catcher, camera on his shoulder, Dave captures Jill's innocuous strut as a hawk swoops over the bridge, and Jill, bless her heart, responds exactly as Allison Pinckney would, pausing, looking up, then blowing the hawk a kiss. It's a fortuitous moment—our budget could never afford a hawk wrangler—and the hawk, as if eager for his screen debut, lands on the railing at the far end, turns its head for a close-up, then dive-bombs the river in search of prey.

Dave jumps to his feet, all that lifting at UPS giving his legs the needed spring. The camera follows the hawk as it skims the water, attacks, and emerges with a fish flapping in its talons as it soars over the tree line. It's enough to shake Veronica from her funk, the four of us watching, transfixed.

"Perfect!" Dave shouts, lowering the camera, he and Jill joining us at the railing. "Absolutely fucking perfect! We could sell that footage to *American Sportsman*."

"A show that celebrates killing animals as 'sport'? I don't think so," Veronica says.

"I said we *could*, if we wanted to. Don't bring me down, V. That was the best cinematography I've done all year."

"Good job, Dave," I say.

Even Jill seems pumped by the moment.

"That was awesome. Maybe we should build a scene around it. It's so primal, almost feral. My skin feels electric, like it's begging for more."

The hawk reappears, circling the river as a pick-up truck crosses the bridge, the driver slowing to check us out before speeding off.

"What if Allison strips down and jumps into the river?" Jill says. "Everything in her life is so tense right now, and that hawk connects with...I don't know...with her primitive longings. She just wants to be free. The hell with everything...Momma and Marty and the baby...she needs to feel that cold water against her skin...what do you think, Kevin?"

"I love it," Dave says. "Maybe she goes fully nude? Tastefully, of course, but enough for a cable sale."

"Well..." Jill contemplates the river, "...okay, but my left nipple is slightly bigger than my right. Can we make sure to shoot it so that we miss the right nipple?"

"You're not jumping into the water," Veronica says. "Our insurance won't cover it."

"The risk is worth it," Dave says. "Jill has too much artistic integrity for a lawsuit."

"I won't sue...unless we see the right nipple."

But the moment passes. A bee swoops near Jill's neck, close enough to damper her primitive longings and send her fleeing toward the car, the day's shoot complete.

"What? It was her idea," Dave says, withering under Veronica's glare. "And it *would* help land a cable deal."

He packs up the camera and heads for the car; Veronica and I hang back.

"Since when are you bothered by nudity? All those Italian films you admire have a nude scene every ten minutes."

"I don't give a damn about her nipples," Veronica says. "But what are you going to do about Henry?"

• • • •

"What are we going to do about Henry?"

I've been waiting all day to get him alone, but for the moment Mike's not interested in monkeys or experiments or the FBI. Instead it's all about the trick. He shuffles the deck and cuts it twice, fanning the cards like an old-time pro, his voice Vegas smooth. "Ladies and gentlemen, it's magic time." He lays the cards in front of me. "Pick a card, young man. Pick a card."

"Can we do this later? We need to talk about Henry."

"Come on, I've been practicing all week. Don't ruin it. Pick a card."

His face sports a two-day growth, his five o'clock shadow dotted with grey whiskers, his eyes tinted a tired pink. He steps closer, the distinctive scent of dill pickles all over him. I reach into the deck and pull out the Seven of Hearts.

"Great. Now hold onto it, and then check the rest of the cards and verify that there's not a duplicate hidden in the deck."

"Jesus, how many pickles did you eat today? You smell like a barrel of kosher dill."

"Stop smelling me. Pay attention to the trick."

"Do we really need to do this?"

"Do I really need to support your film? Yes—we need to do this. Now check the deck and verify that there's no duplicate card."

We're in the den, but through the sliding glass door we can see everyone gathered on the patio, my father in Bermuda shorts and the loudest Hawaiian shirt in history standing by the grill flipping burgers, his wife Gloria stirring a pitcher of lemonade at his side, a baseball cap shading her face, her paisley sundress reaching to her ankles. In adjacent Adirondack chairs Veronica and Melanie sip frozen daiquiris at the patio's edge, their bare toes enjoying the summer grass. Beneath the snack table Henry cradles a tennis ball, and toward the back of the yard, leaning against an old Japanese maple, my mother's ghost, in denim cutoffs and a Budweiser T-shirt, watches it all.

"Stop looking outside and focus on the cards," Mike says.

My brother, the amateur magician; practical and smart, he chose law school, but for three months after college he lived in California and took classes at the Magic Castle. It's where he and Melanie met, the two of them students in a Level II Conjuring class taught by Kid Charlemagne the Great. Give them enough wine and they'll both dream of shucking the daily grind and heading to Vegas, a husband-and-wife magic act being a natural draw.

I flip through the deck, looking for a card I know won't be there. Mike never breaks out a trick until he has it down cold.

"We need to talk about Henry."

"Don't worry, it's under control. Things are in the works."

"What things?"

"I told you, don't worry. Did you see your card anywhere in the deck?"

"You know that I didn't."

"Great. Now give back your card."

On the patio Gloria rubs my father's shoulders, smoke swirling from the grill.

"I don't like her."

"She seems fine. It's not like we have to call her Mommy."

"She's a gold digger."

"He has no gold."

"The house."

"Forget the house...it's going to be fine." He looks at my card. "Okay, the Seven of Hearts...lucky number seven...lucky in love...unless the heart gets broken."

With dramatic flourish he rips the card into four pieces and then tears each piece in two, tossing them in the air like confetti.

"Goodbye Seven of Hearts...now I'll take back the deck, and remember, you've been holding it the whole time."

"She's an actress, or he says she is. I'll have to create a part for her, too."

"Then you'll write her a part. She's cute. She'll look good on camera. Who cares? Now pay attention as I slowly deal the cards."

I know what's coming as he reveals them: Jack of Spades, Two of Spades, Three of Diamonds, Nine of Clubs, and then...the Seven of Hearts.

"There it is, your card, the same card I ripped up thirty seconds ago. How did I do it, you ask? Well, the truth is..." He drops his voice for effect. "...it's magic!"

Mike's smile is genuine and wide, and sometimes I wish he and Melanie would escape to Vegas and follow their dreams, though without an older brother to take care of things, I'd sink like the Titanic.

"Bravo! Letterman should book you immediately. Now can we talk about Henry?"

"Don't worry about it. He'll be out of here in a few days."

"What do you mean? Where's he going?"

The glass door slides open and Melanie enters, still barefoot, her bright pink toes like exclamation points against the hardwood floor. She sees the torn pieces of the Seven of Hearts and scoops them up.

"I do that trick so much better than he does."

"No, you don't."

"I'll do it later and everyone can vote," she says before grabbing my brother's shirt. "Let's go, I need you."

"Here? *Now*?" Mike says. "I thought you said seven o'clock."

"I read the chart wrong. Come on, it won't take long..."

"What did you mean that Henry will be out of here in a few days?" I ask, but Mike is already following his wife as Melanie undoes the top button of her blouse, my brother's face resigned, stoic, and a little bit horny, the scent of dill pickles emanating from them both as they head toward the spare bedroom, Mike's old room, posters of Doug Henning and David Copperfield on the wall for encouragement.

Again, the door slides open; this time it's Veronica's toes that sparkle. "You're hiding. That's not allowed. Come have something to eat."

"I'm not hiding. I'm being anti-social."

"You can't avoid them forever. I spoke with her. She seems perfectly nice."

"She's married to a man who could be her grandfather."

"It happens, and don't be so judgmental. Forty years from now maybe you'll be married to a hot young thing."

"You're not planning on aging?"

"You're planning on marrying *me*?"

"Is that wrong?"

"It's not *wrong*. Stranger things have happened."

Always cagey when it comes to commitments, she drops it fast.

"Did you know your father was in *The Masque of Red Death*? Remember that scene with all the bodies in the ballroom? He's one of them."

"Yeah, I've seen it, he's the perfect corpse."

"What did your brother say about Henry?"

"Not much; he said something's in the works."

"That sounds ominous. I don't like it. Mike understands what the poor thing's been through, right? We need to find out how your father got him. Eventually people will get curious. We need a plan."

"Mike says he has one."

"I wonder. Your brother's a good guy, but he's a lawyer, and while they may be necessary, I'm always wary. Did he and Melanie go home without saying goodbye?"

"They're working on a trick."

"Cool. I hope we get to see it."

"Maybe in nine months."

"It must be a complicated trick." She grabs my hand. "You can't avoid your father forever. If we're going to be an old married couple, you need to start listening. Let's go."

• • •

"...and then Bob Redford said to me..."

My father can weave a tapestry of crap like few others. If "Bob" Redford ever said a word to him, it was probably, "Who the hell are you?"

But his young wife Gloria is eating it up, glowing with starry-eyed love, the same glow my mother wore whenever he came home to grace her with his smooth charm before emptying her bank account. Even now Mom's ghost is entranced, smiling as Dad leans back in his chair to deliver the story's climax.

What kind of ghost watches her husband with his new bride, a 23-year-old corn-fed blonde sitting on his lap feeding him grapes like a Roman slave girl, and doesn't whip up some thunderbolts or at least knock the lemonade pitcher straight to the ground? What's the point of being a ghost if you can't wreck a little havoc when needed? But she seems content to be part of his audience. If anyone is jealous, it's Henry; he tugs at the hem of Gloria's dress as if trying to pull her from his rightful place on Dad's lap. With a plastic straw he bats at her toes, playing them like a xylophone.

"Was Redford invited to your wedding?" I ask. "Since you and he are so close, did you ask him to be Best Man?"

"We eloped,' Gloria says. "It was spur of the moment. A small chapel..."

"Vegas? Did you get the full Elvis package?"

"I've never been to Vegas," she says, shooing Henry away. "We were married in Holt. You've never heard of it, I'm sure. No one has. It's just a little town in Missouri where my grandmother lives. We didn't want anything fancy, but I couldn't tie the knot without Grammy there."

"Grammy and Dad must have a lot in common."

My father glowers but lets it pass.

"She's a doll. Middle America at its finest," he says. "After living on the coast on all those years, everyone so superficial and competitive, it was heartening to be welcomed as family."

Leaving Dad's lap, Gloria hands the grapes to Veronica and pours some lemonade. Henry, not wasting a second, boosts himself onto Dad's knee, the straw sideways in his mouth.

"Grammy and Uncle Ned and Missy Lou, that's Grammy's pig, they brought two bottles of moonshine to the chapel and we jumped in the pickup and celebrated all night," Gloria says, winking at Dad. "Isn't that right, sweet-ums?"

"You bet, sugar plum. Ned dressed up in his Sunday overalls and brought out his shotgun and we all took turns shooting possum right after we said our I do's."

"We do things formal out in Holt. Why, the minister even put on shoes..."

"Okay, okay, I get it," I say. "But all I did was ask about Vegas. I didn't imply you were a Li'l Abner cartoon."

"Holt, Missouri is a charming town," Dad says, "and my wife deserves your respect."

"There's so much of the Midwest I want to see," Veronica says. "I'd love to travel, but all I do is watch movies and work."

"The time is now, my dear, while you're young," Dad says. "The open road is more appealing when your bladder doesn't demand a break every two hours."

"Don't be like that, Brian," Gloria says. "We drove straight through Ohio without stopping once."

"I have this book idea, to write about fifty films, each one set in a different state," Veronica says. "It would be the story of America and its people through these fifty films. I've been thinking about it for almost a year, researching different films."

"You've never mentioned it," I say.

"I have, once or twice. Maybe you weren't listening." She plucks two grapes and hands the bunch back to Dad. "Directors tend to focus on themselves."

Mom's ghost picks a purple leaf from the Japanese maple, tosses it in the air, and watches, fascinated, as it floats to the ground. If her ghost exists only in my head, which is possibly true, (or possibly not—ghosts *could* be real), what am I (or she) trying to say?

Gloria reaches into her bag for a tube of sunscreen and reapplies a layer to her long arms, an unintentionally sexy move at which I look away. Henry, still on Dad's knee, stares with his one good eye at a small rabbit nibbling grass at the patio's edge.

"I realize how we met was extremely awkward," Gloria says to me, prompting an unwelcome flashback, "but I hope we can get past it and be friends. It's important to Brian and me."

"Important to both of us, yes..." Dad says.

"So let's get it out of the way." She takes a long drink. "The elephant in the room, or on the patio, ha-ha, since we're not in a room: I said this to your brother and now I'll say it to you: Brian is much older than me and I'm sure that's concerning."

Again, she calls him Brian—does she know his real name is Edward? Has she ever heard of the bigamist George Gringo?

"But if you love someone, does age really matter? We're all about five seconds from meeting our maker anyway. Lightning could strike, we could choke on a chicken bone, a car could come out of nowhere..."

My mother's ghost nods her agreement.

"...but like The Beatles said, all you need is love. I'm 23 and Brian's 64..." Dad's eyes implore me not to rat him out about being 70.

"...and maybe I have Daddy issues and maybe Brian's robbing the cradle and maybe someday our marriage falls apart like so many do, but that means nothing to me right now. When I'm wrong, I say 'I'm sorry', but I'll never apologize for being in love."

"No one ever should," Veronica says.

Gloria looks straight at me, waiting to be challenged, but my anger feels petty, and it's possible I like her. She and Dad kiss, and even Mom's ghost smiles, leaving me no choice but to smile, too, and grab a glass of lemonade, which I consider dumping over my head before drinking. Henry leaps from Dad's knee and charges the rabbit, but the second the rabbit moves, Henry scurries back to his safe space, jumping onto Dad's lap and hiding his face in Dad's big Hawaiian shirt. Is it the result of all that isolation and men in white coats cutting into his brain, a fear response so heightened that even a rabbit terrifies?

When Mike and Melanie return, the back of Mike's shirt dotted with sweat, Melanie's tousled hair corralled in a scrunchy, Dad and Gloria announce their surprise.

"It's something we worked on this morning," he says, bringing Henry and setting him down between Veronica and me. He joins his wife in the center of the patio.

"We'd like to do a scene," Gloria says. "Brian is teaching me so much about acting."

"Is he teaching her to play dead?" I whisper. Veronica elbow-jabs me as she pets Henry's neck and shoulders with gentle strokes, his useless eye drooping as he snuggles against her hip.

"Kevin, I hope you don't mind," Dad says, "but we couldn't resist."

Melanie and Mike sit on one side, Veronica and I on the other, an impromptu theater-in-the round with my father and his wife center-stage. Gloria lowers her head, centering herself before emerging in a rage.

"How *dare* you show up at the hospital to pay your respects when your whole life has been about disrespect?" she says, the muscles in her neck straining, her cheeks burning red. "Momma waited her whole life for you to come home, and now, when you're finally here, she's too weak to open her eyes and see you."

Dad hangs his head, his body sagging, one leg stepping back as if already headed for his pick-up truck.

"And what's this?" Gloria nearly shouts, shaking an invisible prop. "A Three Musketeers bar? You stop at the vending machine and buy me a candy bar like I'm five years old—I don't need a goddamn Three Musketeers bar—I need my mother to live."

Her tears are sudden and natural, her sobs so all-consuming even her knees shake. Dad plays it exactly as he should, reaching out but keeping his distance, his hands touching air, his face clenched to hold back his own tears, Gloria moving ever so closer, as if her body, in need of connection, has overridden her mind.

It is, of course, the new scene I wrote for *Exit 23*, six pages of legal paper covered in scratch-outs and notes. Dad must have found it on the table and started rehearsing, he and Gloria memorizing the lines and grounding the characters' motivations in their bodies, in their hearts and minds.

"All I can offer is this moment, right now," Dad says, his voice above a whisper, Gloria's head turned, afraid to let him in. "I've lost the right to be her father, to be a grandfather to you...I'm just a man who, for once in his life, wants to do the right thing."

Mike and Melanie are on the edge of their seats. Even Henry is caught up in the moment; he clutches Veronica's hand, says *meek-meek*, his feet hopping in place.

I've never seen my father act before, not really. I've seen him on the screen hundreds of times, always dead or silent, but never acting beyond the demands of drinking a beer at the bar or lying dead on the ground while the rest of the scene ignores him. It's a revelation that he's talented. He plays the scene perfectly, elevating my early-draft dialogue into an authentic emotional moment. Gloria, too, is wonderful, playing Allison with more raw passion than Jill has ever shown. As the scene plays out, my father and Gloria disappear, replaced by Allison and Ralph working through their lifetimes of resentments and regrets. When Ralph offers his hand, a final plea for his granddaughter's acceptance, the expression in Dad's eyes and the hesitant, hopeful tilt of his head captures the turbulence of this troubled man so beautifully, and when Allison-Gloria finally accepts him, stepping into his arms for the embrace she so craves, Mike, Melanie, and Veronica stand up and applaud. Mom's ghost blowing them kisses, and Henry leaps onto the arm of the Adirondack chair, clapping his hands and waving his tail.

I'm shocked, dumbfounded, the director too stunned to direct.

I always assumed my father was a hack, a ham, a crappy actor left in the shadows because he deserved nothing better. How sad and pathetic, dedicating oneself to an art for which one has no skill. But what if the truth is even more tragic—a talent never given the chance to flourish.

Film School Rule #12: there are more talented people, by factors of ten, than will ever make it in the industry. Is my father one of them, a gifted actor dedicated to his craft but shoved into the corner and ignored, doomed to watch lesser actors fall ass-backwards into leading roles while he sips coffee at the catering truck waiting to play dead?

"Too bad you weren't filming," Mike tells me. "That was fantastic."

"Wonderful," Melanie says. "Bravo!"

Even the professional critic is impressed. "Very powerful," Veronica says. "The emotional verisimilitude was tangible. I felt every moment."

Dad takes Gloria's hand, and together they step forward for the traditional theatrical bow.

"Let's not forget the author," Dad says, sweeping his hand toward me. "It's quite a good scene. No one would ever guess that you wrote it only yesterday."

So he's on to me and our plan to save the house, but for the moment I don't care. My only thoughts are about the camera and getting the scene on film. Already I can see the headlines: *Director-Son and Actor-Father Reconcile to Win Top Prize at Garden State Film Fest '99*.

I check on Mom's ghost, hoping that she too is pleased, but the Japanese maple stands alone, Dad raising a glass and toasting his young wife as everyone applauds, except his youngest son.

. . .

I'm in the kitchen, shaking the last of the pretzel twists into a serving bowl when Melanie enters with a red Igloo cooler.

"Your father sure has the gift of gab. He should have gone into sales. He'd be a millionaire ten times over."

For the past thirty minutes Dad has regaled us with his adventures in Hollywood, in Mexico, even in Italy, where he once worked as a donkey wrangler and played three different corpses in a spaghetti western. Forthright and funny, his stories encapsulate his life in a medley of anecdotes reaching back to his film debut. The only thing he doesn't discuss is Henry, dodging the question each time Veronica or I ask how he came to live with a stolen lab monkey.

"That story about his having to pee while playing dead on the set of *The Birds* is classic," Melanie says. "He must be the only person alive who ever raised his hand and asked Alfred Hitchcock for permission to urinate. That kind of publicity could really help you. NPR would jump all over that."

"They're his stories, not mine."

"They're *family* stories. I'm just saying."

I toss the empty pretzel bag and grab a few more napkins, Melanie's eyes following me as I check the fridge for more iced tea. She snaps open the Igloo and lifts out a jar of pickles.

"There's something I need you to do," she says, her voice low. "Before Tuesday night, I need you to soak your testicles in pickle brine."

I wait for the punchline, though she's never been one for gags.

"At least twice over the next few days, for twenty minutes minimum, and then once for an hour on Tuesday before we meet. It'll turbo charge the motility of your sperm."

She slides the jar across the counter, the half-gallon size, a lone pickle floating in the brine. Mike's kosher dill scent suddenly makes sense.

"I'm not soaking my privates in pickle juice. That's ridiculous. We shouldn't even be doing what we're doing."

Her forehead tightens, storm clouds in her eyes.

"You are so selfish, Kevin. Mike has done so much for you over the years. He...*we* practically support you. The brine doesn't have to be cold. Let it warm to room temperature before you start soaking. Really, it's not a lot to ask."

On the label a cartoon duck with a big pickle in his mouth hovers over the brand name, the green-tinted brine reaching to the lid.

"Your brother would do it for *you*," she says.

I pick up the jar. It's a debatable point—writing a check is easier than dunking one's junk in brine—but the sudden slamming of a car door in the driveway diverts any further thought.

There's a second slam, and then another. Mom's ghost appears by the window, peaking through the blinds, her face aghast.

"Are you expecting anyone?" Melanie says.

I rush to the window—two black SUVs block the driveway, a third one in front of the house.

By the time we reach the patio they have already arrived—four men and four women in FBI windbreakers, guns drawn, shouting "Freeze!" and "Federal Agents!" and every other cop movie cliché, Mike shouting that he wants to see a warrant, my father in handcuffs, Gloria too, everything happening so fast it's like a film looped at double-speed.

Melanie and I watch by the sliding glass door, my father and his wife pulled from the patio, a hulking G-Man in a black baseball cap ripping Henry from Veronica's arms.

"Don't say anything, don't say anything," Mike shouts toward Dad, who doesn't struggle as the cops drag him roughly from the yard. In all his film appearances, I've never seen him in handcuffs, and it's worse than seeing him dead.

"Goddamn it, I'm an attorney," Mike shouts.

A female agent shoves Veronica aside when she reaches out for Henry, the monkey's hands shaking as he shrieks, *eek-eek-eek*, Veronica losing her balance and falling back against the Adirondack chair.

"Holy Shit," Melanie says, opening the door and running toward Mike.

I drop the pickle jar, glass and juice exploding over the floor, and the last thing I see as Dad and Gloria are taken away is Henry hanging upside down, his foot in the clutches of a Federal agent, his arms flailing, his one good eye terrified and wide, his mouth agape in a voiceless scream.

-4-

"The old man is tougher than I expected."

My brother bites into a garlic bagel smothered in cream cheese, his sperm-friendly diet abandoned for well-earned doses of salt-drenched fat and carbohydrates. For the past two days Mike has gone head-to-head with the US Attorney's Office and three supervisory agents from the FBI, an experience he describes as playing tennis with a ping-pong paddle against an opponent with a double-sized racquet. He's barely slept, but instead of exhausted he seems charged, eager for more, as if he'd just exited the stage after the best magic show of his life. It's me who's running on empty, frazzled and paranoid and imagining the worst. A week ago, the prospect of Brian Edwards in a prison jumpsuit might have provoked a stupid joke, but now that the chance is real, it's like a sucker punch to the gut.

We're outside the Mercer County Courthouse, sharing a bench beneath a shade tree dating back to the Revolutionary War. A homeless guy sleeps ten feet away, his feet covered with plastic bags, a dingy blanket pulled to his face.

Mike gulps his coffee and frowns at the bitter taste.

"I thought he'd say anything to save his own butt, but he held strong. It's nothing like the movies, with cops pounding on the table making threats. It's mostly repetition, the same damn questions over and over until the subject finally slips up. But he did well. Fortunately, they know he's a minor player. He's not really a player at all, just a well-meaning stooge who needed the cash. His main concern was Gloria. The old man believes in chivalry. He was ready to do time as long as she could walk."

Here it comes, the gut punch. "He's going to do time?"

"He might have, if his lawyer wasn't so kick-ass smart."

Mike raises his hand for a high-five, the smack of our palms scaring off the squirrel eyeing the bagel crumbs at our feet and waking the homeless guy, who turns on his side and curses.

"Do you know how long it's been since I've done anything interesting? Being a lawyer is a slog of dull paperwork, but this was intense. I wish you and Mel had been there. I was like Tom Cruise in *A Few Good Men*. Your next film should be a legal thriller. How about a hot shot lawyer who does magic on the side?"

"Then Dad's not going to prison?" I say, fifty pounds of tension lifting from my shoulders, sprouting wings and flying away. "Thank God."

"Was God involved? That's strange, I didn't notice any deities in the room. I thought it was your brother—"

"Okay, okay—thank *you*. Once again, Mike is the hero. So, what happens next?"

"That's where it gets a little sticky."

The Feds, knowing Dad was merely a courier, had little interest in prosecuting but were hungry for more information on Henry's ultimate destination. Between bagel bites Mike gives me the run-down. Dad and Gloria were living in Indiana when a co-worker at Wal-Mart asked if he was interested in some side work. Not having acted for over a year, Dad was employed as a stock clerk and broom pusher, undoubtably a humiliation for the former George Gringo, but it was where he met Gloria. At first, he was wary of the offer, figuring it involved drugs—an assistant manager sold meth on the Paper Goods aisle—but when all he had to do was keep a capuchin monkey for 60 days and then drop him off in another state, he signed on without a worry. They gave him $3,200 and a crash course in capuchin care. It turned out Dad liked monkeys, having twice been an Extra on *Lancelot Link, Secret Chimp*.

Across the street two vans from Jersey State Prison pull away from the courthouse, a State Trooper patrol car leading the way. The homeless guy looks up as if he's just missed his ride.

"They didn't plan on coming to New Jersey, but their landlord got suspicious, so they took off and figured what better place to lay low for a while than his own house."

"How did the FBI find him?"

Mike sips the coffee, avoids my eyes.

"Yeah, well...as it turns out, my cop friend isn't exactly a friend. I never should have mentioned the monkey when I asked him to check on that gun."

"The raid was *your* fault?"

"It's never the attorney's fault. If he didn't want to get nabbed, he shouldn't have transported stolen property, and let's not forget, I'm the one who's getting him out."

"You turned in our own father."

"I recall a phone call and a panicked younger brother saying, 'Mike, what do I do?' If you'd kept the gun in the raincoat and never called me, none of this happens."

He crushes the coffee cup and tosses it in a garbage can ten feet away, an impressive shot. Immediately the homeless guy gets up and fetches it, shaking out the last few drops of java.

"That's really sad," Mike says, watching as the guy licks the rim of the discarded cup. "It's almost the year 2000, we're the richest country in the world, and some poor bastard has to get his morning coffee from the trash." He reaches into his wallet and pulls out a ten. "Hey Buddy…"

The guy grabs the ten, blesses Mike about fifty thousand times, and wanders away.

"It's not Dad's gun anyway," Mike says. "It's Gloria's. Her cousin gave it to her for protection when she started working nights. They're damned lucky I turned it in. If the Feds had found a gun, it would be a hundred times worse. Everything's a felony when there's a gun in the room, and gun charges are never dismissed."

"But they're not going to prison, right?"

"As long as we hold up our end of the deal, the charges are dropped. The people he's supposed to deliver the monkey to are the ones the Feds want. They're part of the same group who raided the lab. These agents sometimes talk in circles, but there are two people they have a real hard-on for. A man and a woman, some fanatical Bonnie and Clyde. They've raided labs in Utah and Texas. They damaged a fur farm, smuggled cameras into a slaughterhouse and freed about a thousand chickens. Real hardcore terrorists. The FBI knows who they are, but they lack evidence. That's where Dad comes in."

Under the agreement, Dad will make contact and arrange a meeting to turn over Henry.

"The ALF…that's the Animal Liberty…"

"Animal Liberation Front." Over the past two days Veronica has provided a crash course.

"Yeah, that's it. The ALF has a farm somewhere in Canada where they bring these stolen lab monkeys to live. But they'll never make it. As soon as Bonnie and Clyde take possession, the Feds swoop in and make the arrest. They'll arrest Dad too, for show, but then release him and drop all charges. End of story. He can even keep the cash."

"He agreed to it?"

"It's a good deal. If he hadn't, I might have pressed them on the warrant."

"What do you mean?"

"They screwed up the warrant, which reads Brian and Gloria Edwards. Can you believe it? I'm surprised they didn't have one for George Gringo, too. But this deal is the safer route. Some judges look at technicalities and dismiss the case, others could care less, and you never know which judge you'll get. On TV, defendants walk all the time, but the government has virtually all the power, and defendants rarely get a break. This will be cleaner."

"What happens to Henry?"

"The monkey? It's not part of the deal."

"He, not it."

"Whatever. I don't know. The FBI will take custody and I assume return him to the lab."

"They'll probably kill him. That's what they do when they're done with them."

"Legally, they can do whatever they want. He's property. It's not our concern."

From the potential sanctuary of a Canadian farm back to the prison of a Utah lab—too bad Henry doesn't have a lawyer of his own.

The morning after the arrest Veronica hit the library to research the facility where he'd been kept. The facts were grim, but easy to find, the lab proud of its heavily funded work in animal "research." Henry's case was not unique. The bald patch on his head was from a common procedure called a chamber—the experimenters cut into the monkey's skull so they can inject drugs directly into the brain. The indentations were from "head posts," bolts surgically implanted with screws and cement so the head can be held steady for hours or days at a time. In one experiment, performed at the same lab where Henry lived, the monkeys were denied water for days until they were so thirsty, they'd drink whatever bitter liquids or even poison they were given. Another experiment involved pinning the monkey's eyes open and shooting them with water, puffs of air, vinegar, lemon juice, scotch whiskey, etc., just to see how they'd react to an "aversive" event. Henry was lucky he still had his brain. Sometimes the lab techs would leave only the sections they found useful and then suck out the rest, the hell with what the animal might need.

I'd never seen Veronica so distraught and enraged. "For the animals, it is an eternal Treblinka," she said, quoting Isaac Bashevis Singer. After nearly an hour of her listing atrocities, all I could do was hold her and agree to throw out everything on her list of animal-tested products. I'll need to wash my hair with Gatorade until we make it to The Body Shop for replacements.

"Now there *is* one point we need to discuss," Mike says. "Dad has to contact Bonnie and Clyde, and he'll need to meet them somewhere, most likely in upper Michigan, but it could be anywhere. These terrorists are smart, and they could send him all over the country until they feel secure that he's not being followed. Health-wise he can't make that drive alone. He's got an issue with his heart."

"No license, either. What about Gloria?"

"He won't do it if she's involved. He wants her back in Indiana, away from all this. The D.A. suggested someone from the FBI, but the Feds nixed the idea. They thought it might raise too many red flags. These terrorists are sharp. Dad proposed a different option."

I pictured my father hamming it up, the FBI better than no audience at all. "Did he ask for Bob Redford to drive him?"

"No," Mike says. "He requested you."

• • • • •

Thirteen thousand, four hundred and sixty-four dollars for three days, or one hundred and eighty-seven dollars an hour. That's how much it costs to rent the sound stages at Blackstock Studios, the cheapest production house in New York, the only one affordable under the stretched-thin budget of *Exit 23*. Because certain scenes can't be filmed in the living room or the kitchen or staged as an "exterior," (meaning outside, meaning free), we've come to Blackstock for a marathon of set design, adaptive carpentry, and get-it-done-in-one-take scene work with the goal of wrapping principal photography before the money runs out.

Across the street we've booked two hotel rooms, where cast and crew can sleep and shower during breaks. Though I've been up for twenty-six hours, I can't stop until we finish the next scene—Allison outside Momma's hospital room, Dr. Janney telling her that Momma's coma is likely to be permanent. Dave and his brother-in-law, a licensed contractor, have built a mini hospital out of plywood and leftover two-by-fours, and we've scrounged enough equipment (a hospital bed, IV drip, beeping monitors, etc.) to make it all seem real. Jill, too, hasn't slept in a day, but since in the film neither has Allison Pinckney, her exhaustion is in character, giving her eyes a weariness no makeup could fake. In a quiet corner she runs lines with Albert, who plays Dr. Janney. In the world of *Exit 23*, Albert Spencer is a "name," having once played recurring roles on both *The Young and The Restless* and *Days of Our Lives*. Even at SAG Indie rates we can only afford him for another three hours. With the scene already blocked, all that's needed is for Dave to set the lighting before we start rolling.

My father sits in the director's chair, eavesdropping on Albert and Jill. His big scene with Jill is the next one to shoot. Two weeks have passed since his arrest, yet everything is in limbo. The ALF has yet to make contact to arrange for Henry's transport, and so we wait, Special Agent Donna Mahoney calling twice daily to remind my father of his legal obligation and the potential prison stint awaiting if he doesn't deliver. With a directive not to leave the state until the charges are dropped, Gloria has moved into my mother's old bedroom, she and Dad settling in with poor Henry, who's clueless about his fate. At night I wear headphones to block out the squeak of the box spring.

Among the crew only Dave knows I might be called away at any moment to drive my father somewhere, though he doesn't know why. The uncertainty of the looming trip has proven the perfect impetus to finish *Exit 23*, and the reason I've drained the last of Bob's and Monica's check and rented the soundstage to get it done.

"We're ready to go," Dave says, and I call places. Albert and Jill are amazing, the old soap opera pro guiding her toward her strongest performance yet, everyone applauding when the scene wraps. It's a good feeling, diminished only by Veronica's absence and the suspicion that she's back in her apartment sticking pins in a Kevin doll, furious at my complicity in Henry's recapture. But what choice do I have?

"Maybe you should get some sleep," Dave says, checking the clipboard for the shot inventory. "We'll need at least forty-five minutes to break down and set up, and I can do the blocking for the lights. Go back to the hotel and chill."

And so I do, downing a turkey sandwich as I cross the street to the hotel, New York horns blaring as I ignore the yellow lights. I need sleep, badly, but in the hotel room Melanie is waiting with a mug of kombucha and three capsules of horny goat weed.

"How did you know...?"

"I promised your friend Dave fifty bucks if he'd send you over."

She's already undressed, under the covers, a string of quartz crystals around her neck, lavender candles on both sides of the bed.

"We're not doing this."

"One last time—I promise," she says. "You could disappear at any moment."

"I'm not disappearing. I just driving to Michigan. I'll be gone two days at most."

"Mike says they'll have you on the road for at least a week, sending you to different places, making sure it's not a set-up."

"It *is* a set-up."

"Take off your pants and come to bed."

"Melanie, I'm not doing this..."

But I do. Maybe it's the horny goat weed or the pent-up pressures of the past two weeks, but my body responds, and while I have plenty of moral qualms about sleeping with my brother's wife, it's a more pleasurable ethical dilemma than my sell-out of Henry.

When it's over, we forget who we are and share a kiss.

"I think it worked," she says, the smile on her face the happiest thing I've seen in, well, maybe ever. I'm dressed and nearly out the door when she hands me a small box wrapped in Christmas paper and bows.

"It's a little early, isn't it?"

"More like a year late."

It's a cell phone.

"Call the number on the card to activate it," she says. "I pre-paid the first 90 days, unlimited calling. You're going to need it on the road."

"Thank you, but I really don't want it."

"That's ridiculous. It's like saying you don't want the future."

I promise to activate the phone, then step into the hallway, Melanie calling after me, wishing me luck with the shoot. By the elevator, a tall woman in a dark pants suit, maybe around 40, waits next to me as we watch the numbers of the descending floors flashing red on the wall. When the door opens, I follow her in, but instead of pressing the Lobby button, she blocks the control panel and looks me up and down.

"Interesting," she says.

"Excuse me?"

"You're fucking your brother's wife. That wasn't in the file."

She shows me her ID—Donna Mahoney, Special Agent, Mid-Atlantic Branch, FBI.

"We're not—"

"Yes, you are. I can tell by your pupil dilation. We had a class on it at Quantico last month."

Her smile is pure counterfeit as she presses the Door Closed button, sealing us in.

"Don't worry. The information stays in the file, unless we need it. But it does make me curious about your reliability. A man who would cuckold his own brother—"

"It's not like that. I'm doing them a favor."

She nods, jotting a few lines in a tiny notebook. "You care what others think, even a stranger like me. Interesting."

She pockets her badge, shifting her jacket so I see her holstered gun.

"Why are you following me?"

"We follow everyone. We're keeping America safe."

"Look, I'm just a filmmaker. We're selfish narcissists, if that isn't already in your file. I'm just trying to keep my father out of jail."

"Maybe. But your girlfriend has been doing some interesting library research." She flips open a different notepad. "Veronica Merrin: she's very curious about a certain lab in Utah."

"She feels bad about Henry. So do I."

"You mean Specimen 576-A24?"

It's out of my mouth before I can stop it. "Fuck you. He has a name."

"Now that hurts my feelings," Agent Mahoney says. "I'm a public servant, doing a job to protect American lives and property. I don't appreciate that kind of language. It makes me want to tell your brother about your diddling his wife, and maybe kick you in the testicles. We had a class on that at Quantico, too."

Her demeanor is flat, but the threat seems real.

"For what it's worth, your film looks entertaining. I'm not crazy about the bowling scene with Jill and Marty..."

"How do you know...?"

"I've read the script. I don't think you'll win top prize at the Garden State Film Fest, but you've got a shot at a distribution deal, even though this kind of film is on the way out. You should have tried horror, like *The Blair Witch Project*. That girl with the mucus running down her nose conveys a legitimate terror."

"Do they teach snot at Quantico, too?"

Her laugh is a bark and a snort. "We have no reason to interfere with your production as long as you cooperate. You drive the car, period."

She presses the Lobby button and the elevator descends. When the door opens, she steps aside, letting me exit.

"What's that show business expression?" she says. "Break a leg!"

"Or the FBI will break it for me?"

She remains on the elevator, pointing her finger at me and winking as the door slides shut. Because there's neither time nor the budget for me to freak out, I grab the free coffee and a complementary cookie by the front desk and hurry back to the soundstage.

Dave greets me with the clipboard, guiding me toward the set, the hospital hallway where Jill and Dad have their big scene.

"You should have warned me about Melanie."

"She gave me ten bucks to get you over there. Hey, are you and she...?"

"She said it was fifty, not ten. Are we ready to shoot?"

I huddle with Dad and Jill, run through the scene twice, offer suggestions that they don't really need, check the monitors, the lighting, the position of the boom mic, everything a director does to convince the crew he has a vision. If *Exit 23* is ever released, this scene will be the highpoint of my father's career, giving him more dialogue over three minutes of screen time than he's had in a combined forty years. It's more than nepotism—his patio performance on the night of the raid wasn't a fluke. He and Jill have rehearsed the scene twenty times, and each performance reveals new layers to his character, bringing depth and excitement and pathos, and it's a win for both of us, but the complications of his reappearance in my life feel akin to a hostile takeover. Becoming chauffeur for Dad and a stolen monkey was never part of the plan.

Film School Rule #27 – Check your baggage. It's not about you, it's about the film.

With each minute of soundstage time so precious, the director pushes aside the hurt little boy and summons the magic word—*Action!* This scene I shoot myself, the camera heavy on my shoulder as I hold Dad and Jill in a careful two-shot. We'll shoot it at least five times: the two-shot, and over-the shoulder frames for both Dad and Jill, plus the close-ups, the final onscreen version a carefully sliced Frankenstein's monster of multiple takes.

The first three are a bust, but then Dad and Jill find their rhythm, their line readings perfect, the emotional ebb and flow exactly as rehearsed, exactly as I'd written it, until my father changes the blocking mid-scene, grabbing a chair and sitting down instead of advancing toward Jill as we'd rehearsed it. Jill reacts without missing a beat, but the chair is not part of the scene.

"Cut!"

"Looked good to me," Dave mumbles.

Dad slumps in the chair, Jill pacing by the wall.

"Was it my voice?" she says. "I sound like a whiney four-year-old. God, I hate my voice!"

"You sounded great. It's not your voice."

Dad opens the top buttons of his shirt, slipping his hand beneath his collar, rubbing his chest.

"The chair isn't part of the scene."

"I thought it might work," he says. "He's tired. It shows his vulnerability, emotionally and physically."

"It's a nice touch," Dave says.

"But it's not part of the scene. Let's do it again without the chair."

"I liked it," Jill says. "When he sits down, Allison feels stronger—it helps her show more compassion."

Dad stares at his feet, avoiding me, his hand over his chest. In film school we were warned that certain actors like to challenge the director, assert their power to bring the production to a screaming halt if their whims aren't granted. Everyone's right—the chair *does* work; it gives the much-smaller Allison physical leverage over her grandfather. But in the moment, I don't care. It's my script, my film, and my father won't take it from me.

"Lose the chair," I tell them, but when Dave moves to grab it, Dad doesn't budge.

"I *need* the chair," he says.

There's a tremble in his hand as he buttons his shirt.

"I can play this scene however you want, Kevin, but there may be moments when I need to sit. You're the director, and if you want the chair gone, there's nothing I can do. I'll still play the scene. That's what an actor does. But I've been on enough film sets to have watched some great directors accommodate their performers with much more than a chair. It's a simple request. I need to sit—and so does this character."

Of course he needs to sit—he has a bad heart, the whole reason I'm the designated driver for his meet-up with the ALF.

Jill folds her arms, settling in for a battle. "Kevin, if you don't let him sit..."

"Let's shoot it again, *with* the chair," I say. "Places."

Dad catches my eye, and I don't know if it's with gratitude or victory because I don't know what it means to have a father. But I do know how to direct a low-budget movie, and every minute wasted subtracts from the film's potential. We shoot the scene—*with* the chair, with my father's hand trembling, with a wheeze in his voice that could be real or affectation. Over the years Brian Edwards has played so many corpses he could drop dead and I'd think he was acting.

Seven takes later, we've nailed the scene. Jill heads to the hotel for some much-needed rest; Dad wipes clean his make-up and waits for Gloria, his ride home. As the crew breaks down the set and starts building the County Jail, the setting for the next scene, I pour through the production notes, checking off completed scenes, reviewing the scenes yet to be shot. Alex Meserole, who plays Marty, practices reading from the giant cue cards containing his dialogue. Give Alex more than seven words and he struggles to remember, but his face is ruggedly handsome, like a sensitive Marlboro Man who would quit smoking to please his woman, and when he takes off his shirt it's clear why a young woman as smart as Allison Pinckney forgot her birth control that night in her friend Bailey's apartment. As an actor, Alex, on his best day, struggles to reach mediocre, but his chest will look great on the poster. I spend a few minutes with him, explaining the next scene and helping him with motivation. Dave, pulling a long clothes rack filled with orange jumpsuits—the costumes for the prison scene—slides the rack between Alex and me and hands me an envelope.

"I found this taped to the bottom of the chair Brian used in the last scene," he says. "I didn't see anybody put it there, but his name is on it."

There's no stamp, no address, just my father's stage name—Brian Edwards—printed in block letters with a Sharpie. I wave Dad over, and the moment he sees it, we're thinking the same thing. He rips open the envelope and pulls out a single sheet of paper.

"It's an address in Anderson Falls, Michigan."

He hands me the letter, typed like a ransom note with nothing but a date and time, 6:20 PM four days from now.

"Weird," Dave says. "Either of you know anyone in Michigan?"

"My wife's family," Dad says, quick-thinking enough to keep Dave in the dark. "A surprise birthday party."

"At 6:20 at night?"

"They're from the Midwest," Dad says, and being a Jersey boy, Dave doesn't question it; "Midwest" is explanation enough for any number of oddities.

"It's better than Utah," Dad says. "A two-day drive, maybe ten-hours a day."

"A plane will get you there in 90 minutes," Dave says. He pulls a jumpsuit from the rack and steps into it. "My screen debut," he smiles. "I should scrounge up some cigarettes. You can't have a prison scene without smokes."

He heads toward the prop room, zipping up the jumpsuit, the faded letters DOC stamped across his back.

I hand Dad the letter. "How did they tape it to the chair without anyone noticing?"

"If they can break into a lab, a film set is no problem," he says. "I doubt you know everyone here."

"It's a small crew," I say. "But there might be a few unfamiliar faces."

"Four days give you enough time to wrap up here before we leave," he says. "Happenstance or a polite consideration, we'll never know."

He folds the letter back into the envelope and slides it into his pocket. If we dusted it for fingerprints, the only ones found would be ours.

"I recognize the imposition," Dad says. "This is a fine film you're making, and any time away from the production is a risk. Honestly, if I had known we'd be caught, I never would have come to the house. In hindsight I should have avoided the whole episode, but the money was so tempting." He rubs his chest, rolling his neck in a stretch. "Did I ever tell you that I read for the role of Cliff on *Cheers*? I was certain they would hire me. I had it all planned. I'd get a house and your mother would have come out to L.A. to live with me. You and your brother too, of course. But they passed. They wanted a blowhard buffoon, not my interpretation of a put-upon working man demanding respect for the craft of postal delivery. I should have given them what they wanted."

"It's only two days."

"Four days, counting the return trip. An unnecessary interruption to your work. I'd understand if you changed your mind."

Is he offering me an out?

"I was rash to volunteer your participation in this boondoggle without first seeking your counsel. But the FBI is rather good at making one feel cornered and desperate."

"Mike said you were tough."

"Playacting, I assure you." He grabs the sleeve of one of the jumpsuits and holds it against his arm. "A perfect fit. Perhaps I should call the FBI and cancel the deal. Poor Henry is going back to his prison. Why shouldn't I be sent to mine?"

His eyes well up with tears, but even a bad actor can cry on demand.

"Either way Henry is screwed, but that's not your fault. Going to prison won't help."

"It helps *you*. No interruption to your film, no risk to your home. As a father, I've provided you with nothing but DNA. Your debt to me was paid the moment you took a breath."

More playacting? But whatever he's seeking I refuse to give, though I don't renege on my promise.

"It's no big deal. We drive to Michigan, we drive home. Who knows? Maybe the ALF will steal Henry again and he'll get that happy ending in a sanctuary somewhere. For now, all we do is drive to Michigan."

He touches my shoulder, an uncomfortable feeling. "Your mother would be proud."

And if her son hadn't made her back out of the driveway a fourth time, she'd also be alive.

Dad pulls a jumpsuit off the rack and steps into it, zipping up the front and pulling straight the sleeves. "How about I grab a wig and work the scene as an Extra? I'll keep my back to the camera. Prison visitation scenes need bodies. It builds the tension. I was in a jail yard scene once directed by David DeCoteau—"

"Isn't he the guy who directed *Sorority Babes in the Slimeball Bowl-O-Rama*?"

"The very same. Mr. DeCoteau had many eccentricities, but one thing I learned was..."

He continues his story, but I tune him out—Mom's ghost finally appearing on the set, standing behind the fake prison bars watching Dad and me with a blank expression, her hands resting one atop the other over her heart. Worst of all, she's wearing an orange jumpsuit, DOC stenciled across her back, my mother as celestial prisoner trapped behind bars for eternity.

"...and Mr. DeCoteau, who made terrible films but made them with integrity and a dedication to his craft, shared his theory about the grey space between performer and performance, and he praised the way I committed to the role of Prisoner #6."

Mom's ghost leans her face in the gap between the bars, and I approach her as Dad continues his droning, Dave in his prison orange slapping my back, "Almost ready, boss. It's one big jailhouse...," my mother's ghost fading into nothingness the moment I reach the set.

. . . . .

Is this how it felt in the pioneer days before someone hitched up the wagon and lit out for the territories? It's 6:00 AM, but Veronica, Mike, and Melanie have come to wish us well, Mike with a thermos of coffee, Melanie with a pre-paid phone card, and Veronica with a paperback copy of *Animal Liberation*.

My overnight bag is ready to go, and so is Henry's, a shopping bag of peanuts and oranges and the French vanilla protein shakes he loves to drink from a baby's bottle. He sits on the couch playing with a crumbled sheet of paper, unaware that his freedom is coming to an end.

"Remember, they're going to arrest you, but it's just for show," Mike says. "Don't freak out. They'll bring you to the local police station and then release you. It's for your own good. You don't want these ALF nutcases thinking you sold them out."

"Would you have called the abolitionists on the Underground Railroad nutcases?" Veronica says.

"Completely different, and not worth answering," Mike says.

"Did you remember to pack the cell phone I gave you?" Melanie asks. "You really should clip it to your belt. There was a clip in the box."

"Don't let Dad do anything stupid," Mike says. "It's not a movie, and if he gets some grandiose idea about being a hero, remind him that in a real prison you don't leave at 6:00 PM with a check for $100 and a meal voucher for the studio commissary."

"I think we can handle it," I say, and sit next to Henry, tossing him the crumbled paper ball as if we're playing catch.

The plan is simple, Agent Mahoney briefing us the night before. When we arrive in Anderson Falls, we stop at a pay phone outside a diner and call her mobile number. Then we drive to the address in the letter. The FBI will be there, though we won't see them until they want to be seen. We knock on the door, hand Henry over to the ALF, and before we can back out of the driveway, the Feds will swoop in.

Dad and Gloria come downstairs, a backpack looped over my father's shoulder, a ridiculous black cowboy hat sitting on his head.

"It's an exact replica of the one Bob Redford wore as The Sundance Kid in *Butch Cassady*," he says, tipping the hat for Veronica and Melanie. "Bob once told me they made fourteen of those hats and he still had three of them. I'm sorry I don't have one for you, Kevin. If we're going to be outlaws, we should look the part."

"Honey, I'm going to miss you," Gloria says, giving my father a loud smooch. "There's no reason I shouldn't be driving instead of Kevin. I'm not a child."

"I know, I know," Dad says, placating the little woman, "but I'll feel better knowing you're safe, and Kevin and I can use some father-and-son time. Isn't that right, Kevin?"

"You are such a good man!" Gloria says.

As she and Dad canoodle their goodbyes, Veronica steps away. I follow her into the kitchen.

"How much do you hate me?"

"Don't be dramatic," she says. "I get why you're doing this. I just think it sucks."

"We'll be back in a few days and then things will be normal again."

"What if normal is the problem? I'm complicit, too. In my closet I have sixteen pairs of leather shoes."

"You own sixteen pairs of shoes?"

"I ate a goddamn veal cutlet last week and I enjoyed it. Every other day I eat a grilled chicken sandwich...I'm as guilty as you are."

"We didn't create this world. Try not to beat yourself up. You're a good person."

She shakes her head. "I'm what we tell ourselves is a 'good person'. Isn't a failure to act against evil the same as committing evil?"

"Is this really evil? Look, I feel badly about Henry, too, and whatever crap they might have done at that lab is horrendous. But we don't know the whole story. What if they're trying to cure cancer or some childhood disease? Wouldn't that be worth it? If he was in his natural habitat, he'd probably be snack food for a cheetah. I'm not saying what they do there is good, but there's a lot we don't know. It's sad, I get it, but why does this bother you so much?"

She leans against the counter, her eyes distraught.

"Maybe I'm just questioning my whole stupid life, spending so much time thinking about *movies,* 90% of which exist only to sell popcorn and super-sized sodas. I have a master's in film theory. What's next? A PhD in Barbie Dolls? It's so trivial, so pointless. I should be doing something that matters."

"You love movies."

"Yeah, I do, but maybe that's not enough when there's so much suffering in the world."

"Life is suffering. That's Buddhism, right? See? I paid attention in philosophy class."

I hope for a smile, but her face is a black cloud.

"I promise I'll read the book."

"You'd be smarter tossing it out the window," she says. "What good is knowledge if we don't act on it?"

There's so much to say, but I'm not good with struggles of the soul, unless they're in a script, edited down to the essentials, unless I can hide behind a camera and yell "Cut" when needed. All I can offer her is a hug, which thankfully she accepts, returning the embrace and whispering "Be safe" as we break apart.

In the living room everyone wishes us good luck, and I pick up Henry and head for the door, Dad following, tipping his hat a final time and, with a well-honed Italian accent, singing, "Arrivederci!"

"I love you, Brian!" Gloria says, and I wonder again if she knows his real name.

"We should be back on Sunday," Dad says, the "we" excluding Henry, who'll be back in the lab or dead by the time we return. We've dressed him for the occasion in a child's blue overalls, the corduroy fabric pleasing to him as his tiny hands pick at the ridges. If my mother's ghost were here, she might recognize the overalls, pulled from a bin in the attic labeled "Kevin." Yet I haven't seen her since that glimpse of her face behind the prison bars on the set. Henry rests his head against my chest, his bald spot, and the pain it symbolizes, the first thing I see when I look.

Dad opens the front door, and we give our loved ones a final "goodbye!"

Across the street, in a non-descript blue sedan, Agent Mahoney watches us through binoculars, a second agent sitting beside her. They make no effort to hide, their surveillance an obvious warning, and as we walk to the car, Henry hanging onto my shoulder, my father waves to them, doffing his black Sundance hat, his free hand shielded behind the brim flashing a raised middle finger.

"I saw Bob Redford do that once to a state trooper who had pissed him off," he says, returning the black hat to his head as he gets into the car. I strap Henry in the car seat and get behind the wheel.

"And the journey begins, "Dad says. "Come on Butch, let's ride."

PART TWO: JANUARY 2000

-I-

It annoyed the hell out of her that even in church she was thinking about the movies.

Had Veronica ever been inside a cathedral of any denomination without recalling the baptism scene in *The Godfather*, Michael Corleone renouncing Satan while his henchmen dispatched his enemies in an Oscar-worthy montage? (Even after a hundred viewings she still winced when Moe Green got shot in the eye.) Stained-glass made her think of early Scorsese, images of the crucified Christ recalled the Italian Neo-Realists, and the tall ceilings and harsh wooden pews were so Ingmar Bergman it felt like the great director had built them himself, an architectural reminder of God's stony silence. Weddings, baptisms, funerals; it didn't matter—for Veronica, churches felt like film sets waiting for a director to call "Action!"

Though she'd been raised a Catholic, meaning her family went to church on Christmas and sometimes Easter, meaning she'd worn the pretty white dress for her First Communion and suffered through CCD and Confirmation (hoping that the gifts would be worth all those wasted Saturday mornings), her adult relationship with the Church was like her relationship with Wal-Mart. She accepted its ubiquity and importance in the lives of millions but avoided it on principle. Yet when Mrs. Flagler's daughter invited her to attend the memorial service for her mother at Saint Thomas the Apostle Catholic Church, it was an offer she couldn't refuse.

Among the residents at the assisted living facility where Veronica volunteered, Beatrice Flagler had been her favorite. Eighty-six years old, she'd suffered from light dementia, heart disease, and an arthritic knee, yet her long white hair had never lost its sheen, and during her weekly visits Veronica would brush it with an antique silver brush and listen as the old woman sang Big Band hits from the 1940's. "Stardust." "Swinging on a Star." "Boogie Woogie Bugle Boy." Mrs. Flagler often forgot the day of the week, but the lyrics and melodies of her youth she sang without flaw. When Veronica knew the song, and surprisingly, she often did, she'd hum along with her, brushing the old woman's hair in rhythm with the music until it was time for her to leave, each visit ending with Mrs. Flagler squeezing Veronica's hand and saying, in a frail but steady voice, "You're my best friend, dear."

Had such a lachrymose moment appeared on screen, Veronica would have chided the director for the cheap sentiment, but experiences that were hackneyed and gooey on film were often, in real life, cherished moments. "You're my best friend, too," Veronica responded, kissing Mrs. Flagler on the forehead before departing. At first it was a simple kindness to a lonely woman, but in the weeks following Kevin's disappearance, she realized that her life was lonely too, that friends were hard to come by once you left school, and that her time with Mrs. Flagler were the rare moments each week that felt like an authentic human connection. The rest was analysis and busy work and the crazed efforts to bring *Exit 23* to the screen now that Kevin wasn't around to do it himself. That she'd succeeded, that they'd won First Prize at the Garden State Film Festival despite the film's creator being missing in action, that she had a meeting the next day with one of the biggest producers in Hollywood for a potential distribution deal was testament to her fortitude and intelligence but did nothing to make her less lonely. Often it felt like Mrs. Flagler was the only person on Earth who was genuinely happy to see her. Sometimes all she wanted from a day was to brush the old woman's hair, hum a few standards, and forget the rest of the world.

But now that was over—Mrs. Flagler was dead.

Veronica had promised the woman's daughter that she'd be there for the memorial, expecting to pay her respects and slip out during the Benediction. Yet when she arrived two minutes before the start of the service, she'd found the Church empty except for Mrs. Flagler's daughter (she assumed), and a gaunt old man wearing sweatpants, a white dress shirt, and a red bow tie.

At the alter the priest lit a candle, looked at the empty sanctuary, and yawned. Two squirrels chased each other up and down the aisles, darting under the pews and climbing on the organ, their tiny paws just heavy enough to produce a single B flat. Though the Bishop had ordered him to call an exterminator, Father Blank liked the squirrels, who were often the only attendees at his 8:00 AM Mass. Maybe they were responding to God's calling, though more likely they came for the acorns and sunflower seeds Father Blank left scattered under the pews. A few times he had dialed the exterminator's number but had hung up before the first ring.

Candace Flagler, Beatrice's daughter, rushed to greet Veronica, enveloping her in a hug of surprising intimacy considering that they'd never met. She was fifty-two, short-haired and pale, her lipstick smudged at the corners, a powder blue eye shadow applied to only one eye. She wore a white cardigan sweater over a plain black dress and smelled of maple syrup. As the hug's duration continued past unexpected straight toward inappropriate, Veronica counted the days since someone had hugged her, quitting the exercise when the total exceeded one month. At the victory party for *Exit 23,* cast and crew had been all over each other, bodies mingled in celebration, yet Veronica had remained aloof, the person who she *should* have been hugging—the writer/director, in truth her only real friend—having been missing since the day he left with Henry and his father on their FBI sting mission.

Had Veronica known that Candace Flagler's daughter, of similar age, height, and weight to Veronica, had recently become a man and hadn't spoken to Candace in nearly a year, she would have understood the peculiar length of the hug. But she never found out, and when the hug finally ended, Candace Flagler dabbed her eyes with a handkerchief and thanked her for coming, the woman's voice surprisingly loud, her words echoing in the vaulted ceiling. Candace took Veronica's hand and led her down the aisle, the old man in the sweatpants and bow tie turning to watch, Veronica eyeing the empty pews in realization that this was it—no one else was coming.

Poor Mrs. Flagler, she thought, but did it matter what happened after you were dead? During her last visit they'd added "Putting on the Ritz" to their repertoire, and Mrs. Flagler had tapped both feet as Veronica had brushed her long white hair, the two of them clapping at song's end. Didn't that trump a bare attendance sheet at one's memorial?

The priest, a tall, dark-skinned man with greying hair, raised his arms, signaling his readiness, and Candace led Veronica to the front pew, Veronica stepping into the row as Candace followed, Mr. Sweatpants handing her a Hymn book and leaning in for his own hug, a second embrace of awkward endurance, his clammy hands wandering toward the border of her hips, the old man retreating only when the priest said, "Arthur, that's enough." With a triumphant grin—his dentures a string of perfect white piano keys—he winked at Veronica and squeezed her hand. *What the hell*, she thought, and winked back. Arthur straightened his bow tie and glowed.

"We're here today to remember..." Father Blank began, and Veronica's heart broke when he paused to check his notes; he'd forgotten Mrs. Flagler's name. "...to remember Beatrice Flagler, loving mother, caring friend..."

"I porked her! Twice! One time in the back of my Oldsmobile..." the old man said.

"Arthur, that's unacceptable," the priest scolded, his clenched eyebrows conveying the condemnation for which the Church was so well-known. "Please respect the sanctity of God's house."

"Well, I did pork her," Arthur said.

Veronica looked at Candace, who appeared undisturbed by the disruption. Once your mother was dead, did it matter who she had porked?

Father Blank continued, his voice lulling Veronica into a daze, all those words about Jesus's love and God's mercy washing over her like nursery rhymes, her thoughts drifting toward the movies, and how the growing secularization of society might impact the use of religious symbols in American cinema, a train of thought nearly as boring as the priest's sermon, her eyelids drooping until she pinched herself—no, Arthur had pinched her, the old goat, but at least he'd saved her from nodding off.

Or had he? The priest had left the altar and was now standing in front of the pew a mere three feet away, a solemn dignity etched across his face as he offered communion to Candace Flagler, the wafer pinched between his thumb and forefinger.

"This is the Lamb of God who takes away the sins of the world. Happy are those who are called to his supper."

Candace made the Sign of the Cross and accepted the wafer. "Lord, I am not worthy to receive you, but only say the word and I shall be healed."

With a bow of the head she closed her eyes and placed the Host in her mouth. Father Blank stepped to his left and held the wafer out to Veronica.

"This is the Lamb of God who takes away the sins of the world. Happy are those who are called to his supper."

Now this was a problem. She remembered enough from those wasted Saturdays in CCD that one needed to confess before accepting Communion. The familiar litany played in her head. *Forgive me, Father, for I have sinned. It's been...well, forever since my last Confession.*

Before her Confirmation they'd made her say Confession, a mostly phony endeavor for the then thirteen-year-old Veronica, during which she'd repented taking the Lord's Name in Vain (not really), lying to her parents (maybe a little), and being mean to her younger brother (okay—she'd give God that one) while keeping mum about sneaking into theaters to see R-rated flicks (Thou shalt not steal!) and the exploratory masturbation she'd recently begun, not specifically called out in the Ten Commandments, but condemned anyway by the married laywoman who'd taught CCD. (Anything involving pleasure seemed to earn God's wrath.) Her penance—Five Hail Mary's, Five Our Father's—had seemed reasonable enough, though she'd quit after the fourth Hail Mary and had spaced the Our Father's out over the course of a week. Her only other experience with Confession had been a condition of her First Holy Communion. Eight years old, she'd confessed to lying to her parents and stealing one of Sharon Portis's birthday cupcakes at school. Now, at twenty-six, she had a bit more to confess (pilfered cupcakes and masturbation still made the list) but no time to do it. The priest's eyes held a piercing recognition, as if he'd seen her before, her face a normal part of his weekly routine, but she was certain they'd never met. Standing before her, he offered the wafer, the transmogrified Body of Christ itself, and how could she refuse?

"Lord, I am not worthy to receive you..." she said, mumbling the rest. She took the Host and brought it to her mouth but couldn't eat it. Wasn't it disrespectful to engage in a ritual if one lacked belief? With no time to work through the ethics, she palmed the wafer the moment the priest moved on, slipping it into her pocket as Arthur accepted the Host with a hearty, "I'm not worthy, Padre, but lay it on me anyway."

The ritual complete, Father Blank returned to the altar, dodging a squirrel on the way up the steps. Hanging high on the wall behind him was a life-sized wood carving of Christ on the cross. His facial expression always looked so disappointed, Veronica thought, but why wouldn't it, considering that he was being crucified. What was he supposed to do? Smile? The craftsmanship of the carving was impressive, though Jesus resembled a hippie insurance agent from Ohio more than a persecuted mystic from the Middle East. The Church and Hollywood had that much in common: always cast a white guy in the starring role.

Father Blank lit three candles, broke out some Latin, and then it was over, the priest lifting the Staff and descending the alter steps, Candace trailing him down the aisle, followed by Veronica, then Arthur, and finally the squirrel, who dashed to the front, nearly tripping the priest on its way out the door.

After several awkward moments, the four of them standing silently by the exit as if waiting for a dismissal bell, Veronica dropped a $10 bill in the donations box and expressed her final condolences. "I'll miss her," she told Candace, shaking her hand. "Your Mom was always my favorite."

She was almost out the door when Father Blank said, "Miss, if you don't mind..." and grabbed Veronica's arm, leading her to a vestibule to the left of the exit. Confused, Veronica almost pulled away, too shocked by the priest's hand around her elbow to register the violation. Had the $10 donation been too small? But once in the vestibule, the reason became clear. The priest pointed at Veronica's pocket and said, "I need it back."

"Excuse me?"

"You put the Host in your pocket," Father Blank said. "I need it back."

"There's nothing in my pocket," Veronica said, but her hand, unable to lie, dug out the wafer and handed it to the priest. "Oh," she said, "you mean this."

"The Body of Christ."

"Isn't it more like a stand-in?"

"No," the priest said. "During the ritual of communion, the Host becomes the body of our Savior. It cannot leave the Sanctuary, and it's not appropriate for you to save it for later like a snack."

"Sorry."

"Are you?"

Veronica stared at her feet. If he was going to be a jerk about it, she might as well leave.

"It's one thing to refuse to accept our Savior, it's another to disrespect Him by stuffing the Host in your pocket."

"Sorry," she repeated, ready to flee.

"Are you?"

Her temper flared. He had his stupid wafer back. What more did he want?

"I'm here to pay my respects to a lovely woman," she said. "That's all. I didn't want Communion, but I didn't want to interrupt in the middle of your big show, so I accepted it and put it away." She was tempted to stop, but the best way to get rid of any salesman was to be blunt in one's refusal. "If you want to know the truth, I don't believe in God."

Here it comes, she thought, hellfire and damnation, Piper Laurie in Brian DePalma's *Carrie* writhing on the floor in a righteous fury. Father Blank looked at the Host, the body of Christ and the whole reason the church existed, then checked to make sure no one could see them. Veronica braced herself. Was he going to slap her?

"If you want to know the truth," Father Blank said, "I'm not sure I believe in Him, either."

He popped the Host into his mouth, took a few bites, and swallowed.

"Would you like to have coffee with me?"

• • •

After three sips of green tea, she was ready to confess.

Not her sins; those could wait. But since the day Kevin had left with Henry and his father, Veronica had been on edge, ready to burst, and so she told the priest everything: how Henry's story—the senseless cruelty, all that pain and suffering—had her questioning her relationship with non-human sentient beings, her relationships with people, even her relationship with the movies. She understood why Kevin had decided to cooperate with the FBI –he couldn't let his father go to prison—but their betrayal of Henry had made her sick, literally; after their departure she'd spent five days in bed with a headache and chills. And then Kevin had disappeared, Henry too, and while details were sparse—Special Agent Mahoney continued to act like the case had never existed and Kevin's brother had shut her out—it was clear that Kevin *hadn't* cooperated.

Something had changed and he'd made a break for it. She kept waiting for him to contact her, but he never did, and then one morning, weeks later, she opened her apartment door and found three 35mm film reels in a cardboard box with a note in Kevin's handwriting, three words on motel stationary: *Run with it.*

"It", of course, was *Exit 23,* the final cut. How he'd managed to edit it while on the run she had no idea, but Kevin had done it, and done it well—the film was, if not brilliant, the best that it had the potential to be. Now, with the festival win behind them and distribution offers on the horizon, her life was about to change. But shouldn't it be Kevin's life, and not hers, that was changing? (Well, his life *had* changed—he'd disappeared.) How could he have missed the biggest moment of his career? Was Henry already back in that hellhole of a Utah lab? And what were the moral implications of the grilled chicken sandwich she'd had for dinner the previous night? Her brain felt like the crowded stateroom in The Marx Brothers' *A Night at the Opera:* all those questions stacked up against each other waiting for the door to open so they could tumble into the light.

"You're quite the surprise," the priest said when she finished her story. "I never would have guessed. I just wanted to chat about the movies."

Father Anton Blank was thirty-nine, the only son of a Senegalese nurse and a New York pediatrician doing missionary work in the Congo, where Father Blank was born during a long and brutal civil war. When he told people this, he emphasized the violence and the trauma, Americans expecting anyone of African descent to be either starving, victimized, or both, but in truth his family had left the Congo three weeks after Blank was born. He had no memory of it, or of Africa at all, having grown up in Paris, Montreal, and finally Albany, New York, where he'd attended private school and got a brand-new BMW for his 17th birthday.

An avid reader of Veronica's film reviews, Blank had quickly made the connection between the photo accompanying the Friday film column in The Weekly Wave and the young woman playing sleight-of-hand with the Host in his Church. To Veronica's surprise, he'd attended the second of the Festival's three screenings of *Exit 23* and had loved it. Before his time in seminary he'd studied acting but had never pursued it as a career. Well, never *really* pursued it; he confessed to a cameo in a *Friday the 13th* rip-off as the culmination of two years of failed auditions. His mother still had his head shot in a frame on her dresser.

"I once auditioned for the role of a priest in a pilot that never aired," he said. "A small part—seven lines in a single scene—but the casting director hated me, told me no one would ever believe I was a priest. She clearly wanted a roly-poly Irish type with pink cheeks and green eyes, not some mixed-race joker from Senegal, but she was right about the audition: I was dreadful. Four years later I *was* a priest, though it's questionable if anyone believes me in the role."

They shared a table at the back of the Starbucks, Veronica warming her hands over a hot tea while the priest drank black coffee and devoured a scone. It was late morning, the Starbucks quiet except for a trio of stroller moms gabbing by the entrance. The priest wore the traditional black suit and white collar. The top button of his jacket showed a hanging thread that Veronica felt compelled to pluck, but she held back, wary of touching a stranger, and a priest, afraid it might seem rude, or worse, flirtatious.

"I assume you're familiar with Genesis 1:26," Father Blank said. "And let them have dominion over the fish of the sea and over the birds of the heavens and over the livestock and over all the earth and over every creeping thing that creeps on the Earth. Or if you prefer the Good News translation, which I do, 'They will have power over the fish, the birds, and all animals, domestic and wild, large and small'."

"I've heard it once or twice," Veronica said.

The priest placed his hands on the table, Veronica admiring his smooth, pink nails, all of them cut short except for his left pinkie, the curved nail extended an inch above the cuticle like a scoop.

"I appreciate your empathy for this monkey, this Henry, but perhaps his suffering is for a greater cause. Even if the experiments seem marginal, it might lead to something significant, perhaps a new drug that saves thousands of lives. God's design is vast and intricate, and we can't always see it."

"Assuming She exists," Veronica smiled.

"Yes, assuming She exists." Blank reached for his coffee. "I see you're not impressed."

"Considering all the species in the world, God really struck out when he put humans on top. We'd be better off in a world run by alpacas. Alpacas would have never come up with the Holocaust. You know what really gets me? Whenever anyone questions God, the answer is always 'we can't understand God's ways' or 'God doesn't want us to know' or 'you're too stupid to understand the great Oz. It's a cop-out."

The priest added a Splenda to his coffee and stirred.

"Is it better to assume that we live in a cold and indifferent universe, that there is no loving God to offer eternal salvation?" he said. "My faith may not be as strong as I'd like—sometimes it's downright pitiful—but I've never doubted the *need* for faith. Its usefulness, its singular ability to provide comfort to those in need. We can never truly know of all the wonders in the world, as I'm sure you'd agree, and so a leap of faith is required."

She reached into her bag and pulled out her copy of *Animal Liberation*. The priest admitted he'd never read it.

"It's kicking my ass," she said. "Because I agree with every word, and I don't live up to it. It's peculiar—I can't plead ignorance. I've known about the labs, the horrors of factory farms and the slaughterhouses, fur farms...I could go on and on...I've always known, but it's never affected me before...until I met Henry and put a face to it." She sipped her tea, avoiding the priest's eyes. "I'm not a good person, Father," she said.

Blank reached across the table and touched her hand, his one long nail accidentally scratching her thumb. "Your being hard on yourself. We all fall short of our ideals."

"No, it's more than that," she said.

She waited for Blank to respond, but the priest sipped his coffee and didn't say a word.

What am I doing? Veronica thought. In less than twenty-four hours she'd be at the Ritz-Carlton Hotel in Manhattan discussing a deal for *Exit 23* with Harvey Weinstein, producer of all those great movies—*Pulp Fiction, Good Will Hunting, Shakespeare in Love*. She had taken Kevin's film and done what he had asked—she'd run with it, from her apartment door to the Garden State Film Festival all the way to Harvey fucking Weinstein. So why was she sitting with a priest she'd just met, compelled to tell him the worst thing she'd ever done?

If only Blank would pressure her, she could snap out it, get angry, thank him for the green tea and go home, but the longer the priest remained silent, the more she wanted his attention, the dark aroma of his coffee like incense inside a church. Could the back table at a Starbucks make a proper confessional? She didn't believe in Confession, rejected the idea of Absolution, but as she watched the priest move bits of scone around his plate with the tip of his fork, his long, strange nail itching the table, she surrendered to her need to come clean.

"Shit. I guess I have to tell you." She tried to laugh, but it came out a bitter snort. "Forgive me, Father, for I have sinned."

Behind the counter the barista, a purple-haired girl with feathers hanging from both ears, rattled one of the coffee machines, banging the filter tray with a spoon. Father Blank put down his cup and turned his chair. From his pocket he removed a strand of Rosary beads.

"That's okay, Father. I don't need—"

"They're for me, not you," he said, his palm enclosing the wooden cross as the beads lay over his knuckles.

"Sorry." Behind the counter the latte machine hissed and spit steam. "I don't know why I'm telling you this."

"Because you need to tell," Blank said, neither command nor question, a statement of fact.

"I wish this were a movie instead of my life. The thing is, Father..."

The priest brought the rosary to his chest and lowered his head.

"...when I was twelve, I had a crush on this girl, Lizzie Harrow. Nothing sexual, but it was intense, and 'crush' is the only word for it. Lizzie was two years older than me, and she was prettier, more popular, more stylish, more experienced. More everything. She was cool, and when you're twelve, cool is all that matters. There was nothing I wanted more than for Lizzie to think I was cool, too. Because I wasn't, and I knew I never would be, but if I could become Lizzie's friend...some of that cool might rub off...it's stupid, right? But I was twelve."

She paused, again giving Blank a chance to speak, but the priest knew that a confession required silence more than encouragement. The rosary beads dangled over his empty plate.

"One day Lizzie and I were hanging out behind the middle school, and her boyfriend came by. Brian Moser. Jesus, he was a creep, the stereotypical high school jock, two years older than Lizzie, so four years older than me. He was good looking, and popular, and cool...there's that word again...and

Lizzie had already told me she'd given him a hand job in his father's tool shed. So that day, after about an hour, Brian joined us, which right away was a downer since I cherished every minute alone with Lizzie. Such a nerd. I just stood there giggling while Brian and Lizzie made out. I had never even kissed a boy, I'm only twelve...and then Brian said he wanted to show us something over by the soccer field. We followed him out...it was so hot that day...and underneath the bleachers we saw a mother cat with a litter of four kittens curled up in this empty pizza box.

"They were so tiny, maybe a week old, these little grey furballs that could fit in Brian's palm. The mama cat had them all against her stomach, it was the cutest thing I'd ever seen, and I was already thinking about taking one home... and then Brian picked up the smallest kitten and said, "Watch this."

Her heartbeat raced, as if she were back on the soccer field instead of fifteen years removed. She looked at Blank, her confession a whisper.

"He laughed, and then with that giant hand of his, he twisted the kitten's neck and snapped it in two. He killed it. Like it was nothing more than pulling the tab of a soda can. It was just a baby, and he killed it."

Her face grew hot, her shoulders tight as rope.

"Lizzie said something like, "Gross!" but then she started laughing, and Brian grabbed another kitten ...the mother cat hissed and swatted at him, so kicked her, and...what's the point in saying more? He killed all four of the kittens with his bare hands. I swear I heard their bones snap, each one of them. They let out the tiniest cry I'd ever heard right before he killed them, they were crying for their mother, and when he was done, he kicked the mother cat again. He wore these big hiking boots, and he smashed his heel down on her head. There was blood over the grass, and the mama's body kept twitching until he drove the edge of his boot down one last time. He kept laughing, like it was a joke, and Lizzie started laughing, and because she was cool, and I wanted to be cool like her..."

Finally, Blank spoke. "You laughed, too."

"Like a fucking idiot," she said. "I was dying inside watching the whole thing, but I smiled, and said, "Gross!" just like laughing Lizzie fucking Harrow and I didn't do a goddam thing to help those cats. I laughed ...and never said a word, and when Lizzie invited me to the mall with her and Brian the next day, I said, 'Yes'. We left those dead kittens under the bleachers like they were trash and I said yes to a trip to the mall." She grabbed *Animal Liberation* and rifled through the pages. "How do I reckon with this knowing what I've done?"

During his tenure as a priest Father Blank had heard worse confessions, but the casual brutality of Veronica's story shook him. He knew his role was to reassure her that God's forgiveness was available to all who asked for His loving mercy, but first he wanted to find this Brian Moser character and kick his kitten-killing ass.

"Father, I condemn the people in that lab who torture Henry, but how is that worse than my laughing while Brian murdered five cats?"

"Frankly, what you described is far worse than anything done in a lab," Father Blank said. "The motivation behind those experiments is valid, even if the means are illegitimate. The killing of those cats served nothing beyond satisfying the violent urges of a troubled young man and the need for acceptance by two weak-minded girls."

Not what she expected. Weren't priests supposed to offer solace? But why should he when she didn't deserve it?

"I saw Lizzie at the mall two years ago. We talked for maybe ten minutes and didn't say a word about those kittens. I had just gone for a haircut and all I could think was, 'I hope Lizzie likes it.' How pathetic. I'm a grown woman worrying that this terrible girl won't think my new haircut is cool."

"It's terrible, but also human," the priest said. "Terrible and human— those words mingle much too often." He reached across the table and touched her hand. "I can offer absolution through the sacrament of Confession, but if you don't believe in His grace, will it matter? All we'll have is an empty ritual."

"I'd like to believe ..."

"Do you? I have my doubts, but since I only know you from reading your film column, it's unfair to say. Not even the Pope could determine spiritual intention from a review of *Happy Gilmore*."

A pair of new customers approached the counter, and for a moment Veronica thought it was Brian and Lizzie. *What the hell...?* But they looked nothing like them. They were middle-aged, both women, African American. The purple-haired barista slid her hands over her apron and took their order.

"I'd love to continue...whether or not you believe in Christ, you're facing a true spiritual crisis," Father Blank said, "and that's my game. Does that sound ridiculous? I worry it does, but I like how it sounds. More urgently, I'm due to visit a parishioner this morning, and she gets quite distressed if I'm late. Perhaps you might come along? It seems more than coincidental that you told me this story before my visit to Melissa."

He shifted in his seat and pulled out his wallet.

"You want me to visit one of your parishioners? Is that even appropriate?"

"I believe so. It's more of a wellness check than a religious one. This morning is turning quite interesting, connections are starting to form. None of that will make sense to you, but every time my faith wanes, the Hand of God reveals itself, this time in your unexpected presence and that atrocious story."

He pushed the coffee away and left two dollars on the table. Though short of funds, Veronica did the same, thinking that, if the meeting with Harvey Weinstein went well, it could be a long time before she worried about money again. (Or maybe not. Her financial stake in *Exit 23* was vague. She trusted Kevin, but was he ever coming back? Perhaps it was time to negotiate her cut of the profits, but with who? Herself?) They stood from the table, Father Blank surprising her by holding out her coat like an English butler.

"Let's share a ride," the priest said. "I'm coming back this way and the drive to Melissa's can be confusing. I'd hate for you to get lost."

"What if I'm already lost?" Veronica said.

"Oh, I do like you," Father Blank said. He surprised her again by hugging her, his long arms drawing her in for a comforting embrace.

•　•　•　•　•　•

The house was an old ranch, weathered and ramshackle, accent on *shack*, the type of house that, when people passed, they immediately thought *why don't they tear that place down?* The white siding was covered with a film of green moss; shudders were missing from half the windows; the front and side grass reached to a visitor's calf, and a small tree appeared to be growing inside the house, the top branches protruding from a gash in the roof, spotted leaves bunched along the gutters.

"Not what you expected, is it?" the priest said.

"Are we location scouting for a remake of *The Texas Chainsaw Massacre?*"

"We're doing the Lord's work," the priest said. "Melissa is homebound and I help when I can. My faith in God may be weak, but my faith in this..." He gestured toward the wreck of a house. "...is rock-solid. There is no higher calling than helping others." He reached into the glove compartment for a tube of hand sanitizer. "Bring it along if it makes you feel better."

She slipped the tube into her bag as she exited the car and followed Father Blank to the front stoop, jagged cracks in the concrete of every other step, weeds growing through the crevices, the cracks snaking across each step like a weird signature. As they walked, Blank pulled a key ring from his pocket, a single tiger-striped key dangling from the fob. The priest knocked twice before sliding the key into the lock.

The door turned and Blank entered the dark house. Veronica, lagging behind, clutched her bag, her fingers tingling as if she were in a horror movie, another clueless female heading to her doom. They stood in the unlit foyer, the air sour and still, an unwashed armpit of a hallway.

"Melissa, it's Father Blank, and I've brought a friend," the priest said, reaching for the light switch. Something brushed against Veronica's leg and she jumped back, ready to bolt, but when the lights snapped on, she saw it was only an orange tabby, the cat's tail raised high as it circled her legs and rubbed its big head against her toe.

"Hello, Oscar," the priest said, pulling a bag of cat treats from his jacket pocket. The effect was immediate: a stampede of cats, Veronica's counting twelve as they swarmed the hallway, meowing and squealing as the priest rattled the treat bag, a fat grey cat dropping to the floor and rolling against the grimy hardwood, a trio of black and white kittens standing on their hind legs as they leaned against Blank's shin, stretching toward his hands. The priest scattered a fistful of treats and tossed a second handful down the hall, the cats racing after them, except for the orange one, Oscar, who sat patiently at the priest's feet until Blank kneeled to feed him from his palm.

"I get it," Veronica said. "This is my penance."

"Not at all," Father Blank said. "Cleaning the litter boxes—*that* will be your penance. Plus a few Hail Mary's, since I'm Catholic and Hail Mary's are always required." He smiled, enjoying the moment. "But first you need to meet Melissa."

They headed for the living room, Veronica watching her feet, afraid to step on a cat tail or the occasional clump of poop strewn about the floor. The deeper into the house they went, the more pungent the smell. The windows along the back wall were boarded up with cardboard, old grocery receipts pinned to each board.

Veronica waited, anticipating the arrival of a crazy old cat lady. The priest turned on a lamp—there was no lampshade, only a bare bulb atop a cracked base—and moved an abandoned plate of mac and cheese from the sofa to the end table, the plate dotted with litter pellets and a regurgitated hairball.

"Really, Melissa, the cats shouldn't be eating macaroni and cheese. It's not good for them; it's not good for *you*."

Who is he talking to? Veronica thought, but then she saw her: the crazy old cat lady.

Only she wasn't old. In the corner of the room, sitting cross-legged on a pile of bath towels and throw blankets, was a woman of Veronica's age dressed in an orange Halloween cat suit, the long fabric tail curled on her lap, face-painted whiskers on both sides of her nose, her long fingernails polished in tiger stripes. Wavy brown hair reached her shoulders, wild and uncombed. Blank approached and they touched fingernails, the priest's long nail clicking twice with each of the cat lady's claws.

"Melissa, this is Veronica," Father Blank said. The cat woman repositioned herself onto all fours, moving from her towel pile and crawling across the floor, rubbing her cheek against Veronica's leg before turning back, twitching her butt so that her tail swished from the side to side before she settled back in her lair.

"Hello," Veronica said, a black cat walking by and swatting her with its tail. "You sure have a lot of cats."

Idiot, she thought, but what else could she say? The priest patted her shoulder, his hand providing the slightest nudge forward.

"Now let's see what needs to be done," he said. "You two get acquainted; I'll be in the kitchen."

The orange cat, Oscar, followed Father Blank as they disappeared around the corner. The cat woman, Melissa, stretched out on her towel-bed, her cat suit surprisingly snug as she rolled onto her back and looked up at Veronica, strands of hair flopping over her eyes.

"Why are you here?"

Her voice was strong and deep, not the weak purr Veronica expected.

"Father Blank asked me to come along."

"He did that once before. It didn't end well." Melissa shimmied to the edge of the nest. "But I like you. I think. Maybe not. No, I like you."

Four cats came out of nowhere and jumped on the couch, then jumped into the nest, pushing their heads beneath the towels and blankets, burrowing. Two were grey, one had orange stripes, and the fourth was a pure, perfect white. Melissa petted each one, the cats rubbing and purring, dander flaking from their coats. To the left of the nest, a shabby rocking chair swayed back and forth, two cats batting the chair's legs with their front paws, nudging it with their heads.

"I'm not delusional. I know I'm not a real cat," Melissa said. "But this is how I identify. How do *you* identify?"

"I watch movies," Veronica said, by reflex. It sounded dumber than wearing a catsuit.

A grey striped kitten jumped on the rocking chair and scratched at its arms, tearing into the fabric. Melissa crawled from her nest toward a water bowl in the far corner. *She's not going to...*Veronica thought, but she did. The cat woman lowered her head and drank, her tongue lapping up the water as strands of her hair dipped into the bowl. When she was done, she wiped her chin and crawled back to her nest, petting each cat as it crossed her way.

"I think Father needs me," Veronica said, clutching her bag as she rushed toward the kitchen.

The priest stood by the sink, hot water running as he scraped food from ceramic plates.

"Dried oatmeal may be the world's strongest adhesive. I've been scrubbing this bowl for five minutes and it still won't give."

"I know what you're doing," Veronica said. "I can't help those kittens, but I can help care for these cats."

"Not at all. These cats are fine, very well cared for. You could help, certainly, but that's not where you're needed."

"This is an invasion of her privacy, like you're showing her off in the circus freak show."

"Not at all. She likes visitors."

"She's mentally ill. She should be hospitalized."

"Why? Because she's not cool? That's Lizzie Harrold talking."

"Lizzie Harrow," Veronica said. "That has nothing to do with it. This woman is not well."

"Perhaps not, by certain standards. But she has food and a roof over her head. This was her grandmother's home. Her siblings pay the utilities and the taxes; she has a small inheritance for cat food and vet bills. What would you propose for her? Medication? Locked doors in an institution where she couldn't be with the cats that she loves, and who love her?"

"You enable her delusions."

"Isn't that the job description, for a priest? Christ's divinity may be nothing more than two thousand years of myth and public relations, but to live a life of compassion and care in His name seems a worthy pursuit."

He stepped back from the sink, drying his hands on a dishtowel, and offered her a sponge.

"You wash, I'll dry," the priest said.

Her copy of *Animal Liberation* jutted from her bag as she placed it on the counter and took the sponge. She approached the sink and began scrubbing, her hands darting in and out from under the hot spray, the dried mac and cheese refusing to budge. *This is nuts*, she thought. Why wasn't she preparing for her meeting with Harvey Weinstein instead of helping a weird priest clean up after an even weirder young woman? She used her fingernail to scratch off the final bit of hardened cheese and handed the clean plate to the priest, who toweled it dry, Oscar the cat standing between them, fascinated by the running water.

"There's nothing you can do about those kittens, is there? But there's something you can do right now, and that's to be a friend to Melissa."

I should have never told him that story, she thought. "I don't even know her—"

"Before you object," Blank said, "consider what's happened today. At the church, when I confronted you about the Host, you could have lied. What would I have done, strip searched you until I found it? No—you could have left with the body of Christ in your pocket and gone your merry way. Then, when I asked if you wanted to have coffee with me, you could have refused. Why would someone who takes meetings with Hollywood moguls have coffee with a priest she just met? It doesn't make sense even to me. But you said yes. Even stranger, when I asked you to accompany me on a chore, you didn't ask for any details. You just got into my car and came along. Curious, right? I'm sure Melissa and I seem strange to you, but from my perspective, it's *your* behavior that seems the most unexpected. I'm sure if you asked the last thousand people who met with Mr. Weinstein to negotiate a film deal, none of them spent the day before accompanying a priest on his daily rounds. So why am I telling you this? Because you *want* to be here; otherwise, you'd be somewhere else."

Veronica grabbed a dirty mug and let the hot water stream over her hands, closing her eyes as her heartbeat quickened.

"You can never go back and change the past, but today, right now, you can act in a way that adds to the storehouse of human kindness. Hey, I like that." He put down the towel, produced a small red notebook from his pocket, and jotted down the phrase. "For Sunday's sermon. You'd be surprised how tough it is to come up with something new each week. The storehouse of human kindness...I can use that."

The priest stepped to the sink, turned off the faucet, and set his hand on Veronica's shoulder.

"You're probably thinking, 'why is this guy preaching at me?' But it's part of the job. I may not convert many people to Christ, but if they become converts to kindness, I'll take it, every time."

Veronica put down the mug and took long, deep breaths, the tension in her body like a million termites gnawing on her skin. Everything had happened so fast. Was she *really* expected to meet with Weinstein and act like she knew what she was doing? Kevin had asked her to run with it, not run smack into a brick wall. Since he and Henry had left, she'd either been working on *Exit 23* or beating herself up with questions that *Animal Liberation* made unavoidable. The priest had a point. She was there of her own volition. Maybe some time with a crazy cat lady was exactly what she needed.

She turned and faced the priest. "Okay."

"Okay? Really?" He touched her arm gently, then stepped back. "I expected a debate. You certainly do surprise me."

She headed to the living room, where thirteen cats, one of them human, sat staring as only cats can stare, as if the stare might last forever. Slipping off her shoes, she walked over to the nest.

"May I join you?" she asked, knowing cats were territorial. Melissa flexed her nostrils, then scooted toward the edge, patting the vacated space. How long had it been since the towels and blankets had been laundered? Too long. But when she thought of Henry in his cage, forced to live in his own feces, the towels seemed exactly what she deserved.

Veronica settled in as Melissa groomed her face, licking her hand cat-like before rubbing it over her cheek. From the hallway Father Blank observed with a hopeful smile.

How do I talk to a crazy cat lady? Veronica thought, but the answer seemed obvious: the same as with anyone else.

"Is that just for show or is that really how you wash your face?" she asked.

Melissa paused, her hand in mid-air, studying Veronica, calculating a level of trust. She gave her hand another lick and said, "Both."

Veronica, all in, gave it a try: she licked her hand and brought it slowly across her chin.

"Feels good, doesn't it?" Melissa said.

"I have a facial scrub at home that feels better. It's made from coconuts."

The cats, curious about the strange new visitor, gathered around the nest, some approaching with trepidation, others rubbing against Veronica, walking across her lap or, as one black cat did, jumping onto her shoulders and batting her hair. Eight cats, not counting Melissa, swarmed and circled over the blankets and towels.

Oscar, clearly the cat in charge, watched from ten feet away.

"Lady Di, stop that!" Melissa said, shooing away a grey kitten who had mistaken Veronica's leg for a scratching post. Oscar ran over to investigate.

"That one is adorable," Veronica said, pointing at a white and orange longhair.

"That's Chandler. He's a nightmare when I'm trying to sleep."

She offered her hand for Chandler to sniff.

"So, what's with the cat suit? I like cats, too, but I don't pretend to be one."

For a moment she thought she'd blown it; it was too much, too soon. But Melissa kept grooming, undisturbed, as Oscar joined them in the nest.

"I have psoriasis," Melissa said. "Pretty bad. I don't want anyone to see my skin. I'd prefer to be a cat."

"I'd prefer to be blonde," Veronica said.

If Lizzie Harrow could see me now, she thought. Could anything be more uncool?

Father Blank watched the two women conversing, wondering, as always, whether it was the Hand of God or pure coincidence that had brought the three of them together, along with twelve cats, on a cool January morning. He'd long given up on flamboyant expressions of God's presence—the one burning bush he'd seen was the result of some idiot's tossed cigarette—but he still hoped that God's machinations might be visible in the tiny victories of everyday life.

"That's Gretchen, and that's Alex, and that one over there is Mr. Snuffles," Melissa said, naming each cat as she pointed. "Everyone is here except Miles. He's too shy, but he'll come around, and when he does, he's a real lover. Now that you and I are best friends, we'll be seeing each other all the time. When you come tomorrow—"

Best friends? Veronica thought. *I can't come tomorrow. I'm meeting with Weinstein.*

"—I'll show you the tree that's growing in the guest bedroom. The cats love climbing it. Me, too, on really bad days when my skin is out of control."

By the foyer Father Blank held Veronica's bag in one hand and a litter scoop in the other, the paperback spine of *Animal Liberation* sticking out as if it too were observing. There was nothing in the book about women who pretended to be cats, but there was plenty about compassion, dignity, and respect. She could never bring back those murdered kittens, or even atone for all the chickens and cows and pigs that had been killed for the benefit of her plate, but this she could do.

"...that's Horace...he's terrified of the doorbell, so you'll need your own key..."

Though straight-faced, Father Blank was giddy inside. *This just might work*, the priest thought.

Rolling onto his back, Oscar waited for Veronica to pet him. She reached over and stroked the side of his head, his purr growing stronger, Melissa rubbing her face against Veronica's arm with her own soft purr, and soon Veronica was petting them both, her hand moving between Oscar and the cat woman, undoubtably the strangest moment of her life.

It felt like an ending. *Fade Out*, she thought. No—*Fade In*. A new beginning.

—1—

PART THREE: AUGUST 1999

-I-

"Look at it this way," Dad says, the brim of his black Sundance hat pulled low over his forehead, "we get to hit the open road and see America, and Uncle Sam's paying for the gas."

Not quite. In three hours we've gone exactly forty-five miles, the only "America" on view being the rusted back fender of the Ford Taurus in front of us and the yellow Roadwork signs spaced every hundred yards as a reminder of why exactly we're in gridlock Hell. In the backseat Henry plays with a tangerine, content to rub his fingers over the smooth rind. He's strapped into a car seat, dressed in blue overalls, and any onlookers would assume he's my son, his grandfather in the passenger seat, three generations on the drive back to grandmother's house for dinner.

"That's one sweet hog," Dad says, eying the Harley Davidson two lanes over. "I rode one of those in *Race with The Devil.* Did you ever see it? Peter Fonda and Warren Oates. I played one of the dancing Satanists, though you can't see my face because of the mask. I *almost* got cast as the Gas Station Attendant. Man, I could have really brought that part alive. It would have been a game changer."

In the cupholder between us he's stashed a roll of breath mints, a can of soda, and a tube of pineapple-scented lotion. For the tenth time since we've left, he squeezes a dab from the tube and applies it to his neck, gently massaging beneath his chin. He pulls down the sun visor and checks his face in the mirror.

"We were on location in Texas, a real wild set. Whenever Pete was around, the pretty ladies were close by; he'd open a case of champagne, share a little smoke, and let's just say the ladies were generous with their affections, even with the extras. Good times."

I've never seen the film, a mid-Seventies slice of exploitation crap.

"Weren't you married, with a wife and two kids back home? Did you share that fact with the pretty ladies?"

"I shared *everything* with the pretty ladies," he laughs, nudging me with his elbow like a good-time Charlie bragging at the neighborhood bar, and then he remembers. While he was chasing after Fonda's groupies, Mom was working full-time and raising two kids alone.

"Hell, things were different back then," he says, his face flush as he flips the visor upright. "It was important for your career to socialize with the stars, and as you know, an actor needs to experience life. It's essential to the practice of one's craft."

Infidelity as a job requirement. It's artful bullshit par excellence, and I'm ready to lash into him. Though she's dead (and I'm to blame), I will be my mother's champion and scold him for his marital sins, but in the rear-view mirror I see Henry with a tangerine, moving it back and forth between his hands, playing catch with himself, his attention rapt, and my anger wanes. A few times he's winced when we raised our voices, shutting his eyes and biting a toe until we stopped.

"It looks like traffic is breaking," Dad says, popping a breath mint. He points ahead, cars accelerating toward open lanes.

It's clearly a conversational dodge, but he's not wrong. Suddenly everything is moving, and for the next twenty minutes we drive without speaking, a welcome silence interrupted only by Henry's occasional squeak.

On auto pilot, I think about *Exit 23;* with principal photography wrapped, the grind of post-production awaits. If only we had the funds for a professional editing suite. As I start crafting a pitch to Monica and Bob for an infusion of cash, the rear-view mirror fills with an approaching grey sedan. It slows and hangs four car lengths behind, but something feels off. I change lanes, and so does the sedan. I speed up, slow down, speed up, and like a mirror image the other driver never leaves my rear-view, the windshield close enough for me to see the driver: a single man in dark shades and a buzz-cut, a G-man type for sure. When the left lane clears, I slow down again, but he doesn't pass.

"I think they're following us."

Dad checks the side-view mirror. "We're small potatoes. They'll be there in Michigan, but why follow us now? They've got real criminals to track."

"I'm going forty on the Interstate, and the guy behind us isn't passing or shooting me the finger. Seems strange."

"It's just nerves. Totally understandable, for a beginner. Back in '84, three cops trailed me for a hundred miles..."

"That was an episode of *The A-Team*. You were in the backseat and didn't say a word."

"Believe me, it's more nerve-wracking being followed when it's a network show. You're doing fine, Kevin. If you want to test him, pull off at the next exit for a bathroom break."

"We're behind schedule. I'm not stopping for another fifty miles."

"The last sign said there's a Wa-Wa at the next exit. We can use the restroom, and if this joker is tailing us, we'll know. I think it's a good idea." He slides off his hat, resting it on his lap. "Give your prostate another forty years and you'll think so, too."

"You can't wait fifty miles?"

"I was once on set with the legendary Mr. Fred Astaire, and he said—"

"Do you have any stories that don't involve name-dropping? I get it. You need to pee, so we'll stop. I don't need to hear that the 'legendary Mr. Fred Astaire' also needed to pee. Who are you trying to impress? I don't care about Fred Astaire and neither does Henry. He's more impressed by a tangerine."

At the sound of his name Henry perks up, his legs kicking at the sides of the car seat. In the rear-view mirror I see his smile.

"I'm not name-dropping," Dad says. "I can't help it if my life intersects with the lives of so many famous people. Bob Redford once told me..."

"Bob Redford told you nothing. Every conversation between us sounds like a bad segment on *Entertainment Tonight*. I'm sick of it."

I'm about to go off on him when the tangerine hits me in the back of the head. Chastened, we drive in silence for another two miles. When I flash the turn signal for the exit, the sedan signals too. Dad peeks over the seat for a better view.

"Okay, he's definitely a Fed, but so what?" he says. "We're working *with* them. For the next few days, we're Feds, too."

"I'm not a Fed...I'm just helping you stay out of jail."

"And it's appreciated. But you're still a Fed. One time..." He stops, saving me a story about his gig as a gangster's flunky on the old series *The*

FBI. "I've heard those animal rights people can get rough. Maybe they're following us for protection."

The sedan continues its tail, making the same right at the exit light and following for 1.7 miles until we reach the Wa-Wa on the left, but instead of turning when we pull into the lot, the other car keeps driving down the road, signaling for a right as it moves out of view. I find an empty spot as Dad rolls down the window and pounds the hood, whooping it up *Dukes of Hazard* style.

"Smooth driving, Butch. You lost him."

Since it's too hot to leave Henry alone in a parked car, I shift into Neutral and wait while Dad heads for the restroom. I grab the tangerine from beneath the brake pedal, but Henry has fallen asleep again, his eyes shut, mouth half-open, the pink palms of his hands resting on the car seat buckle. He looks peaceful, innocent, words I know are projections but still feel true. If he were a human baby, would I be turning him over to an uncertain fate?

I reach into the bag of snacks Veronica packed and chomp a few pretzels, imagining Dad trying to bullshit the cashier that he's on "a government mission" and worthy of a free Decaf.

When I turn to check on Henry again, suddenly the sedan is back, Mr. Dark Sunglasses maneuvering into the adjacent spot. My stomach turns queasy as he shuts the engine and exits the car, a 40-year-old guy in a short-sleeve dress shirt, the yellow fabric stretched over his paunch, striped tie hanging loosely, dark shades halfway down his nose.

I consider a quick getaway, squealing tires, burnt rubber, the chassis scraping pavement, but it only reminds me of my mother's death. Dad is right: we're already caught, already working for the man. What's he going to do? Rough me up for giving my father a pee break?

I roll down the window. "You're following us."

"I'll neither confirm nor deny that." He removes the shades and drops them into his shirt pocket. "Lower the back window, please. I'd like to see the animal."

He leans through the window and touches Henry's head, as if confirming I didn't switch him with a Cabbage Patch Doll. Henry stirs, rubs his good eye, makes his *meek-meek* sound and turns his face away from the G-man, who steps back, checks his surroundings, then opens the passenger door and gets in the car.

"Hey, don't you need a warrant, or probable cause?"

"Relax, I'm not here to hassle you." He gives Henry a quick scan. "You've dressed him as a child, which is smart, but understand that he's an adult, a mature capuchin."

"I'll buy him a beer with dinner."

He offers his hand. "I'm Wally, though that's not my real name. You'll never know my real name. I both am and am not who you think I am. I'm with the Bureau, but not always."

"I appreciate the confusion."

From his pocket he pulls out a baggie of pumpkin seeds and peanuts.

"They're for the monkey. You're calling him Henry, right? We have a lot invested in his welfare, in giving him the chance for a peaceful life."

"We? You're with the ALF?"

"There is no ALF, not as you see it. We don't have membership cards or pay monthly dues. The Animal Liberation Front is just a name utilized whenever well-meaning people take action to alleviate the suffering of non-human sentient beings." He shifts in his seat and watches Henry sleep. "Are you aware of what he's been through?"

"I've seen the scars."

"That's the least of it," Wally says. "He was part of a study on isolation and sensory deprivation. Taken from his mother at birth, locked in a metal cage, kept in darkness and fed through a tube. That's the first six months of his life, and those are the *good* months. He's one of the lucky ones. They got him out before he was broken. What you're seeing now, in his behavior, is the work of some very good people. Their anonymity was jeopardized, and that's when your father got involved. We needed a way to transport him fast."

He looks out each window, his eyes catching every corner of the parking lot, then exits the car, leaving the door open as he reaches into his sedan and grabs a DVD. He slides back into the car and shuts the door.

"Stop at a hotel and watch this," he says. "Within a minute you'll be crying. Give it two minutes and you'll be sick. After three minutes your life will change, unless you're a monster."

My instincts say not to trust him. If he's with the ALF, why not take Henry and disappear? With his striped tie and military hair, he looks too much the G-man not to be the real thing. Unless it's intentional—a rouse so obvious that it raises doubt. It's a test, but of who?

"I joined the Bureau to protect America and keep bad things from happening, not to hunt people whose only crime is compassion" he says. "I understand why you're doing this—I've read the file—but I know your heart is with us."

It's flattering to hear someone acknowledge my goodness, but how could a stranger know what's in my heart? Am I good? *I* don't even know.

"I'm just a filmmaker. We're selfish control freaks."

"I'm a Federal agent. We're bureaucratic and heartless. But people change. Watch the DVD and know that you're not in this alone."

Turning again, he sees my father walking toward the car, a six-pack of Pepsi in one hand, a bag of chips in the other, the black hat angled on his head.

"I watched the tape of your father's interrogation," Wally says. "Does he really know Robert Redford? He must have been a fun dad."

I ignore him. "I don't get why you're here. What am I supposed to do?"

"Don't deviate from the plan, but know there's another plan, *our* plan. That's why I'm here. So that you know we're working to save him."

"Why not take him now?" I say, though the idea of turning Henry over feels like a mistake.

"It's not part of the plan, yet."

He reaches back and touches Henry's feet. The monkey turns in the car seat, scratches his head, *meek-meek,* Wally's face transforming, his clenched mouth opening to a grin.

"Isn't he wonderful?" he says.

The passenger door opens; Dad leans in, tipping his hat.

"Have I been replaced by the understudy?"

Wally turns, scans my father, then offers me his hand.

"Have a good day, Kevin," he says. "We appreciate what you're doing."

"I'm sure you do," I say, but which "we" does he mean? And what exactly am I doing? He exits the car, stepping aside as Dad takes his seat.

"And who might that have been?" Dad says, closing the door. "Friend or foe?"

Behind the wheel of the sedan, Wally offers a salute, then backs away.

"Both, I think."

"I'll be glad when this is over. I miss my wife."

It feels like the first honest thing he's said. I give Henry the tangerine, shift into Reverse, and once more we're on the road.

• • • •

We stop for the night at a hotel outside of Youngstown, Ohio. I could have kept driving, put another hundred miles behind us, but it seemed wrong keeping Henry strapped in a car seat for hours on end. His face in the rear-view mirror is a near-constant presence, his dead eye staring into nothingness while his good eye watches me. Perhaps his smile is a capuchin's normal expression—I know absolutely nothing about monkeys—but he seems to be enjoying the trip.

Dad's gone to the hotel bar, proclaiming a need for a cocktail before sleep, though what he really wants is an audience. Since my outburst, he's kept his tongue, his stories and name-dropping stripped from our conversation, leaving us zero to talk about except the traffic, the weather, and mundane observations about Henry. The first hour was bliss, a respite from his Hollywood hogwash, until the boredom of the open road kicked in, each stretch of interstate pretty much the same, and I yearned for another Bob Redford story, bullshit or not.

Growing up in the shadow of his absence, imagining my father's show-biz life had been a favored activity; in school I'd daydream tales of his on-location antics and celebrity shoulder-rubbing. I craved his voice, his attention, the aura of celluloid success. So why are they now an annoyance? Once Henry's gone, chances are he and Gloria will head back to Indiana and I'll never see him again. Why not enjoy now what I wanted so badly as a child?

"I should be more forgiving," I say, but Henry's not interested in hearing my plans for self-improvement. Relishing the space of the open hotel room, he's created a makeshift obstacle course, and with tangerine in hand, he jumps from one bed to the next, leaps to the floor, jumps on a chair, then grabs the lamppost and swings around it before jumping onto the desk, scurrying across the bureau and hopping back onto the bed, where he rolls in a somersault before starting the whole routine over, from bed to bed to floor to lamp. It's an impressive feat, and while maybe it's nervous energy, I suspect it's just play; he's having fun, and I'm tempted to join him, the hours in the car leaving me tense and sore, too, but sudden movements seem to freak him, and he's entitled to his playtime. I've changed him, fed him a plate of orange slices and lettuce leaves, and freed him from the overalls, leaving him in nothing but a fresh diaper for the night.

The DVD from Wally, or whoever he is, sits next to the TV, almost daring me to view it. The footage will be brutal, and since I'm already sympathetic to Henry's plight, what's the point in watching?

In film school we studied documentary footage shot during the Allied liberation of a concentration camp, Bergen-Belsen, I think, though the name doesn't matter. We watched stone-faced as the film played in our cramped screening hall, the professor sparing us her usual incessant commentary, Veronica sobbing, maybe all of us sobbing at the image of a bulldozer pushing hundreds of emaciated corpses into an open grave. When the film ended, we remained silent, in the dark, everyone ruminating on the historical awfulness, swearing that such an atrocity could never happen again, until the professor uttered a single word: "Srebrenica."

It was 1995 and it *was* happening. We were film geeks, worlds away from the poly-sci students with their seminars and deep analysis of foreign affairs, but we still caught glimpses of starving men on the newsstand covers of *Time* and *Newsweek*, their ribs protruding, their faces hopeless behind barbed wire. We knew about Rwanda the year before; details were vague, except for the word *machete*. Dave and I signed a petition in Bryant Park that had something to do with UN peacekeeping forces, and we'd felt righteous and involved, but when had a petition ever stopped a machete?

"Srebrenica," the professor repeated, and we discussed the imperative to bear witness, the ethical trapdoors of filming human suffering, and whether as filmmakers we had a moral obligation to put down the camera and act.

We left that screening room shaken and depressed, then headed to our next class, a workshop on lighting.

"Srebrenica, that's some real fucked-up shit," Dave said, and for a moment we were somber and thoughtful until someone (My God, I think it was me) said, "Let's send Rambo," and suddenly we were back to what we knew and loved, the movies, everyone's energy rising as here was a conversation we knew how to have. Dave countered with sending Schwarzeneggar instead, and the debate began: who was tougher, Rambo, Arnold, or Bruce Willis from *Die Hard*? If you were stuck in a concentration camp, who you gonna call? So much for thoughts of bodies in open graves; so much for thoughts of it happening *now*.

Humans have a great capacity to acknowledge horror and then make a joke about it, an observation I shared with my classmates, and then made a joke. But what could you do? Whoever ran the camps in Bosnia didn't care what a bunch of film students thought. We didn't even know if Srebrenica was a country or a city. I still don't.

Henry, enjoying his obstacle course, again makes his circuit from bed to floor to bed, *eeka-eeka,* the tangerine still in hand.

Is there a moral obligation to watch the DVD? I grab the phone and call Veronica, who doesn't answer, so I call Mike, but again no answer. This seems right. Moral issues should be wrestled with alone, even if I'm left in a philosophical half-nelson, my face flat against the mat. If I watch the footage of monkeys being tortured, I will vow to my core never to turn Henry over to the FBI. Yet when the moment arrives, that's exactly what I'll do. Does it make me a monster, the same way everyone who bites into a chicken sandwich is a monster, the horrors of the factory farms and the slaughterhouse killing lines hardly a secret?

And if we're all monsters, maybe none of us are, and the imperative to act is negotiable.

I could pack Henry into the car and take off, but to what end? Where would I go? If there is no good answer, am I still required to act? The seminar in my head could go on all night and I'd never resolve it. What I want is for someone to tell me it's not my fault. But that's exactly what they told me when my mother was killed—*Kevin, it's not your fault*—but I knew otherwise, and even if in some complicated chain of causation I was absolved, Mom was still dead.

Henry doesn't care about fault. He just wants his tangerine and someplace to live where no one implants electrodes into his brain.

He completes another somersault, but instead of jumping to the floor he hops onto my shoulders and rubs the tangerine in my hair. *Meek-meek.* Sometimes it seems that he craves connection, the touch of another body, confirmation that he's no longer alone. I listen to him breathe, his head against mine.

He trusts me, I think. A definite mistake.

· · · · ·

Dad sits at the hotel bar, chatting up the waitress, a middle-aged blonde in black slacks, a waitress's smock, and flat-soled shoes. She appears amused by his banter, smiling and touching his shoulder, her tolerance for bloviating old guys and their eventual tips a key part of her weekly pay. I scan the room for my mother's ghost but doubt she's made the trip. Dad's in his element, holding court, and his smile shrinks as I approach the bar, his eyes switching from the waitress's warm face to the grim countenance of his youngest son, but he is nothing if not a pro who can play a scene.

"Consider this your lucky day," he tells the waitress, swiveling his bar stool to greet me. "Liz, this is my son, Kevin Stacey. Remember that name. You're gonna see him on the TV one day winning an Oscar for Best Director."

The waitress, Liz, offers her hand, beaming as if I've arrived with a red carpet and swirling spotlights. My father, the old goat, will say anything to impress a woman. Or is it me he's flattering, hoping to win me over with predictions of my future success? The possibility of his sincerity is a thought that doesn't stick.

"Hon, what can I get you?" Liz says. To be called "hon" by a Midwestern barmaid seems a milestone. I order a rum and coke. "Be right back, sweetie."

I take the stool next to Dad.

"Good to see you out and about. A single guy in the proximity of a hotel bar shouldn't be spending the night with a monkey. Not without appraising the local talent first."

He raises his glass in salute, nodding toward two women in a booth by the jukebox.

"Not bad, right? Should we send them a drink?"

Two blondes, one chubby, the other bone thin, both too young to drink, share a plate of French fries in the corner. The chubby one's T-shirt displays a dark green four-leaf-clover image stretched over her cleavage. A sign?

"When it comes to women, first impressions often change after the arrival of a cocktail. In ten minutes that plump one might seem delicious."

"Will you stop? It's not charming or rakish...you sound like a dirty old man."

"Just trying to embrace life. And she's not for me; I'm married. I'm looking out for your welfare, son."

Liz reappears with my rum and coke, Dad continuing his spiel, the obligatory "Bob Redford" reference impossible to miss, my father winking as he says it, Liz all giggles and grins until a table of six waves her over for a second order of drinks. I sip my watered-down cocktail.

"We need to talk about Henry. What we're doing is wrong."

It's not what he wants to hear. He swivels the stool and faces the bar.

"He's stolen property, being returned to his rightful owners. It's not wrong."

"You know what happens in those labs."

"I have an idea, but I don't really know, and neither do you. You're a smart kid, Kevin, but you know about movies, not science. Me, too. I'm an actor, not a technician. Should we really make decisions on matters we know nothing about? I like Henry, but it's rather arrogant thinking you know better than the National Institute of Health."

"Maybe..."

"I've seen his scars. It's one of the reasons Gloria and I agreed to hide him. Yes, I did it for the money, but I wanted to help, too. I hate thinking about him suffering, but I can't say for sure, and neither can you, that whatever experiments they're doing don't serve the greater good. It's bigger than us."

He grabs a handful of free peanuts, tossing them into his mouth one by one. "And I don't want to go to jail."

I can't fault him on that. "Maybe you won't. Mike said there was a problem with the warrant. We could go back and fight it on a technicality."

"I find that strategy the equivalent of a Hail Mary. I'm not a football fan, but I know that whoever throws the Hail Mary usually loses. But even if it works, Henry remains stolen property. No technicality can change that."

On the TV screen above the bar someone hits a home run, the three truckers to our left clinking their beer mugs with hearty chants of 'fuckin' A!' Dad's right. Banging my head against the ethical wall won't alter the facts, and any decision toward action implodes in the absence of a plan. For Henry, there's only one good ending: that Wally really *was* with the ALF and liberates him before we arrive in Michigan for the sting.

"I admire your wanting to help him, sincerely," Dad says, "and I'm grateful for your company on this lousy boondoggle. You didn't have to agree...but I wanted time with you, even if only a few days. The way you carried yourself on the set was impressive. You're a damn fine director, or will be, once you believe in yourself. I never got that one break, that chance to realize my dream beyond standing in the shadows while the real actors worked, but Kevin, my God... you've got a shot to be someone special."

He squeezes my shoulder and pinches my cheek like he did when I was six. Even then I hated the pinched cheek, but his attention was gold. During his rare visits home he'd promise me a bedtime story, pinching my cheek before waving me upstairs, and I'd curl under the covers, counting down from two hundred to one and then back to two hundred as I waited, but he never came for the promised story, usually falling asleep on the couch hoping for a glimpse of himself in some B-movie on cable, and when Mom came to turn off the lamp and leave her four-leaf-clover beside me, I'd wonder what played on TV that was so much better than me.

The pride seems real as he praises my filmmaking skills and the wit and emotion of my script, but is it acting? The two blondes with the French fries watch us, the chubby one with the four-leaf-clover T-shirt, who's kind of cute, flashing a friendly smile, and for a moment I'm tempted, by the blonde *and* my father's flattery, until I remember Henry and that goddamn lab.

"I get that it's bigger than us. But don't you feel like we're turning in Anne Frank?"

Dad nods, his eyes growing soft as he embraces me, then bursts out laughing.

"Such a melodramatic mind! He's a monkey...a stolen monkey we're returning to his rightful owners." He shakes his head, still chuckling. "My

God...with that kind of mind you'll go far indeed! Anne Frank...that's ludicrous, Kevin, and insulting to six million Jews. We're talking about a monkey!"

He hops off the stool and walks toward the center of the bar, his mug and his voice raised as he addresses the crowd.

"Ladies and gentlemen, if I can have your attention, please."

It's 10:00 PM in a hotel bar in Youngstown, Ohio where nothing ever happens. Maybe there are thirty people here, most of them truckers or retirees, weary and bored souls whose attention is rarely sought. Dad puffs his chest as if delivering an Oscar speech and every eye focuses on the two of us, anticipation high that maybe the old fool will buy a round of drinks.

"Friends, this young man standing next to me..." He lifts my arm as if I've just won a heavyweight bout. "...is the writer-director of a new film called *Exit 27*..."

"*Exit 23*," I whisper.

"...*Exit 33*. It won't be released until next year but when you see it, you'll love it, and you'll tell your family and friends that you were once in a bar in Youngstown, Ohio with the film's creator. Yes, that's right...imagine telling someone you met Orson Welles before the release of *Citizen Kane*. Consider yourself lucky..."

Behind us the bartender mumbles, "Who the fuck is Orson Welles?"

"When you see the film, he won't be there for you to give him the standing ovation he deserves, so why don't we all raise our glasses..."

Welcome to the most embarrassing moment of my life.

"...and give him the applause he so richly deserves. Ladies and gentlemen, the writer-director of *Exit 43*, my son, Kevin Stacey!"

If I start running now, can I make it back to the room before I hear the word 'asshole'? But the people of Youngstown are gracious. Liz the waitress starts clapping, followed by the chubby blonde and her anorexic sidekick, and a bearded guy in a trucker hat pushes back his chair and stands to applaud. Others follow, my father waving his arms in encouragement, and suddenly I'm in the middle of my first standing ovation. A middle-aged couple enters the bar, looks around, and starts clapping, too, the man whistling through his fingers, the woman standing on her toes for a better view, and at the back of the room Mom's ghost claps along with the crowd. She's dressed for the occasion in a short black dress, bare-shouldered, her lucky pendant laid against her smooth, slender neck, and when she reaches out with her upturned palm, I'm drawn to her, but the name on her lips is my father's, not mine. It's him she's come to see. Can I blame her? He may have abandoned her, but directing her death scene was all on me.

The applause continues, the crowd eager to share in my assumed glory. If only they knew that *Exit 23* is an unedited mess. If only they knew I'm transporting a monkey to his doom.

"Thank you," I say, waving, and for the moment, it feels good, however undeserved.

"Remember everyone," Dad says, "*Exit 33*...coming soon to a theater near you."

As the applause fades, four people approach me for an autograph, which I graciously provide, scribbling my name and *See You at the Movies* on the backs of napkins and credit card receipts, Dad fighting the urge to offer his autograph, too. I downplay the moment, it's just a bar in Youngstown, Ohio and no one knows who the hell I am, but the energy and enthusiasm is strong, and I lean into the moment as if I've been signing autographs for years. When the chubby blonde touches my shoulder, she's close enough for me to see the French fries salt in the corner of her lips.

"Sometimes all we get is Chuck Norris around here," she says, "but I'm gonna see your movie the day it's released even if I have to drive to Cleveland."

"I love Cleveland. Maybe I'll see you there," I say, just like my father would. It's cheesy but being him is more fun than being me. "We're negotiating with Robert Redford for my next film. Bob loves the script, and if we get Meryl Streep for the female lead..."

Blondie hands me a napkin with her room number written in magenta lipstick. Someone sends us a drink, and Dad puts his arm around my shoulder, whiskey breath hot on my neck.

"Do you really want to throw this all away for a monkey?"

•   •   •   •   •

When we return to the room, Henry is gone.

We look everywhere—under the bed, behind the curtains, in the closet. We call his name and pull up the bedding, check behind the mini-bar, look in our bags, even make that *meek-meek* sound in a foolish attempt to speak monkey —but there's no sign of him, and when I rattle his baggie of nuts and seeds, he doesn't come running.

"It must be the ALF. They saw their chance and grabbed him."

Dad punches the air, barely missing the TV. "Goddamn it. No way will the Feds believe this. They'll think we're in on it."

"But we're not. They can't prove anything."

"They don't need to prove it. They can prosecute on the original charges. There's no deal if we don't deliver." He paces the room, his shoulders hunched like a man on death row. "My God, I'm going to prison."

Henry's blue overalls remain on the dresser along with his water bottle. Why didn't they take them? I look for evidence of a break-in or a note left behind, but there's nothing except the flashing red light on the bedside phone. I hit the button for voicemail.

"This is Special Agent Donna Mahoney," the message plays. "We expected you to be further west. You'll need to be on the road by 7:00 AM to get back on schedule. Call my number at 6:30 AM for further instructions. Everything is set for the arrest tomorrow. Remember, you need to be there at 6:20 PM, Anderson Falls. Arrive at the designated location with 576-A24. That's it. We'll handle the rest."

576-A24. She still won't say his name. Dad sits on the bed, head in his hands, his right leg shaking.

"I'm an old man. I can't handle prison. They'll make an example of me. Forget minimum security, they'll send me to a Supermax. I won't survive the first month."

"Don't jump to conclusions. Let's call Mike and get some advice."

"Your brother is a real estate lawyer. I never had proper counsel."

He paces again, rubbing his chest. A tuft of white fur stands out against the dark rug.

"Maybe we can locate another monkey and turn it over in Henry's place," Dad says. "No one will ever know...they all look alike, don't they? We need to find a pet store."

He pulls open the end table drawer, tosses the Bible and some stationary onto the bed.

"Where the hell is the phone book?"

"Dad, try to calm down."

He yanks open the top bureau drawer, the middle one, and then the bottom, and suddenly there's Henry, curled in the wooden drawer hugging a roll of toilet paper, the tangerine between his feet.

"Oh, thank God," Dad says. "Thank God!" He turns his face, his nose wrinkling. "He smells like shit!"

He lifts him out of the drawer, Henry's diaper askew, three turds dropping to the floor as Dad's face curls with disgust. Shaken from his torpor, Henry starts shrieking, his tiny legs kicking as he bites down hard, his teeth clamping onto the fleshy skin between Dad's thumb and forefinger.

"You goddamn monkey."

Henry doesn't let go, his teeth drawing blood before Dad tosses him onto the bed; Henry, five pounds at most, crashes against the headboard, the tangerine dropping. It rolls off the bed as Henry screams, slapping his head wildly, repeatedly. Dad grabs a towel and wraps it around his hand and Henry, spotting the tangerine, leaps from the bed and grabs the fruit, sticking it in his mouth as he climbs up the lamp stand and clings to the lampshade with both hands, the tangerine between his lips. His face is a mask of fury, a capuchin remake of *Planet of the Apes.*

"He's crazy," Dad says.

Henry slides down the lamp pole and runs toward the bathroom, shrieking like a jungle ape, the loose diaper falling off as he hides behind the door.

"He bit me. That son of a bitch...what's wrong with him?"

"He's scared."

"So am I, but I didn't bite *him.*" He shows me his hand. "He broke the skin. I'll need a rabies shot."

"He doesn't have rabies."

"How do you know? Maybe they were cooking up some killer virus in that lab. I heard they inject monkeys with the blood of serial killers."

"That's a Vincent Price movie from 1962. They don't really do that."

"You don't know that for sure. He could have killed me!"

My father's hand shows two small puncture marks, dots of red bubbling toward the skin. It doesn't look serious, but then it's not my hand, and I'm not the one Henry attacked. I stuff the diaper and the turds in the trash bucket and call the Front Desk for some First Aid cream. Dad sits on the bed, staring at his wound, the bleeding already stopped. In the bathroom Henry crouches in the cramped nook between the toilet and the sink, moving the tangerine between his hands. He watches me with his good eye, the other unfocused and dead. He's the same old Henry again, his anger gone, but for how long?

"And you wanted to rescue him. Ha! He belongs back in the lab, behind bars, locked up so he can't terrorize innocent actors."

My pulse races as I stand in the doorway. Again, I'm in over my head. I move one step closer, Henry watching me carefully.

"Sometimes I want to bite him too," I whisper. A second step, then a third, and Henry tilts his head, rolling the tangerine toward my feet. I roll it back and Henry grabs it, rubs it against the top of his head, then rolls it back. After a dozen rolls back and forth, Henry's eye never leaving the tangerine, Dad leans in the doorway, watching.

"Is he normal again?"

"He's better, I think."

Henry smiles each time the tangerine returns, stroking it with both hands before sending it back. It's a game, clearly, and when I pause too long before returning it, he gives me an impatient *meek-meek*.

"Why in the world did he bite me? He's never shown a hint of aggression. If he had, I would have dropped him immediately. Imagine if he had bitten Gloria."

"You scared him."

"I thought he liked me."

"It was a fear instinct. Veronica said they keep them chained in cages with their brains wired up and then approach with these giant snakes to scare the crap out of them so they can measure the fear response."

"I hate snakes," Dad says. "They were on set during *Race with the Devil*. Pete Fonda said..."

There's a knock on the door—a hotel staffer with a First Aid kit for Dad's wound. I close the bathroom door and wait with Henry while Dad answers the door.

In the small bathroom, which to Henry, after all those years in a cage, must be a palace, we continue the tangerine game, the fruit rolling between us, again and again. He seems pleased, and I sit on the floor across from him. PTSD. If people can have it, why not capuchins? If I were him, I'd bite, too.

And there it is, the question I can't avoid. *If I were him...?*

What makes us different? He uses language, just like me. *Meek-meek* can't compete with a Shakespearean sonnet, but maybe to another capuchin it's beautiful. He plays games, experiences fear, expresses affection, eats, sleeps, breathes, thinks. Maybe I'm anthropomorphizing, but I suspect he might even love. I'm smarter and can read, but so what? If I got whacked on the head with a boom mic and my cognitive ability plummeted, would it be right to stick me in a cage and threaten me with snakes and electro-shock? Stephen Hawking is a hundred times smarter than me. Should he have the legal right to inflict pain and suffering on me because he understands the history of time and I'm not even sure why it's three hours earlier in California? Should Hawking shoot bolts into my skull and cut open my brain? Someone once wrote that the only difference between humans and animals is that humans use money and exploit each other for profit. Two hundred years ago slavery was legal, accepted as the normal order. There was nothing wrong with buying a person and keeping him in chains. Black-skinned humans were property. When we think of it now, we're disgusted. *How could they?* But two hundred years from now, when the history books describe how we treat animals, will readers be disgusted, too? *How could they...?*

"What's the answer, Henry?" I ask, but he doesn't know either. He just rolls the tangerine, and when I roll it back, he claps.

Dad opens the door.

"He should sleep in here tonight, in the john," he says, a dab of white first aid cream in the crook of his thumb. "With the door closed, and a chair against it on the other side." He watches Henry, the apprehension clear. "I slept in the same room with him for weeks and didn't think twice, but not anymore. He may be calm now, but I'm not waking up with him eating my face."

Considering Henry's previous digs, a hotel bathroom seems a fair deal.

"I'll get him a pillow and a blanket." I give the tangerine a final roll. "Be right back, Henry."

"Meek-meek."

Dad grabs my arm as I step out of the bathroom.

"We *are* handing him over tomorrow, right?"

"Right," I say, but the better answer is: *how could they...?*

That night, while Henry sleeps on a pillow in the tub, while Dad snores under hotel sheets, I sit on the edge of the bed and watch Wally's DVD, undercover footage shot in a lab. Monkeys, but rabbits too, and mice, kittens, and beagle puppies, the experiments different, the pain and fear the same. The question is simple.

How could they?

116

-2-

My father sings in the shower, that strange song "MacArthur Park" with its oddball lyrics about cake left in the rain. It's a *long* song—he's been in the shower for nearly ten minutes—yet Henry is enthralled. He sits outside the cracked bathroom door listening to my father croon, his beloved tangerine beside him as he taps the floor. Whatever instinct drove him to attack last night is gone; he and Dad are friends again, Dad sharing his room service eggs and letting Henry steal a few sips coffee. Just what we need—a caffeinated monkey, but for now, Henry is content.

I knock on the bathroom door. "Can you hurry, please? We should have left a half hour ago. We need to be there by 6:20 PM."

He doesn't respond, though I'm sure he hears me. Raising his voice, he brings the song home, Henry standing up and dancing, or something like a dance—he moves up and down like he's doing squats in gym class, his lips pulled back in a crazed grin.

Ending with a flourish, Dad holds the final note and says, "Thank you very much," the water shutting off, Henry spinning before jumping to the bed, where he pets the tangerine.

Dad steps out of the bathroom, stark naked, toweling off his hair.

"Jesus—put on a robe!"

"Bare skin requires exposure to natural air," he says. "Twenty minutes of nudity each day maintains healthy skin. It's never too early to establish a routine. Go ahead, try it."

I turn my back. "I'll pass."

He laughs. "It appears my son is a prude."

"I'm not a prude. I just appreciate boundaries, underwear being a good one."

"When you were a baby, your mother and I walked nude around the house quite often. It's perfectly natural. Sometimes she and I would spend the whole day nude. You were too young, but your brother might remember. He was nude, too."

"I really don't want to hear this."

"I assumed that, when I wasn't home, your mother continued the practice."

"Ah, no, thank God."

He slides deodorant under both armpits. "My apologies, sincerely. I should have been there to guide you toward body acceptance."

"You should have been there to...I don't know, teach me to hit a baseball or ride a bike or help with my math homework, not walk around with my junk hanging out."

"It's not junk, son. Be proud of your testicles and penis."

"Please get dressed. The FBI is waiting."

I grab my phone and leave the room, finding a quiet alcove near the ice machine. Melanie was right about a cell phone—it's a useful gadget to have, and I hit the number pre-programmed for Mike. It's still early, but he answers the third ring.

"What's wrong?" he says, skipping the greeting. "What did he do?"

Does he remember the nudity? I consider asking, but why ruin his morning?

"We're about to leave Youngstown, Ohio. Nothing's wrong." A half-truth, at best. "Henry freaked out last night and bit Dad, but the wound isn't serious, and Henry's back to normal."

"Good thing you're getting rid of him soon. You can never trust a wild animal."

"He's not 'wild'. He's the exact opposite. If he was raised in his natural environment, he'd be better adjusted."

"You know what I mean. Everything's still on schedule, right?"

I've always trusted my brother, but I hold back about my second thoughts and even about Wally. "It should be over by the end of the day."

"Good. Remember, they're going to arrest you, but it's just for show. You'll be back on the road within an hour. Call me if there are any problems."

"Remember what you said about the warrant for Dad being in the wrong name?"

He packs maximum suspicion in a single syllable. "Why?"

"I'm thinking of writing a spec script for *Law and Order*. It might be a good hook: an actor gets arrested under his stage name. Would he walk?"

"It could go either way. I'd have to ask one of the other associates, someone who practices criminal law. I could show them the script, but you'll get charged for the billable hour."

It's not the free pass for Dad that I'd hoped. "I'll let you know when it's done."

"Fine, but keep it in a script, Kevin. Playing that card could backfire on both of you."

"I'm not playing any cards."

"Good." His tone shifts. "Hey, we got the news yesterday. Melanie's pregnant."

"Terrific."

"We're keeping it quiet until she's through the first trimester, but we wanted you to know."

Because I'm the father? Melanie swore I'd never know for sure.

"You know, I was starting to wonder if she was cheating on me."

"Mel would never do that."

"I don't know. She was frantic about conceiving. Another few months and it might have gone that way. Not that I don't trust her. I do. But sometimes I got a funny feeling..."

"No way. You're the father, absolutely. Congratulations."

"Don't tell Dad he's going to be a grandfather."

"He barely knows he's a father."

A man walks by, slowing down to check me out. He's non-descript, unmemorable, a guy in sweatpants heading toward the lobby for the free morning coffee, but something about the way he pauses and makes eye contact leaves me wondering. I smile, offer a friendly wave, and he nods and keeps walking. The head nod—was it a signal? Is he with me? Against me? Nothing more than a stranger being polite? My stomach turns queasy. I wasn't cut out for intrigue.

"I'd better get back. We're already late."

"Stay cool, Kevin," he says. "I know how you think, but don't go down the rabbit hole. Just go with the flow and you'll be home working on your film by the end of the week."

On the way back to the room I pass the chubby blonde girl from the bar. She's dressed in a hotel robe and flip-flops, a towel over her shoulder as she heads to the pool for a morning swim, something my parents never taught me to do. Dad was never around, and Mom was afraid of the water. She'd have been smarter to fear driveways and her son with a camera.

The blonde's name eludes me, though she told me last night.

"See you at the movies!"

"Or maybe before that," she winks. Is it a come-on or is she part of the ALF? *Please take Henry*, I think. *I don't want to turn him in.* Her hips sashay as she struts toward the elevator. If I were Dad, I'd follow her to the pool for a skinny dip. Maybe I *am* a prude.

At least he's dressed when I return. Six pill bottles are lined on the dresser; he shakes out one pill at a time and swallows without water.

"It's the magic formula that keeps me alive," he says, downing another pill. "Who knows what half of them do, but I'm still here, so they must be working."

After the last pill he caps each bottle and tosses them one at a time into a plastic grocery bag, which he ties in a knot and drops into his suitcase. All those pills seem a bad sign.

"Is there anything I need to know about?"

"Yeah, I'm old, but don't worry. When the director calls Action, Brian Edwards is ready."

Henry's dressed in his overalls, waiting on the bed with the tangerine. His fixation is fascinating—is it a toy, a baby, a surrogate monkey? Maybe it's just the scent or the texture, but either way it calms him, and when I pick him up, I make sure the tangerine is safe in his hands.

"Action," I call, and Dad, always the pro, grabs his bag and follows me to the door.

"I like the sound of it," he says. "There's nothing better than action."

•　　•　　•　　•　　•　　•

There's no traffic on the Interstate and we're making good time. Henry has discovered the joy of the car window, the 18-wheelers amusing him as they thunder past, each one worthy of its own *meek-meek*. Dad's stories have reached a tolerable level of braggadocio and balderdash—though I will never believe that, as Harvey Keitel's stand-in in *Mother, Juggs & Speed*, he made out with Raquel Welch. On the surface, everything is fine. Only my conscience is screaming.

What if... I think, but every "if" ends the same...with Henry back in the lab and me in prison. Does the impossibility of a successful ending let me off the hook? In college we read about Henry David Thoreau and Ralph Waldo Emerson. One of them, Thoreau I think, was in jail for not paying taxes in opposition to a war. Emerson went to visit him and said, "Henry, what are you doing in there?" Thoreau responded, "What are you doing out there?"

The lesson is clear: a moral obligation requires action and sacrifice, consequences be damned; otherwise one is complicit. But for Thoreau the stakes were low. He was alone in a small-town jail cell in Massachusetts for a single night before his mother paid the taxes and Thoreau went home to his pond and his virtue.

The one outcome I don't consider is that I pull it off, that I avoid the FBI and ferry Henry to freedom. So I drive on, hoping Wally and the ALF arrive in time to save us.

"On the way back, do you think we could stop so I can visit an old friend?" Dad says. "It's out of the way, but I haven't seen him in years. You'll want to meet him, too. A great guy!"

"How out of the way?"

"A few hundred miles."

Just what I need—another day of driving so my father can shoot the shit with a fellow Hollywood nobody.

"I need to get back and start editing *Exit 23*."

"Of course. We don't want any delays." He shakes a few breath mints from the container. "I hear the actor who plays the grandfather has a powerhouse scene."

He smiles, his tone sincere, and I feel like a jerk, the mean father who won't stop for ice cream on the way home from the hardware store.

"We'll see how it goes. If we have time..."

"I'd love for you to meet him. He's got a great place, a ranch. Henry would love it there."

An 18-wheeler powers past us in the left lane. *Meek-meek*, Henry calls. Even if we do stop at Dad's friend's ranch, it won't matter to Henry. He'll already be back in the lab.

• • • •

We break for lunch at a rest stop, the day warm and sunny with a fresh breeze, one of those days when you think, "The world is really great, I should enjoy it more," before you go back to obsessing about your troubles. Though we can still hear the engine hum of the Interstate, the rest stop is shielded on both sides by a patch of woods, a stand of evergreens bordering the highway, the other side an incline dense with maples and small conifers.

"Good choice," Dad says. "I was worried you would stop at the Weigh Station. In my experience, the port-o-johns at weigh stations are the seventh circle of Hell."

Three other groups have stopped: a retired couple from Kentucky (according to their license plate), two guys and a woman, leather-clad, their Harleys sharing a parking spot, and a family of six with an RV: Mom and Dad, three kids, and an older woman who must be grandma. They all watch us, curious about the two men (father and son?) walking toward a table with a capuchin monkey between them, each man holding one of the monkey's hands. Henry, whose experience of the natural world is limited, pivots his head in fascination, taking it all in, his nostrils sniffing double-time as we leave the pavement and walk across the lawn, his bare feet tickled by the cool grass.

Wee-ah, Wee-ah, he says, a new vocalization that must mean happy.

"I should have taken him outside before," Dad says, "but I was afraid of being seen and worried he might run away."

On the second point we're prepared. The FBI, experts at restraint, gave us a pair of link straps before we left. One cuff is around my wrist, the other around Henry's. A six-foot cord binds us. I always thought it was dreadful when I'd see parents tied to their kids at the mall, but now I understand. If Henry opts to climb a tree or hide from the hawks circling overhead (he senses that the hawks mean trouble) he can only go six feet before I'm there, too.

"When they gave him to me, they said to keep him inside unless it was absolutely safe. I never felt that it was, so we kept him hidden," Dad says. Henry sits in the grass and runs his hands through the blades. "I regret that now."

One of the kids points at us, and the senior couple waves. Unsure of rest stop etiquette, I return the wave but keep distant. We settle at the table farthest from the others; I distribute the sandwiches while Dad fills a plate for Henry with orange slices, celery, and pumpkin seeds. Henry puts the tangerine on the table, keeping it in view as he paws at his food.

I wait for a story about Dad shooting a highway rest stop scene with the legendary (Fill-in-the-blank), but he's almost contemplative as he chews his turkey sandwich and studies the trees.

"Before you were born, I quit the business for three months. I think it was 1966. I worked as a fire watcher in a state forest in Oregon. Three months in the middle of nowhere keeping an eye on the trees. All I had with me were food supplies, a notebook, and *The Tibetan Book of the Dead.*"

"I don't believe that for a second."

"Then don't, but it's true. In certain ways it was the best three months of my life. I almost signed up for a year's commitment, but your mother came out and convinced me to go back to California. You won't believe this either, but my career was as important to her as it was to me. Maybe more. She loved being married to an actor, even a nobody like me. I was ready to join the rat race plenty of times, but she always steered me back to the biz. No complaints—I've had an interesting life—but that time in the forest was special."

"Meek-meek."

"At least you believe me, Henry," Dad says, petting his head.

"Mom told me plenty of times that she wished you were home," I say, though really, she only said it once. "But she did love seeing you on TV."

"Fame through osmosis, even if my fame was paltry. Better to say you were married to an actor than to a truck driver or an insurance agent, but that's all behind us now. When your career takes off..."

"If it takes off..."

"It will, and it *will* overwhelm you. Remember that there's more to life than the movies." His voice lowers. "Somebody's coming."

My heart quickens. The ALF? But it's only the mother and her two kids. The boy is about eight, the girl six. Mom wears stretch pants and a flower-print blouse.

"Excuse me," she says in a slight Southern twang, "but my kids would be so darn happy if they could say hello to your monkey."

Is this her opening gambit, coded language to indicate her ALF sympathies? I look around for Wally but there's no sight of anyone except the other couples.

"Certainly. He'd love to say hello," Dad says.

The two kids approach cautiously; Henry is nervous too, looking over his shoulder to check on his tangerine. The little girl holds out her hand like she's approaching a pit bull and Henry scurries onto my lap, leaning back into my chest.

"Go ahead, he's friendly," Dad says, a minor leap of faith. What if Henry bites again?

The little girl takes one small step at a time, but the boy, suddenly emboldened, lunges with both hands out, and I brace for the worst. Henry makes himself big, stretching his arms overhead, the cord between us straining as he yells, "Oka-oka eee!"

Both kids hide behind the safety of Mom's hip, and I tighten my grip on Henry, who grabs the tangerine, touches it to his forehead, and then, inexplicably, holds it out for both kids to see.

"He wants to play," Dad says, and he's right; Henry tosses the tangerine to the boy and girl, neither of whom move, the tangerine flopping onto the grass, Henry flashing a wide smile.

The boy looks at Mom, who gives the okay. He picks up the fruit and hands it back. "*Meek-meek*," Henry says, and both kids, even Mom, start to laugh.

"What's wrong with his eye?" the girl asks. Do I tell her about the DVD, the footage of long syringes and eyelids pinned back, chemicals shot into the sclera?

"He's fine. He was born that way," Dad says. "He can see you as well as you see him."

After three more rounds of tangerine toss, Mom says thanks and leads her brood back to their table. Dad sips some Coke and slaps the bench.

"Now here's an idea," he says. "We buy Henry from the lab and start a children's act. Birthday parties, school assemblies; with my acting and Henry's natural charm, we'll rake it in."

"Last night you wanted him locked in a cage."

"That was adrenaline. The bite really hurt, but I'm over it." He ruffles Henry's head. "What do you think, pal? If it goes well, maybe we'll get a children's show on PBS. I'm seeing lunch boxes, stuffed toys, action figures, maybe a video game. I'd make a great action figure, don't you think? This could be huge."

He paces around the table, dollar signs floating in his head.

"They'll never sell him to us."

"Why not? This is America, everything is for sale."

He almost trips on a divot but regains his balance. Henry scoops pumpkin seeds into his mouth, his one good eye following Dad.

"You don't want him back in the lab and neither do I. This is the perfect solution. We go through with the set-up and the FBI makes their arrest. That's all they want, and then they're off our case. We contact the lab and make them an offer. What's the point of getting him back? They already did their experiments. I bet we could get him for a hundred bucks at most. I start a new career, and Henry gets his freedom. It's a win all-around."

"It's crazy."

"It's not. I'll take a class in monkey care or hire some unemployed vet tech...this could be the third act my career's been waiting for. I'll talk to Gloria, but she believes in me. It's a no-brainer. Kids love monkeys and parents love their kids and every kid in America has a birthday party. We do two a day on Saturday and Sundays, maybe $300 per show, that's..."

He does some mental math.

"...a hell of lot more than Wal-Mart wages and Social Security. That's not even counting school appearances, libraries, county fairs..."

Has my father actually come up with the solution? Maybe he's right. Why would the lab want Henry back? Could it be as simple as asking if we can keep him?

"Maybe we should call Mike" I say, Dad's enthusiasm starting to catch. "He can negotiate with the US Attorney's office, make our cooperation dependent on getting Henry back."

"Forget your brother. I love him like a son...well, he *is* my son...but he's not a showman like us. Trust me, Kevin. This is the answer. It's a win-win-win."

Henry agrees. "Meek-meek-meek."

Dad picks him up and sets him on his shoulders. "What do you say, Henry? I've worked with the great ones...how about we add your name to the list?"

From Dad's shoulders he leaps from the table, grabs the tangerine, and jumps back into my father's arms.

Three tables over, the family of six applauds, and my father bows, Henry clinging to his shoulder to avoid falling off, the six-foot cord between him and me stretched to its limit, a strange umbilical binding the three of us.

• • • • • •

Maybe it's a pipe dream, but my father's plan to buy Henry from the lab lightens the remainder of the drive. The mind-numbing boredom of the Interstate begins to lift as our destination approaches. I'm still on alert for trailing cars, but anytime a vehicle materializes in the rear-view mirror, it disappears within a few miles, switching to the off-ramp or swinging to the passing lane, blowing by us in a burst of acceleration. If the ALF or the Feds are trailing us, it's a masterful job.

Stay on the road long enough and every car and driver look the same. Only one car sticks: a brown Buick Skylark in the left lane, my mother's ghost in the passenger seat waving as the Buick passes. Why do I keep seeing her? If her ghost is real, meaning she's traversed the border between life and death, perhaps the greatest feat of all, why can't she choose something better than a brown Skylark? And if she has a message for me, why is she always silent? I assume the only message is that she's dead and I'm responsible.

I hit over 80 mph chasing the Skylark, but when I finally reach it, her ghost is gone, the passenger seat occupied by a tall, bearded man.

We drive, and drive...and drive.

Though I've stopped paying attention to road signs, the next one is a jolt: Anderson Falls, 2 Miles Ahead.

Anderson Falls—we've arrived.

I shake my father from his half-sleep, and he wakes with a start.

"What?"

"This is it. Anderson Falls."

"Anderson who?"

"We're here. We need to find the Tick Tock Diner and contact Agent Mahoney."

"Jesus, already?"

Henry sleeps in the car seat, the tangerine in his lap.

"I was in the middle of this wonderful dream," Dad says. "I was playing a scene with Deborah Kerr. She and I were—"

In the dream he was Burt Lancaster's stand-in during the notorious beach make-out scene in *From Here to Eternity*, but I tune him out the moment I see the exit number on the final sign for Anderson Falls.

Our destination is a mile ahead. Anderson Falls—Exit 23.

-3-

"The location is under surveillance and everything is set. Your role is minimal. Knock on the door, hand them the monkey, and let us do our jobs."

Special Agent Mahoney peers through the car window at Henry, who paces the backseat moving the tangerine from hand to hand, *meek-meek*, his head bobbing nervously as he watches us, his one good eye wary of Mahoney and her partner, an agent named Smitherson, who stands ten feet away, his hand inside his jacket as if waiting for commandoes to attack.

We're in the parking lot of the Tick Tock Diner, ten minutes from our destination. As instructed, we've contacted the Feds, and while Dad heads to the diner restroom, Mahoney opens a folder, showing two photographs, both taken at a distance, the subjects unaware of the camera. The first is of a woman with a tired blonde perm wearing nursing whites; she carries a grocery bag as she walks through a supermarket parking lot.

"Susan Zander, female Caucasian, age 52."

Mahoney flips to the next photograph: a bald man with a grey mustache pushing a broom inside a warehouse.

"Richard Carlos, male Caucasian, age 56. This is who we want. We've confirmed that they're at the location waiting for you, but if someone else opens the door, we might hesitate before we enter. Hang on to the monkey until you see at least one of them. It's important that Zander or Carlos take physical possession of it."

"Not it, him."

I study the photographs. Susan Zander and Richard Carlos. In less than an hour, their freedom will be gone, because of me. "They look like nice people."

"They're criminals."

"They're just trying to help animals."

"Then they should donate to the Humane Society and adopt a cat. Do you want me to read the charges against them?" She doesn't wait for an answer. "Destruction of Property, Breaking and Entering, Theft, Harassment, nine felony counts for Terroristic Threats."

"You made your point."

"These aren't nice people. Do you want to live in a safe, stable society or in an anarchist hellhole where everyone does whatever they want and everything turns to shit?"

"Gee, let me think about it."

"They belong behind bars."

"Does Henry belong there, too?"

"He's property," she says. "You might dislike how I store my shoes in the closet, but you don't have the right to steal them and call it liberation."

"Your shoes aren't tortured."

"After a twelve-hour day on my hot, sweaty feet, my shoes might disagree." She smiles. "That's funny. Why didn't you laugh? It was better than your sarcastic 'let me think about it' comment. Maybe I should be the filmmaker instead of you."

A car swings through the lot and parks beside us. Two men get out. One of them is Wally.

"Everything is in place," he says to Mahoney.

When he looks at me, there's no recognition or acknowledgement—his face is as blank as a post-it note. Is that part of the plan? Or was the plan just to fuck with me? The other guy carries a black doctor's bag. He's tall, heavy-set, his eyes squinting behind wire frames.

"I need to see 576-A24," he says, and reaches for the door handle. I block his way.

"This is Dr. Doremus, from the Lab," Mahoney says. "He needs to identify the animal."

Wally, or whatever his name is, grabs my hand and removes it roughly from the handle. As he leans into me, I wait for him to whisper that this is all part of the ALF rescue plan, but he doesn't say a word, and Henry, seeing two strangers ready to enter the car, jumps to the floor and crawls under the front seat. Though he's small, he can only fit halfway, his tail and legs still visible. Wally tightens his grip, and Mahoney clamps my bicep and yanks me away.

"The FBI appreciates your cooperation," she says, and slams me against the car hood. Wally opens the door and Doremus climbs into the backseat. He grabs Henry's tail and pulls him out, Henry shrieking as he clutches the tangerine. Doremus, one arm wrapped around Henry's neck, steps back from the car, Mahoney pinning me to the hood as Doremus hands Henry over to Wally, who yanks open Henry's mouth, Doremus shining a flashlight down Henry's throat, searching for the ID number.

A few onlookers approach, but Smitherson intercedes. All I hear is "Federal agents" and that's enough to turn anyone away. The sun begins to set, the metal hood hot against my face. Henry screams but can't move as Wally restrains him, one arm around his legs, the other across his neck. Doremus pries the tangerine from his fingers.

"Let him keep it. He loves it..."

Doremus gives the tangerine to Smitherson, who shoots it like a basketball into a trash can. Henry's cry is a terror-scream, his one good eye connecting with mine, his pupil wide and desperate as Doremus injects his leg with a large hypodermic.

The effect is immediate. Henry's body slackens and stills.

"Confirmed. It's 576-A24," Doremus says, shutting the flashlight. Wally puts Henry back in the car seat and snaps the buckle, Henry's body as limp as a ragdoll.

"He'll be immobile for an hour. It's easier that way."

Mahoney releases her hold.

"You all suck."

"I believe the FBI can withstand your criticism," she says. "If your objections are legitimate, refuse to cooperate. Your father will have a fair trial."

As if summoned, Dad hurries across the parking lot, his gait unsteady; his fly unzipped. Smitherson moves to block him, but Mahoney calls him back.

"What's going on?" Dad says, checking his fly and zipping up. He peers into the car and sees Henry unconscious. "What happened to his tangerine?"

"Sometimes they claim objects as toys or surrogate friends," Doremus says. "But he has no need for enrichment now."

Wally checks his watch. "It's time."

"Are you clear on the instructions?" Mahoney asks. Dad approaches Doremus.

"You must be from the lab," he says. "Brian Edwards, it's a pleasure to meet you. If you're thinking, 'where have I seen that face before?', it's likely you've seen one of my many TV and film appearances."

"I don't watch TV," Doremus says, "except for golf. Do you play golf?"

"Not currently."

"Then I've never seen you before."

"Perhaps in one of the commercials that played during the golf broadcast?"

"We don't have time for this," Mahoney says.

"Of course, of course," Dad says. "But I have a proposition. After this incident is complete, would you be open to an offer for Henry, for the monkey? I believe you refer to him as 576-A24. My son and I have established a bond with him, you see, and I'm confident he has a promising career in entertainment. My references are outstanding. You'll recognize many of them, for example, Mister Robert Redford."

"Is this joker for real?" Smitherson says.

"You want to use 576-A24 for entertainment?" Doremus says. "That's an abomination."

"Excuse me?"

"To use a conditioned laboratory animal for show business, that's outrageous."

"He'll be cared for very well. Perhaps five hundred dollars as an asking price?"

Doremus turns his back and walks away.

"Make sure the subject is returned to me as soon as you make your arrest," he tells Mahoney, and he and Wally get back in their car. I try to catch Wally's eye, desperate for a nod, a glance, anything except the stone face on view. Was it all bullshit, a test of my reliability? His car starts, reverses, then drives away.

"It's time to move," Mahoney says. "Are you clear on the instructions?"

"Will you slam my face into the hood again if I'm not?"

"She did what?" Dad says.

"You won't see us again until we engage, but we'll be watching. You're almost done. Another hour and you can get back to your lives."

In the backseat Henry is limp, perfectly still, his breath reduced to a weak inhalation. It's nothing like the peacefulness of sleep. He's unconscious, his heart still beating, but every muscle in his body is slack, as if he were already dead.

•   •   •   •   •   •

"Such arrogance," Dad says. "If $500 is an inadequate offer, where's the counter-offer? He has every right to negotiate, but to dismiss the idea outright is disrespectful. It's small-minded! Henry would excel at children's entertainment and my professionalism is beyond reproach! Ask anyone!"

My hands grip the steering wheel, knuckles turning white.

"They don't care. It's not about you or even about Henry."

On the DVD, that goddamn DVD, men and women in white lab coats mocked the different monkeys as the capuchins writhed in pain.

"They're *proud* of sticking electrodes in his brain so they can measure the results. He's their property and they want him back. Case closed."

As each intersection approaches, I slow the car, squinting to read the street signs, our destination looming. My gut feels like I've swallowed a bowl of flathead screws. The DVD footage, captured by a smuggled camera, was crude and amateurish, sometimes blurry, the shots poorly framed—in film school we would have torn it apart—but every second demonstrated the lack of compassion and empathy, the absence of basic decency. Lab techs blowing cigarette smoke into cages, laughing while a monkey huddled at the back of his cage, paws covering his eyes as he rocked himself endlessly; a doctor slapping a monkey with the back of his palm when the monkey dared to turn his head. A monkey screaming while a doctor drilled into his skull, and when the doctor realized that no one had bothered to administer anesthesia, he kept drilling anyway.

"Why did that woman have you face down against the hood like some common criminal? She's drunk with authority, a fascist soul! All of them. Police brutality."

Dad turns and checks on Henry, who's still immobile in the car seat.

"We should turn around and go home. The hell with them."

"Easier said than done."

"I'm serious." He grabs his black Sundance hat from the backseat, brushing crumbs from the brim before setting it on his head.

"Argentina, Butch. Let's make a break for it."

"Do you remember how that film ended?"

"With a beautiful freeze-frame."

"And a thousand gunshots in the background."

"They won't shoot us. We're not drug dealers or bank robbers. This isn't the Old West. They know we're not armed. Where's your outlaw spirit?" He flips the visor and checks himself in the mirror, admiring the hat. "If they want to send an old man to prison, let them do it."

"You don't mean that."

"Maybe I do. What's my future? Going back to Wal-Mart and waiting for my wife to run off with someone younger? Taking ten pills a day until my heart gives out? I'm sure prison is hell, but they leave old men alone, don't they? I'll wind up in the hospital unit, get out in six months for good behavior."

He frames his profile for the mirror, his jawline arched, the black hat cocked at an angle, his eyes gazing out the window toward his future, the martyred animal activist released from prison feted at a PETA gala with Hollywood's elite.

"If I play it right, going to prison could open some opportunities. This country is desperate for heroes. What do you think? Is this the face of a hero?"

He turns, a visage like an aged Marlboro Man waiting at the senior center for his free Bingo card.

"It won't make a difference. They'll still get Henry back. We can't hide him forever."

"We could if we make it to Argentina, or even just to my friend's ranch." He grabs a sheet of paper from the cupholder. "I've got the address right here. It's out in the middle of nowhere, five hundred acres. We'll hide out until some big-shot attorney cuts us a deal and finds a loophole that frees Henry. There's always a loophole!"

"Will you stop? There's no loophole."

"That's negative thinking." He stuffs the address in my shirt pocket as if he's giving me cash for the Good Humor man. "The public would eat us up. A father and son fighting to save a monkey. People love monkeys!"

If it were anyone else, I might believe, but my faith in my father disappeared before I left high school: he probably thinks Bob Redford will ride to our rescue and Gregory Peck as Atticus Finch will lead the defense. My neck still aches from Mahoney's slam-down as I turn left at a traffic light, our destination less than five minutes away.

It comes down to this: somewhere in their house, Susan Zander and Richard Carlos are going about their business, doing laundry, making dinner, maybe watching a *M*A*S*H** re-run on TV, unaware that the storm clouds have gathered, the FBI ready to strike. I am one of those clouds.

How did it start for them? Did they see a woman walking down the street in a mink coat and start thinking about the mink instead of the price tag and the fashion thrill? Did they read an article about conditions in a slaughterhouse and decide to stop eating meat? Maybe they were volunteers with a local shelter who decided that it wasn't enough to help only the cute ones, that if a person encounters suffering in the world, he or she must take action or share culpability. What is it that turns someone from the comfort of routine, and its myriad compromises, to that giant leap in which the safety of one's own ass no longer outweighs the pain and suffering of another sentient being?

I didn't ask for any of this, but from the moment my father and Henry barged through the front door, was any other ending possible? After this is over, what happens next? I go home and finish *Exit 23*. Maybe it's successful and I make another film, and then another...watch me drive my Mercedes to some big-shit Hollywood power lunch to discuss my next deal. Will Henry's suffering still matter, and if it doesn't, am I a monster? Henry's suffering...forget Henry, the suffering of hundreds or thousands...there could be millions of animals in labs for all I know...the knowledge of that suffering is mine, forever, the only unknown being what will I do with it? Things happen in your life and they change you. I was a kid with a camera who wanted to impress his absent Dad and so I asked my mother to back out of the driveway while I filmed the scene. Take 2... take 3, take 4...and while I know her death was an accident, if I hadn't asked her for another take (*just one more, Mom, okay?*) ...if I hadn't asked her, she'd still be alive. We never ask for the things that change us the most.

That has nothing to do with Henry, I tell myself, and maybe I'm right. But it has everything to do with my need to atone.

We drive another half-mile and I stop at a red light. Film School Rule #4 – the protagonist must act. I imagine myself on the screen, the audience booing as I knock on the door and hand Henry over to Zander and Carlos, Mahoney and her goons jumping from the bushes with their guns and handcuffs, the film's final shot—Henry back in his cage, his head in a vice, wires implanted in his brain, a blank expression in his lone shell-shocked eye as he awaits the next jolt. The audience leaves the theater despising the main character. *That piece of shit! How could he do it?*

The traffic light turns green; horns blare, cars pass, but my foot remains still.

"The light is green," Dad says.

"I know."

Green–the universal color for *Go*. I open the car door to a two-lane road in a small town, hardly Manhattan at rush hour or the Garden State Parkway, but I'm almost clipped by an approaching Chevy the moment I get out, the driver shouting, "drug addict!" as he drives away. The setting sun casts a pink-orange glaze on the horizon, and I see my mother's ghost on the other side of the street. She stands in front of a small grocery store smoking a cigarette, watching me, and I run toward her, my father calling, "Kevin, what the hell...? Get back in the car!"

For years I've glimpsed my mother's ghost without ever making contact, her appearances inscrutable, dismissed as daydreams that pop like soap bubbles the moment I approach, but this time she doesn't vanish. She turns, the automatic doors sliding open, and steps inside the store. I sprint across the parking lot and rush through the doors. The cool air strikes me, and a clerk straightening shopping carts gives me a startled look before offering me a cart.

"In a hurry?" he says. He's sixteen, acne-scarred but bright-faced, and jumps away upon seeing that I'm not just another customer; for the moment I am an authentic crazy man, a wounded adult son chasing his mother's ghost, and if only the kid knew my backstory, he might cheer. Mom's ghost stays twenty paces ahead, and I follow her down the canned food aisle. Green Giant corn, asparagus, peas, store-brand beets. God, I hate beets. No one else notices her, a slim, attractive woman in her late thirties who's been dead for more than a decade. Her hair is 1980's big, a super-permed brunette with frosted streaks wearing black pants, a white blouse, and a dark blue blazer, her law secretary uniform. I would sit on the couch watching *Gilligan's Island* reruns while she prettied herself for work, ignoring calls for me to get myself ready, a wedding photo on the TV stand, Mom and Dad, young and in love, my mother gazing adoringly at Dad, both of them convinced he was destined for stardom. Had they known that one day their youngest son would be chasing a ghost through a grocery store in Michigan totally out of his mind, would they still have said, "I do"? I dodge the other shoppers and Mom turns the aisle, the physics of it all so confusing, I'm running and she's walking—I've seen hundreds of movie ghosts, and they never run—yet I don't catch up with her no matter how fast I move until she stops on the fruit aisle, reaches into a bin, and grabs a tangerine.

"I know you'll do the right thing," she says, and hands me the fruit. In a moment, she is gone.

I feel a hand on my shoulder.

"I know who you are. Come with me."

She's neither my mother nor her ghost, but the resemblance is spooky. A slim, attractive woman in her thirties, big hair, out-of-style red glasses, baggy jeans and white tennis shoes, she grabs my arm and leads me toward a rack of onions against the wall.

"I'm here for your friend. We can get him to safety."

I knock against the rack, flakes of papery onion skin dotting my hands, a single onion rolling to the floor.

"How do I know...?"

"You don't," she says, "but you have to trust me. Go to the car and bring him to me. Let's meet by the cold cut aisle. There's a back exit."

When I hesitate, she shoves me forward.

"Hurry. We've got five minutes at most before they realize something's wrong. Go get him. Wrap him in a blanket if you have one. If the manager sees you, she'll give you crap about an animal in a grocery store. Just ignore her, ignore everyone, and meet me by the cold cuts."

I'm holding a tangerine, my feet surrounded by the fallen onion, its layers peeling. Did my mother's ghost hand me the fruit or did I blank out while grabbing it? Either way, there's no time.

"Move," the woman says.

I rush through the aisles even faster now, not thinking; the shopping cart kid sees me coming and jumps to the left as I collide with the carts but don't lose a step. Having moved the car, Dad stands in the parking lot waving his black hat, the back door open.

"They're here for Henry," I tell him.

He cocks his head as if not hearing. "The Feds? We just talked to them."

"There's a woman by the cold cut aisle."

"There's *always* a woman by the cold cut aisle," he says. "What are you talking about?"

I reach in and unbuckle Henry from the car seat. He's still sleeping, zonked on the lab guy's drugs. There's no blanket, only the towel my father stole from the hotel, the logo folded under Henry's chin, every bit of him obscured except for his face, his mouth drooped open, a bead of saliva on his lip.

"You're handing him over to some stranger?" Dad says.

"She says she'll get him to safety."

"And you believe her?"

His skepticism is warranted, but I can't share it. Maybe it's the bat-shit crazy chance that my mother's ghost led me to her or maybe it's the cold-hard calculus of having so little choice, but between the FBI and the woman from the produce aisle, I trust the woman as Henry's best chance.

"I need to hurry."

"So that's it? We just hand him over and never see him again? What happens to us?"

He turns his back and kicks at a stone, his shoulders sagging.

"Isn't this a joint decision? You're my goddamn son...who put you in charge?"

"Look, I hate this too, but where's the choice? Do you want to turn him over to the FBI? I don't. You don't need me to drive you anymore. The meeting spot is a mile away. If you want to make the decision, go ahead."

A police car pulls into the lot and double-parks by the entrance. Two local cops exit the cruiser, sturdy guys with mustaches and too-tight pants. It's probably nothing but a dinner break—they don't even glance in our direction—but how long will it be before the Feds issue notice that we're not where we should be?

"Maybe I'm wrong, but if we're going to help Henry, we need a leap of faith."

My father nods. "Like Butch and Sundance, right? The leap off the mountain top?"

I know the scene—a great one—in which Dad's so-called buddy Redford confesses that he can't swim, but he and Butch leap into the river anyway. And survive, inexplicably. Should I tell Dad that, like Sundance, I can't swim either, having grown up without a father to teach me?

The local cops head into the grocery store, hitching their pants as they swagger through the automatic door. Dad rubs his chest, grimacing, but steps toward me and reaches for Henry. I hold tight, fearing the worst, my father and I wrestling for control of an unconscious monkey in a Michigan parking lot, but Dad's touch is gentle as he unfolds the blanket and tickles Henry's chin.

"Take care, my friend. I wish we had time for a proper goodbye."

His eyes are heavy as he pats Henry's cheek, and while there's no time to spare, it feels right, and deserved, considering the weeks that my father took care of him. I drop Henry into the cradle of his arms, Dad rocking him twice before kissing his forehead and whispering, "Be safe."

He hands Henry back, but before I can leave, he leans over and kisses my cheek, his hand squeezing the ball of my shoulder.

"God speed, son."

He's on the verge of tears, but there's no time.

"I'll be back in a minute. Then we'll call Mike and decide what the hell we're going to do."

I walk fast but don't run, trying to be as inconspicuous as one can be carrying a drugged monkey through a supermarket. I get a few looks, but they're kind ones, fellow parents appreciating a father holding his baby with such care. On the cold cut aisle, there's no sight of the woman. A pair of teenage girls, a mother with a toddler, an old man sampling a slice of salami complaining that it's too thin; it's business as usual, my eyes scanning desperately for the ALF woman. Did I imagine her the same way I imagined my mother's ghost?

I'm almost ready to give up when, thank God, the woman materializes, this time in a loose windbreaker and a Detroit Pistons hat, waving for me to follow as she heads toward the double doors between the gourmet cheese and specialty breads. Snuggled inside the towel, Henry stirs, his foot giving a weak kick.

"So nice to see you again, Brad," the woman says. "And this must be the little one. I can't believe how big he's grown."

Her eyes urge me to play along.

"Yeah, the pediatrician says he's two months ahead of schedule."

"That's great. Can I hold him?"

"Sure."

But when it's time to let go, I hesitate. Am I sending my father to prison? Am I sending myself? Henry is light in my arms, his chest rising and falling as he sleeps, his fate about to leave my hands.

"Can I hold him?" the woman says, nervous eyes checking over my shoulder. "We need to hurry."

I don't want to let go. "Goodbye, Henry," I whisper.

But it's too late.

Mahoney and Smitherson turn the corner from the fish counter, hands at their holsters.

"Let's not do anything stupid, Kevin," Mahoney says. "You've got a film waiting for you at home. A solid future. The woman next to you is a terrorist. You're in over your head."

"Give us the monkey," Smitherson says, swinging to Mahoney's left, blocking the aisle. The salami guy sees that somethings up, maybe this won't be just another boring day at the Anderson Falls Shop-Mart. A crowd gathers.

"It's time to yell 'cut' and shoot a different ending," Mahoney says. "Come back with us and we'll finish this like we planned. You'll be on the way home in an hour and this very stupid decision can stay on the cutting room floor."

Smitherson approaches in a half-crouch, chewing a wad of gum. *If I ever direct a film again*, I think, *I can use that,* the main character focusing on the banality of the chewing gum over the dread of being caught.

"I like you, Kevin," Mahoney says. "If you ever need a technical adviser for a film, you can call me anytime. I want you to get through this unharmed."

She moves closer, Smitherson's eyes mean and hungry. The ALF woman is frozen, except for her shaking legs. The two local cops appear on the aisle, gawking like bystanders.

"Maybe in your next film, I could do a cameo," Mahoney says. "Directors sometimes use real people. Did you know Martin Scorsese uses his mother in almost every film?"

I answer by reflex, name-dropping like dear old dad. "I met him once, at NYU."

"Do you know how many people envy your life?" She nods to her partner. "Alex, wouldn't you love to make movies instead of all the crap we have to deal with?"

"It's a sweet life," he says.

The perimeter tightens, Mahoney and Smitherson twenty feet away.

"I heard your sister-in-law's pregnant. We both know what that means." Her smile is sly and condescending. "Congratulations. You've got a lot to live for."

"Don't throw it away," Smitherson says, "over a monkey."

Beside me the ALF woman (when this is over, will I learn her name?) stares at the floor, her face ashen, terrified, hardly the look of a terrorist. She resembles a head teller at a small bank who folds the moment a customer complains. Mahoney comes another step closer, and I realize it's over. Thank God Henry is still sleeping. At least I tried to do the right thing, small consolation for Henry, though—my lame attempt to save him won't matter the next time a wire gets inserted into his brain.

"What's the saying?" Mahoney says. "No harm, no foul? Come on, we're all tired. Let's get this done."

There's nothing I can do, only this: I pull the tangerine from my pocket and tuck it inside the blanket, Henry's hands instinctively closing around it.

"Okay," I say, and Mahoney and Smitherson move, Smitherson reaching for his handcuffs, but suddenly there's a cry, a wild call of pain and fear, my father in his black Sundance hat staggering down the aisle clutching his chest.

"I'm...having a heart attack!" he cries, stumbling against the deli case. "I think I'm dying!"

It's pure Brian Edwards ham, and there's not a director alive who wouldn't fire him on the spot for the scenery-chewing performance, but no one knows this but me. He's creating a distraction, he's *stealing the scene* like he always wanted, my father the focus of every eye, and for once, it works. The local cops rush toward him, Mahoney and Smitherson too, the reflex to help a citizen in distress baked in during training, and in that momentary interim counted off in seconds, the survival brain kicks in. It snaps the ALF woman from her fog, and she grabs my arm.

Dad falls to the ground, kicking his legs.

"Hurry! Call a doctor...now!"

He knows that I'll recognize the words—his only spoken dialogue from *The Guns of Philadelphia*.

"I see the blue light. Hurry! Call a doctor, now!"

All those years playing corpses in the background have prepared him for his death scene. Everyone surrounds him, and in the last second before I'm gone, I see my father's face contorted with pain, and the momentary wink of his eye.

And then I'm running, Henry tucked in my arm like a football, the ALF woman leading me through the double doors as we dash through the warehouse, crates of bananas and tomatoes, bags of Idaho spuds and boxes marked cereal, toilet paper, Bush's Baked Beans.

"Don't look back," the woman tells me, and this I know from all the horror movies we analyzed in film school. Look back and you'll fall, the boogeyman will always be lurking. But there's no boogeyman, just a pair of high school kids unloading a pallet of frozen chicken cutlets, and we're out the door and into the light, Henry still safe in my arms, a dark blue minivan waiting in the lot with the engine idling.

The van door slides open and someone yells, "Get in."

We're almost there when suddenly Wally appears, his gun drawn.

We freeze, his face 100% tough-ass lawman, until he melts into a human being.

"Hurry," he says. "I'll tell them you drove off in a red pick-up."

Into the minivan we jump, the doors sliding shut, the driver ordering us to the floor. The woman—I still don't know her name—pulls a sheet over us as the van begins to move, and as I sit on the floor, adrenaline surging through every pore, Henry finally awakens, his one good eye searching for me, and all I can think as I curl beneath our shroud is the classic film transition, *fade to black*.

-4-

I've learned something new: because yeasts lack a nervous system and don't experience pain, it's okay to eat bread. The guiding principle: don't consume anything that once had a face.

Rita (I've finally learned her name) unwraps a sandwich from the cooler and sets it on a plate, assuring me that the peanut butter is vegan, too.

"Wouldn't it have to be? I've never seen a peanut with a face. I have a cousin who resembles a hazelnut."

My attempt to lighten the stress falls flat. Rita is all business.

"You need to check the ingredients. Some commercial peanut butters include bone char."

Isn't it obvious that I've never read a label in my life?

"It's a porous, granular substance made by charring the bones of pigs and cows," she says, unwrapping her own sandwich and shaking some carrot sticks from a baggie. "It's unnecessary, but God forbid they don't make a buck from every part of the animal. Start reading labels and learn the terminology. They hide the cruelty behind obscure names. Who in their right mind would buy something with 'scorched pig bone' as an ingredient? But bone char? Hey, why not?"

It's 2:00 AM, and despite my exhaustion, I'm wide awake. After eight long, bumpy, nerve-wracking hours on the road, we've stopped at a motel somewhere in Iowa or maybe Illinois. It's possible we're still in Michigan. I haven't seen a road sign since we left the grocery store, having spent the entire ride on the van's floor hidden under a sheet, Rita's legs on top of mine, Henry and his tangerine hiding in the pockets between us. We stopped once to pee in the woods and twice to drop Henry's soiled diaper in a rest stop trashcan. Otherwise it was a steady 55 mph, lane changes at a minimum, obscurity the goal. I've been told we passed hundreds of state troopers without arousing any suspicion, but covered by the sheet, all I could see was Henry, Rita, and my aching legs. Thanks to Wally, they're looking for a pick-up truck, but I can't help feeling that the net is drawing tighter, the long reach of the law ready to nab us.

The initial plan—apparently there *was* one—involved a safe house an hour from Anderson Falls, but the anonymity of the location became jeopardized and we couldn't chance it. If there's a new target destination, I'm still in the dark. Neither Rita nor the driver (*his* name I never learn) seems to trust me. I'm a dilettante who's never heard of bone char, some meat-eating impulsive fool who lacks commitment. All true, and yet I've seemingly tossed my life away to help a monkey I've known for two weeks. Shouldn't that count for something? All I have are the non-vegan clothes on my back and $77 in my wallet. Welcome to shit's creek.

Rita finishes her sandwich and makes two more, offering me a second one before I've finished the first. The motel room is clean but spartan, decorated thirty years ago and never changed. On the wall between the two double beds is an oil painting of a hunter shooting a duck. The lamps are all fake brass, and the coffeemaker on the table offers two paper cups and a single pack of roasted grounds.

Though the driver left as soon as we reached the motel, his part of the mission complete, a new car will be waiting outside in the morning, or so we're told. Now all that's needed is a destination.

I'm desperate to find out what happened to Dad. Is he already in prison or did his fake heart attack earn him a night in the hospital? But any call, even from a phone booth, would be a gift to the Feds. We've monitored CNN but there's been no word on us, an earthquake in Greece the big story.

Rita sits on the bed across from me, the most tired person I've ever seen. She's kicked off her tennis shoes but still wears the windbreaker, her pink socks like cotton candy against the dim brown hue of the carpet. Despite eight hours with our bodies intertwined beneath a sheet, we've barely spoken. At least she smells good, her lavender scent no doubt cruelty-free, whereas Henry and I are a combined funky monkey.

"They didn't tell me much about you," Rita says, "and it's best to keep it that way. If one of us is arrested..."

"I ain't no stool pigeon." It's my best Cagney impression, but she only yawns.

"Some of us have pledged ourselves to the movement and are prepared to go to prison. You've never made that pledge. It takes more than a single action to earn the group's trust. Don't get me wrong...we appreciate what you did. You saved Monty's life."

"We call him Henry."

"Okay. You saved Henry's life. You stood up to the FBI and put your freedom at risk to help another sentient being. Do you know how rare that is?"

"Hooray for me, but it was pure reflex. I'm not sure I'd do it again. I'm no hero."

"Few people are," she says. "Certainly not me. If my daughter was still alive, I would never have become involved. Frankly, I'm terrified, even of you. Spending the night in a motel with a strange man is not something I do. Don't take it personally if I sleep in the bathroom with the door locked."

She stays quiet about what happened to her daughter as Henry pushes the tangerine across the floor, his tail swishing as he follows the fruit until it rolls under Rita's bed. *Meek-meek*, he says, pawing at the spread, unable to grasp that he can reach under the fabric and grab the fruit. I drop to the floor and help him, my hand moving around the rug until I feel the fruit's round shape. Before I can stand, Henry jumps on my back and taps my head as if demanding a ride. For once Rita smiles, clapping "Oh, that's precious!" as I crawl around the floor, taking Henry on a piggy-back ride until my knee bangs the desk and I shake him off and hand him the tangerine.

"He loves that damn thing."

"They are fascinating animals. Do you know his history?"

"Just what happened in the lab. I watched a DVD."

Her face shifts, as if I've just cursed out her mother. "I've seen it, too. It changes you."

"I wouldn't say that I've changed."

"You're hiding from the cops with a strange woman and a monkey. Trust me, you've changed."

The air conditioner rattles and wheezes, pushing out air not much better than the room temperature. Rita unzips the windbreaker and lays it on the bed.

"When they drop off the car, I'm hoping there'll be directions to the next stop. The goal is Canada, a farm in Manitoba, though no one expects you to cross the border." She folds the windbreaker into a neat square. "No one expects you to do anything, really. You can stay here in the morning and pursue your own plan. All I ask is that you give me a head start."

"You mean I should turn myself in?"

"I'm not telling you to do anything, but the longer you elude them, the angrier they get. I'm not even sure if you've broken a law yet. Evading arrest, maybe, possession of stolen property; such a sickening word for a living being—*property*. But if they let you transport him, is he still considered stolen? I don't know. When they can't nail you on anything specific, they call it "conspiracy to commit whatever.' You'll need an experienced lawyer."

"My brother's an attorney."

"Is he good?"

"He's my brother, I never thought about it. Mostly he does real estate."

"You'll want a criminal attorney. Don't mess around—it could cost years of your life."

There's a bag on the bureau, and Rita removes a plastic baby bottle and unscrews the cap. The moment Henry sees it he jumps and spins, clapping his hands. He follows her to the bathroom as she fills the bottle, boosting himself onto the toilet so he can watch the water streaming from the faucet. It fascinates him, and even when she shuts the water, he stares at the last few drips, not leaving until she shuts the light, taps his shoulder, and hands him the bottle. He jumps on my bed, crouching on the pillow as he sucks the rubber nipple.

"We should try to sleep," Rita says.

"I'm exhausted but wide awake."

"Nervous energy is the hardest to shake."

She grabs the bag and enters the bathroom, emerging a minute later in green pajama pants and a football style nightshirt, Number 99. In her palm is a red canister of bear spray.

"Don't take it personally. My instincts tell me you're a good person, but if not, I'll use it."

She pulls off her socks and climbs into bed. I lean back against the pillow, desperate for my mother's pendant and the lucky four-leaf-clover.

I don't even have a cigarette to light. How great it would be to breathe in her smoke, fill my lungs with her memory no matter how toxic the tar. But as Rita shuts the lamp, all I can smell is the stale motel air, all I hear is Henry sucking on his bottle, and all I can see is neon lights through the dingy curtains, the motel sign flashing Vacancy.

•

In the morning there's a new car parked in the lot: a '95 Ford Explorer with Nebraska plates. I wait outside while Rita showers and changes into fresh clothes, my own clothes sleep-wrinkled and crusty with sweat, the day's first and only planned stop being the Wal-Mart the motel manager says is only sixteen miles away, and wouldn't Veronica howl if she saw me decked out in Wal-Mart jeans and a Hanes T-shirt? It's a beautiful day, the sky an open plane of blue, the grass around the parking lot glistening with morning dew. If only I had a camera to capture the scene; if only Jill were here to be Allison Pinckney in a plot-driven pickle instead of the real-life crunch in which I'm stuck; if only Veronica could analyze the situation and tell me how Hitchcock or Truffaut might have handled it.

I've never been more immersed in real life. Isn't one supposed to feel "alive" no matter how dire the straits? Instead I yearn for a camera and crew, a script in which, if something goes wrong, I can strike the pages and start again. I've thrown it away for a worthy reason—helping Henry—but standing in the parking lot in whatever the hell state we're in, waiting for a stranger to shower and dress before we embark on the road to nowhere, my first and last thought is that I'm Dorothy in *The Wizard of Oz*, tapping my shoes, chanting *there's no place like home*.

Since the car arrived without an address or a map, we've decided to head toward my father's friend's ranch, the address, scrawled in Dad's chicken scratch, still tucked in my shirt pocket. It could be a grave mistake—another of my father's pipe dreams, like his imagined friendship with Redford—but for now it's all we've got, and it provides a destination while we wait for the ALF to make contact.

The room door opens, and Rita joins me outside, her hair still damp, a fresh T-shirt and hiking shorts her new ensemble.

"Morning, honey," she says, and pecks my cheek. No one's watching, but if they are, we're a happy couple on a road trip.

"Do we need to stop for gas?" she asks.

"We're on Full."

"Good." She thumbs through the wad of bills in her purse. "Just over $400 but we need to make it last." She circles the car, checking it out. "I should drive, and it's probably best that you and Henry stay hidden under the sheet. They know what you look like, but they might not have an ID on me yet. There were no cameras in that grocery store, we made sure of it, and no one in that town knows me. I'd like to keep it that way."

"You want me to hide under the sheet, again?"

"Would you rather be in handcuffs?"

As if planned, a local cop car passes on the road. It doesn't slow down, doesn't turn into the parking lot—it's doubtful the cop even saw us—but it still chills me, and we head back to the room to get Henry, outlaws in name only.

• • •

In times of crisis, people learn about themselves, and this is no exception: I've learned that clean clothes make a difference. I've changed into my fresh-from-Wal-Mart pants and shirt, socks and underwear included, and feel ready for Day Two of my accidental odyssey. In film school they taught us to compartmentalize, one scene at a time, one shot at a time, and this is what I do, staying focused on the moment to alleviate the lingering dread. Something terrible *could* happen, and most likely will, but for now I'm okay, though when I root through the Wal-Mart bag and see the twelve-pack of underpants Rita bought for me, it's clear we're in this for the long haul. My goal: return home before I step into that final pair of briefs.

Before we leave, I pick up a twig, giving Henry a second toy to accompany the tangerine. It's twelve inches long, as thick as my middle finger, and he's fascinated the moment he touches it. In his hands it's a drumstick, a spear, a backscratcher, even a toothbrush when he rubs the bark against his teeth. The first time I reach for it he's possessive, holding on like a soldier protecting his rifle, and his new favorite pastime is using it to slap the back of the passenger seat. After five minutes of hard whacking, the twig splits in two and I brace for a freak-out, but instead he's curious, studying the split before he resumes whacking, only softer now. He's problem-solved, used his intelligence to preserve something he cares about. A simple thing, but heartbreaking considering all his time in isolation locked in a cage without stimulation or enrichment. It's not only the pain and fear that makes what happened to him so wrong, but the stifling of his intelligence and need to interact with his environment through something as simple as a stick.

Perhaps I need a stick, too, as hiding under a sheet while Rita drives is like watching a three-hour movie in which a blank screen never changes. There's Henry, but while it's pleasing watching him play with his twig, by the five hundredth time he's whacked the seat, its charm is gone. To help pass the hours, I read *Animal Liberation*, its spine cracked, the page tips bent, every other paragraph showing sentences highlighted in yellow and pink. The chapter on becoming a vegetarian seems the easiest to swallow and I read about B vitamins, proteins, and amino acids, thinking that falafel and hummus are both pretty good, better than a ham sandwich or some other meat-based meal that I've consumed my whole life without thinking. By mistake I read a few pages of the chapter on factory farms. It's all gruesome, as expected, but what hits the hardest is the kill line at the slaughterhouse.

Imagine pigs stunned by electro-shock and then hung upside down on a conveyor belt, their legs locked in a metal clamp as the belt moves them around the kill-room floor like luggage on an airport carousel. Sometimes a pig falls off the belt and regains consciousness before he's hoisted back up onto the line, throat slit while still aware, the next stop a pot of scalding water, and yes, sometimes the pig is still alive when it's dumped into the cauldron. All for the glory of a ham and cheese sandwich or pork chops shake and bake.

Imagine working on that line, standing for eight hours a day slitting throats at three hundred pigs an hour, five days a week. Add in the cows, the chickens, the turkeys, the lambs, a mountain of dead bodies repeated every day, every year, every decade. Consider a cow being herded onto a truck, packed into a box car with a hundred other frightened cows, bodies prodded, branded, shot with a stun gun or an electric wire inserted into his or her anus, strung up on the conveyor belt, the noise of the machines and the workers shouting in English and Spanish; imagine the cries of the still conscious cows as they start the journey toward the knife.

When I watched the DVD, the clandestine footage of capuchin monkeys being tortured in the lab, it shocked me, disgusted me, angered me, lit a fire inside me that led to my current trouble. But I didn't feel guilty. I had nothing to do with those labs or those experiments. But how many ham sandwiches have I consumed in my life? Chicken cutlets, chicken strips, chicken chow mien, chicken nuggets, chicken cordon bleu, chicken soup for the soul, but what happens when the soul understands the plight of the chicken who wound up as the soup? That conveyor belt and scalding pot leads straight to my open mouth. I keep reading, every page an indictment. If only Rita had handed me a Kurt Vonnegut novel or the latest issue of *Good Housekeeping*.

But she didn't.

· · · ·

"Everyone's story is different but the ending's the same. You reach a point where you can't live with yourself anymore unless you do something."

For Rita, it began with a mink stole.

"It was a gift from my mother-in-law," she says. "Mary's a lovely woman. Even after Jim and I divorced, we remained close and we still talk almost every week. Do you know how rare that is? When a couple splits, the in-laws usually circle the wagons around their child, especially the mother's-in-law, but Mary sensed that it wasn't anyone's fault, that Jim and I just grew apart and the marriage died. I wish it hadn't, but it did. After what happened to Lisa, how could it not? Are you married? Wait—don't tell me. The less we know about each other, yada-yada-yada. Do you watch that show? In the early seasons Elaine spoke out against fur. Remember that? Most people don't, and they dropped that aspect of her character and made her more self-involved as the show went on. The executives at NBC got nervous, I bet. Macy's or some other sponsor that sells fur complained, that's my guess. Anyway, that's a tangent. Our marriage was strong when Mary gave me the mink. It was right before our tenth anniversary. Let me tell you, it was gorgeous, a dark grey mink fur with these tiny white hairs interspersed...is that a word? Interspersed? I think it is. It was so soft...I'd hold it against my neck and my cheek, roll it against my skin...it was just so decadent for someone like me. Growing up, my family struggled, believe you me, so that fur wasn't just beautiful and luxurious and made me feel like a Hollywood star; it was proof of how far I'd come in life. We'd been a hand-me-down family. I even wore my brother's hand-me-downs until I reached puberty. Understand? That fur was important to me, and I loved Mary for giving me not only the fur, but that feeling of being special whenever I wore it."

Her voice is like a radio broadcast, all I can see being the inside of the sheet, and Henry, of course, my fellow refugee. We've pushed back the seat, clearing space on the floor to extend my legs, though every pothole and bump is a super-charged kick in the ass. Henry busies himself tapping my leg with the stick in a 1-2-3 pattern, keeping the beat.

"Now I'm the last person to show off and, believe you me, had I worn a mink stole around town, people would have talked, and it wouldn't have been *nice* talk, if you know what I mean. Jealousy...I can't stand it. So I didn't wear it much, mostly in the house, but every now and then, on special occasions, I couldn't resist. Like for our tenth anniversary we went to dinner in...well, I won't tell you where we went, the less you know, the better, but we went to this classy restaurant and had tickets for a show, and Jim was in a good mood, which was rare...it's not the alcohol, if you ask me, it's the depression...but that night he was funny and relaxed and pretty close to romantic, for Jim at least. It was a good night, a *great* night, right until we left the restaurant and started walking toward the theater.

"I didn't see them coming, and who knows what I would have done if I had, but out of nowhere these two kids, punks absolutely, a boy and a girl with Halloween masks, clown faces, but *ugly* clowns, and they ran up to me with spray cans and started shooting red paint all over the mink stole. One of the kids yelled 'Murderer!' and the other yelled, 'How would you like it if a mink walked around wearing *your* skin, bitch?' It was chilling...they were so close the paint got into my hair and on my face and in my mouth and it was so violating, so frightening. It was five seconds, at most, but the time stretched like eternity. I've never been raped, thank God, but it felt like it. When they turned and ran, laughing like monsters, Jim chased after them, and he caught one of them, the girl, not the boy. Thank goodness because Jim would have pounded the crap out of the boy and probably gone to jail, but he would never hit a girl and that saved him. The police came and arrested her; she was a minor, so nothing happened to her or the boy, but I stood there crying and shaking, and I was so upset the police drove me to the hospital. They gave me some sedatives before sending me home, but it was weeks before I felt safe again. The fur was ruined...not because of the paint...the dry cleaner restored it like new, but I felt such anger whenever I looked at it. How could those kids have done something so vicious to someone like me? I was a good person. I gave to charity; I was Class Mom three years running and that is *not* a fun job. I volunteered at the senior center; I fed the birds every morning. How dare they do that to me? The court made them both write letters of apology...you should have seen the grammar and the spelling, my God, it was atrocious, and though the letters said the right things, I didn't believe a word. I was so furious and nervous and couldn't sleep. No one diagnosed it, but it was PTSD. I'd look over my shoulder every time I turned the aisle at the Pathmark, and Jim was angry all the time. At those rotten kids, but at me too for still being so upset. I won't say it ruined our marriage, because it didn't, but it sure didn't help.

"Then one day there's a knock on the front door. The story made the local papers, so people knew who I was, and there on the stoop were two college kids wearing PETA shirts. Why I didn't slam the door in their faces I still don't know, but something made me hesitate. I braced for the abuse. *Animal killer. Bitch.* But they were both polite, and the first thing they did was apologize."

She pauses, and I feel the van changing lanes. "Are you still awake back there?"

I pull down the sheet, stealing a few deep breaths before slipping back under. "Still here."

"I'm probably boring you, but what else are we going to talk about?" Rita says. "Even though they apologized, I kept waiting for the attack, but those kids were sincere, and explained that those two punks with the spray paint were vandals looking to cause trouble and it had nothing to do with the movement to ban fur. They didn't work for PETA, but they said that the ethical treatment of animals included the ethical treatment of *human* animals too, and that no one seriously working for animal rights would engage in violence against another person. Let me tell you, I was skeptical, and kept waiting for the spray paint to reappear, but they didn't proselytize, they just apologized, handed me a pamphlet, and walked away. I stood at the door for ten minutes, staring at the front lawn, wondering what the hell had just happened.

"We had a table by the door where we kept the mail, and I put the pamphlet down, thinking I'd throw it out later. When Jim came home and saw it, he flipped and called the cops about a restraining order, but the more I thought about those two polite students apologizing for someone else's actions, I thought I owed them the respect of reading their pamphlet. If they had called me a bitch or a murderer, I wouldn't be here driving this van, that's for sure. I'd probably be wearing a fur coat *and* a fur hat. You can scare me, but when I dig in my heels, I'm a stubborn one. But I didn't want to be one of those close-minded suburban women who thinks the world starts and ends with the PTA and a fine set of china. So I started reading. Well, I don't have to tell *you* how it changed me. After I finished, I looked at the fur and didn't see the paint or the luxuriousness that had made me love it so much. I saw a mink instead. I saw an animal who'd been anally electrocuted just so I could wear its skin and feel pretty. After that there was no turning back. But you know that. That's why you're here, with Henry. Something happened and it changed you."

I'm tempted to shout *damn right*, or *you know it, sister*, but have I really changed?

I couldn't stand the idea of sending Henry back to the lab, so I followed my mother's ghost into a supermarket and made a split-second decision to defy the FBI. Granted, this is a giant leap forward on the ethics scale from trying to impregnate my brother's wife and cajoling money from my dead mother's friends to finish a film that might be a piece of crap, and that must count as change. But what happens next? Once Henry makes it to safety (or returns irretrievably to the lab), how do I live the rest of my life? It's something I never really thought about before: how to live one's life. Growing up, you do what your parents and teachers say, what your friends expect you to do, what you expect of yourself based on what you've seen and heard, so much of it in movies. If there's anyone with a master plan, I've never met them. Life is like an improv skit, only in Improv you're supposed to always say "Yes, and..." whereas in life half the time or more you're responding "No, but..." Why can't Veronica be here to help me unravel it all? I finger-flip the pages of *Animal Liberation* while Henry crouches and squints, a sure sign I'll be changing his diaper again soon, and I hear Rita say, "...it's all worth it, isn't it?" and I wish I knew the answer but suspect that even when you're 95 and dying, the long thread of your life unwinding from the spool of your memory, the question is still tough no matter how much you want to answer, "Yes."

· · · ·

It's risky and stupid but I do it anyway. While Rita hits the restroom in the 7-11, I run to a pay phone and call my brother. When he hears my voice, his response isn't comforting.

"Are you in prison yet?"

"We're on the road, somewhere. I'm not sure. Most of the time I'm hiding under a sheet."

"Jesus...what the hell were you thinking, Kevin?"

Though it's unlikely the FBI would wiretap a law office over a stolen monkey, I can't be sure, and if Rita sees me on the phone she'll flip. There's no time for banter.

"How's Dad?"

"Critical but stable. Gloria's flying out to see him."

"He's critical? What's that mean? Did they arrest him?"

"He had a massive heart attack."

"No, he was faking...to create a distraction."

"I don't know what you're talking about, but after you made the stupidest decision of your life, the FBI had him and he collapsed. He's in the hospital in Michigan. Supposedly he's stable, but with his prior conditions it might be a while before anything's clear."

It's hard to take in, my father experiencing something that *isn't* acting, a real coronary following his fake one. Did my decision to run off with Henry and Rita, leaving him alone to face the consequences, cause his heart to fail?

"Shit."

"Make that shit's creek, which is what you're up," Mike says. "My suggestion, as a lawyer and your brother, is to turn yourself in...now. The

U.S. Attorney's office won't tell me a damn thing, and that's not a good sign. The best course forward is cooperation."

"We need to get Henry to safety."

"Will you forget about the monkey? Do you think he'd risk his ass to help *you*? In the jungle he'd probably eat you."

Through the 7-11 glass, I see Rita at the register, checking out.

"I have to run. Tell Dad..."

Is it possible I'll never see my father again? What last words do I have? *Thank you. I love you.* Or should I make him happy with something he cares about. A deathbed scene, always a weeper...the son leans toward his dying father and whispers.

"...tell him he was great in *Exit 23*. It's the best performance in the film."

Mike isn't impressed. "There is no *Exit 23*, not unless you give up this ridiculous..."

But there's no time. I run back to the van, to Henry and the queen-sized sheet that's starting to feel like a shroud.

.   .   .   .   .

Somewhere (and from my under the sheet perspective, the entire world has become *somewhere*) Rita pulls to the side of the road and stops, the engine idling. Is this it? I wait for the sound of a car door slamming, the clomp-clomp of dark boots on pavement, the rote "license and registration, ma'am" before we're both face down on the highway shoulder, hands cuffed behind our backs.

Instead, I hear Rita crying.

Henry is asleep, and I pull down the sheet and squeeze through the gap between the front seats, twisting my knee as I climb over the Emergency break and land in the passenger seat. Rita's head leans against the steering wheel, sobbing.

"Get in back," she croaks. "Someone might see you."

My hand finds her shoulder. "So what? No one knows who I am. That sheet is ridiculous."

"We made it this far."

She lifts her head, runs her sleeve across her eyes, turns her head and exhales.

"I'm sorry."

"It's okay...don't worry, it's going to be..."

Her hand covers my mouth, her head shaking. "Don't say anything, okay?"

She's right. Comforting cliches seem a mockery of what's almost certainly our fate. We look back at Henry, curled sleeping on a towel on the floor. Maybe Mike is right—in the jungle he would eat me. (Probably not—he's only five pounds, I could take him in a fight.) But it's not just Henry or the other monkeys at the lab; it's not the mink that died for Rita's fur or the pigs and the cows and the chickens on the kill line. There's the world as it is, and the world as it should be, and since my mother died, since I killed her with that doomed fourth take, the only one that's mattered is the world as it should be, as I want it to be. Why else make movies to recreate reality? In the world as it *should* be, monkeys live free in the jungles and forests; they live their monkey lives with other monkeys like they should, like New Jersey mothers of 14-year-old boys with cameras should back out of their driveways and not be killed.

If getting Henry to safety is a fool's errand likely to cost everything, it's not a battle against the FBI or some university lab; it's a raised middle finger to the world as it is, the world where animals suffer and mothers die, but I don't say a word of this to Rita. I just hold her hand until she stops crying, until she shifts into Drive and we get back on the road, back toward the world, not as it should be, but the world as it is.

•　•　•　•

"I think we're here."

Instead of the run-down shack in the forest that I expected, (think: Unabomber), the long drive toward the main house is paved and bordered by immaculate white wooden fencing, an open pasture on one side, on the other a paddock with three brown horses trotting in a circle. Behind the house mountains loom over the horizon, the slopes covered in aspen and pine, a hawk floating over the tree line.

"Your father's friend lives here?" Rita says, incredulous. "Wow."

A barn sits to the right of the house, bales of hay stacked along the side, a tractor parked in the clearing between the barn and the paddock. The house itself is huge, a ranch with separate wings attached at each end, a circular driveway at the center, a detached garage toward the right, a roof covering the breezeway between the garage and the house. Parked in front are two pick-up trucks and a shining black Mercedes, and as we approach, the landing strip carved into the grasslands becomes visible, a runway extending toward a hangar where, if I squint hard enough, I see a small jet plane being hosed down by two men in white jumpsuits.

"Does he know we're coming?"

He doesn't know we exist, but I don't share that with Rita, who'll find out soon enough when we're kicked off the property. For the moment, I focus on the beauty of the landscape, the open plains stretching toward the horizon, the elk grazing in the field. I'm from New Jersey, which is not as ugly as most people think, but shopping malls, diners, and billboards are my world. This is like stepping into a postcard. The amber waves of grain are missing, but that's about it, and should an invisible chorus start singing "America, the Beautiful" I'd join right in.

We roll down the windows and breathe the warm evening air which, after so many hours hiding under a sheet, reinvigorates my lungs, clears the sludge from my brain. The van slows, and a man on horseback gallops toward us, a rugged, sun-bronzed man twice my age in a brown cowboy hat and T-shirt, a plaid kerchief in hand as he wipes the perspiration from his neck.

Rita stops the van as the man jumps off the horse and approaches, his eyes polite but stern.

"This is private property," he says. "If you're lost, go back to the main road and drive about five miles. There's a gas station and a convenience store. They can help you out."

Rita looks at me, flummoxed, ready to shift to Reverse and speed away. In the backseat Henry starts whacking the seat with his twig.

"Um, my father is a friend of..."

Why didn't Dad ever tell me his friend's name? *Because it's bullshit,* I think. There *is* no friend.

"My father...Edward Stacey, his stage name is Brian Edwards..."

The cowboy's face tightens, his eyes peering into the van looking for trouble.

"...sometimes he went by George Gringo..."

His demeanor brightens as if I've said the magic word. "You're George's son?"

"Yes!"

"Damn. Nice to meet you. Is George with you?"

"No, we're..."

Running from the FBI with a stolen monkey.

"Is Mr. Redford expecting you?"

Mr. Redford?

I stare out the window, stunned. The beautiful house, the private plane, the horses, the acres of open land. All those Bob Redford stories...*they were true?*

"Yes, he's expecting us," Rita says, because what else can we say, and that's all the cowboy needs to hear.

"Then welcome. Mighty glad to meet you. I'm T.C."

"I'm Rita and this is..."

"Kevin Gringo," I say, and Henry jumps onto my lap with his stick and his tangerine, giving T.C. a *meek-meek* as he waves the stick in my face. "This is Henry, our monkey."

The man's smile fades, suspicion creeping back into his eyes, but he tips his hat and waves us forward. "Well, all right, pull on up and I'll let Mr. Redford know you're here."

Somewhere my father is laughing.

·   ·   ·   ·

"I first met George in '68 on the set of *Butch*," Robert Redford says.

Robert Redford—*Bob Redford*—my father's friend. The Sundance Kid. Johnny Hooker in *The Sting*. Bob Woodward in *All the President's Men*. The director of *Ordinary People* and *A River Runs Through It*. It's all I can do not to giggle or stare like a fool.

"Your father played one of the riders in Joe LeFors posse. Did he ever tell you that? You only see them from a distance, but George was in those scenes, in the third row of horses, I think, but that was so long ago, I can't be sure. Ask him someday—he'll remember. He worked the catering crew, too; Coffee George, we called him. One day we started talking about horses. We both loved horses. There's so much downtime on a movie set, we'd shoot the bull and wait for the next call. He's a good guy, your father. Somehow he always wound up on my sets."

Redford stands by the open glass, looking out at the stables, where the horses trot in circles, dust kicking up, a black crow perched on the wooden fence, watching. The far wall is all glass with a stunning view of the vista. We're in the main room—the great room, I think it's called; Henry sits on Rita's lap, drinking a bottle of coconut milk, white drool dribbling from his mouth, his trusty stick beside him. *Please Henry,* I think, *don't ruin the couch of an Oscar winner.*

T.C. waits by the door, just in case we're trouble, but Redford is relaxed, cordial, every bit as cool as his screen presence, dressed in jeans and an open-collared white shirt.

"So how's George doing? Is he coming by? It's good to meet you but seems a little strange that he'd send you here without calling. He's always been great at maintaining our privacy."

Rita flashes me a look, ready to run, but I feel strangely confident, as if I'm back on the set of *Exit 23* and Redford is just another actor waiting for my direction. If my father could cultivate a friendship with a legend, anything seems possible. There's a piano in the far corner and a glass case with an Oscar statue I'm dying to touch, but I keep my eyes on Redford.

"He's in the hospital. He had a heart attack recently."

"I'm sorry to hear that," he says. "Is the prognosis good?"

"He's stable, but there's still some risk."

There's a Matisse on the wall, a bridge covered in flowers framed above the bar, and it's not some $20 mall replica, it's the real thing, probably worth more than every house on our block back home. The oak bar looks right out of a movie set for an old West saloon, except for the crystal wine glasses in a wrought-iron rack.

"Send him my regards," Redford says. "If there's anything I can do..."

"We appreciate that."

He turns, looking over his shoulder like his character in *Legal Eagles* questioning a witness. "So George is in the hospital, but you decided to drive out here anyway with your girlfriend and your monkey?"

"Rita and I are just friends."

"George really should have called. I'm sure you appreciate our need for security here."

A guy walks into the room and whispers to T.C. Henry grabs Rita's arm, climbing onto her shoulder.

"So who's Elizabeth Winkler?" T.C. says. "If you're Kevin and she's Rita, why is the van registered to someone else?"

"That's my mother," Rita blurts, but no one believes her. T.C. inserts himself between Redford and me, any sense of hospitality gone. We're screwed.

"It's nice of you to stop by, and give my regards to George, but maybe it's best that you get going," Redford says, still cool. T.C. grabs my arm, his hot breath in my face.

"I really am George's son..."

Suddenly T.C. has me in a chokehold as three guys rush into the room, the biggest of them shielding Redford while one guy grabs my legs and the other blocks Rita. They lift me from the floor, T.C. with one arm around my neck, the other arm like a shelf beneath my back, his partner gripping my ankles, stretching me out like a corpse. Redford, his back to the scene, focuses on the horses galloping outside the window as I'm carried toward the door, pain shooting through my neck, and it's all so violent and quick I can't really think, but Henry does. How many times has he been grabbed, poked, restrained, thrown into a cage? His voice is like a chainsaw cutting glass—EEE-AAAK!—as he jumps from Rita's shoulder and whacks T.C.'s knee with the twig. The stick breaks in two, but Henry isn't done. He bites T.C. on the calf, and I'm dropped to the floor while T.C. reaches for his leg, the other guy grasping after Henry, who's too fast for them as he darts across the room toward the cabinet with Redford's Oscar, two more guys rushing into the room heading straight for Henry, who jumps onto the piano, a cascade of notes playing as he runs across the keys, and when a guy with a rifle enters and aims, both Rita and I shout, "No!" Redford dodges his bodyguard, yelling "Hold it," and of course everyone listens, even Henry, who stands on top of the piano staring at Redford, whose legendary presence can even charm capuchins.

"Just hold it," Redford says. "No one is shooting a monkey in my house."

Rita helps me off the floor, and I walk to the piano and scoop Henry into my arms.

"I really am George Gringo's son," I say, "though that's not his real name. Mostly he's Brian Edwards, but he was born Edward Stacey. The heart attack is the truth, but we're not here by accident. He gave us the address in case we needed a place to hide."

T.C. and his goons look ready for a second shot as us, but Redford, still calm, walks to the bar and pours a glass of wine. I expect him to down it, Sundance Kid-style, but instead he offers it to Rita, who's so nervous she might finish the whole bottle. She mumbles her thanks before drinking.

"My father always bragged about knowing you, but honestly I thought it was bullshit because...my father was never a good father to me. He was never *any* kind of father. He was always away on a film set somewhere, in California or Mexico or anywhere except home. The only time I saw him was on TV. I hadn't seen him for years until he showed up a few weeks ago with Henry."

Rita finishes the wine, handing the empty glass back to Redford. "Can I have another one, please? My god, you're so handsome!"

T.C. jumps forward but Redford waves him back and pours the second glass.

"Henry was stolen from a lab by animal rights activists. We had nothing to do with it. My father agreed to drive him across the country because he needed cash. My involvement is completely accidental but I had to make a choice, and once I learned what they do to lab animals, I couldn't let Henry go back to that. If you don't believe me, check the roof of his mouth. There's an ID number tattooed on the back of his gumline."

"How fucking Auschwitz is that!" Rita shouts, the wine kicking in hard and fast.

"We're here because we have no place else to go. There's a sanctuary, somewhere, but we have no idea where it is, and we'll probably wind up in prison. Oh yeah, *Quiz Show* should have done better at the box office, and three times I got rejected for a fellowship at Sundance but I don't hold that against you because the reel I submitted was crap."

I'm out of breath, pain shooting through my neck, my back throbbing.

"If you let us go, we'll forget your address. You'll never see us again."

"Okay, that's enough," T.C. says, but Redford raises his hand, stopping him.

"I want to see the tattoo," he says.

. . . . .

Though Redford leaves the next morning, flying out to Utah in his private plane, he orders his staff to treat us as guests. We're set up in adjoining suites in the west wing, each room with a private bath and kitchenette, the window gifting a priceless view of the Rocky Mountains.

The night before, while Rita slept off her wine-buzz, Redford knocked on my door and invited me to join him outside. It wasn't the first time I talked with someone famous—at film school I met Spike Lee and Scorsese, Susan Sarandon and Haskell Wexler—but this was different. He wasn't required to spend time with me as part of his honorarium. He handed me a beer, and we sat behind the house in Adirondack chairs watching the moon against an endless plane of black. There was no light pollution, no background noise from cars or trucks or anything beyond the cicadas and the occasional yip-yip of a coyote.

When he asked about Henry, it was hard to explain.

"If you look closely, you see the indentations from where they bolted his head. His scalp is covered in scars where they cut into his brain and implanted wires. I'm not too sure about the science, but I've seen footage of the experiments. They keep them in isolation, and sometimes they sew their eyelids shut. He's blind in one eye from God knows what.

"Growing up, we never had pets. I'm not even sure I like animals. But when Henry showed up, my friend Veronica got really upset about what they had done to him, and she got me thinking about things I usually ignore. None of this is planned. I'm just trying to help another sentient being."

Sentient being. A month ago, I would have checked the dictionary for the definition. The night wind moved low through the grass, and Redford told me about his work for the environment and for Native American rights.

"Your father showed me your picture once," he said. "You were a toddler. We were on the set of *The Great Waldo Pepper* so it must have been around '74."

"I was born in '72."

"You were in overalls, wearing a cowboy hat and holding a toy lasso. It's strange that I remember it, but I do. People show me things all the time, like it's an honor if I look at their snapshots, but George was so excited showing off that photo."

My mother kept the same picture in a small frame on her dresser.

"What I liked about George was that he never asked for anything. When you're someone like me, everyone wants something from you, always, and it's hard to maintain relationships that don't feel transactional. You're always waiting for someone to ask for money or a film part or for me to read their brother-in-law's script. On a film set, when you're the star, the perks are incredible, but it's lonely, too. George was just another extra, but he'd talk to me like I was an extra too, like I really wanted to see a photo of his son. Most extras treated me like I could grant their every wish or condemn them to Hell. Not George. He had something real and decent about him. It's too bad his career never took off. He got a lot of auditions, but someone else was always a little better or the director wanted something different. In this industry, that's a familiar story."

Though I hate beer, I drank with him anyway. Only a fool wouldn't share a beer at the foot of the Rocky Mountains with the Sundance Kid. We clinked bottles, the moon throwing slivers of light across the grasslands, something big and dark moving in the distance, a grizzly according to Redford. Since he wasn't worried, neither was I, and we followed the red taillights of a plane heading west, Redford telling stories about he and Dad on the set of *Jeremiah Johnson*, and though I wanted to hear more, every story a revisionist history of the father I'd never known, the effects of the beer and all those miles in the van turned my eyelids into falling shades, and when I woke, it was sunrise, a coyote staring at me from fifty yards away, my father's friend Bob Redford already gone.

•　•　•　•　•

After lunch the next day Rita leaves too, heading back to Michigan to coordinate with the ALF. We can't stay at Redford's place forever; once she learns the details on getting Henry to the sanctuary, she'll come back for him and finish the journey, leaving me to head home toward whatever consequences await.

"It could have been anyone in that supermarket," she says before climbing into the minivan. "I'm glad it was you."

Henry and I wave goodbye as she shifts into reverse and heads for the main road. Does Henry know what it means to wave or is he just mimicking me? With a new, stronger stick in hand, he moves his arm up and down, the conductor leading the band.

Though the staff view him with equal parts resentment and fear, Henry loves Redford's ranch, and I take him outside three times a day to play in the grass, Henry hesitant at first, the natural world beyond the cage and the backseat of the van still so new to him, but soon he is running and rolling on the ground, swatting flies, throwing rocks, *meek-meek*, and while I stand guard in case a coyote should view him as a snack, I let him experience the world without me. The warmth of the sun on his back, the fresh air, the crunch of grass beneath his feet, the open spaces so different from the three-foot cage that was the totality of his world until he was rescued.

Day one, day two, day three...the time passes slowly, but how can I complain? I think about my father and my film, about Veronica, about Mike and Melanie and the child that could be mine, and about how I should conduct my life once this is over. Redford's house has an impressive library, but instead I finish *Animal Liberation* from front to back. I've already made my stand. Shouldn't I have the ethical foundation about why it matters? Chances are I'll be in court one day, pleading to the jury for my freedom.

On the fourth day, a car arrives, nothing special, the staff drive in and out frequently, but this time it's a visitor, and I listen as T.C. gives the guy the third degree before granting him access. I'm in the hallway, watching, when I recognize him.

It's Wally, the FBI agent, most likely a friend, but I'm still not sure.

Henry's playing in the bathroom when Wally knocks on my door. He doesn't mince words.

"I'm not here to arrest you. For the record, I'm not even here. I'm 75 miles outside of Cheyenne investigating a counterfeiter. But I've got something for you."

Before we leave, he peeks in at Henry doing somersaults in the tub, the bar of white soap his latest toy as he alternates between batting it and putting it in his mouth. It's all-natural, orange scented, at Redford's place it's only the best.

I follow Wally down the long corridor to the front driveway, T.C observing every step.

"Your father is still in the hospital but seems to have stabilized. From what I hear, he's going to recover. We're still waiting for the US Attorney to give direction. Things could work out okay for you. This whole episode makes certain people appear foolish and that's never good for a bureaucrat's career. They might prefer to let it drop. We're getting chatter about a domestic attack by Al-Qaeda. It's probably just noise but it's a higher priority than a stolen monkey and two civilians with no idea what they were doing. Don't get your hopes up...they could still drop the hammer and probably will, but it's not as clean as you think."

Once outside, he opens his car trunk and pulls out two duffel bags.

"Take a look."

The first bag is filled with tagged reels of 16mm film in metal canisters, the tags showing a familiar handwriting, my own. The second bag is the same. It's the raw footage of *Exit 23*.

"I thought you might need something to do," he says.

Before he left, Redford showed me his private screening room and the three editing decks in the adjacent studio space, the equipment the best I'd ever seen.

"How did you get this?"

"Thank your friend Dave for gathering it together. Hopefully he'll keep his mouth shut."

He shakes my hand before leaving.

"We appreciate what you've done."

Later that night, I carry Henry to the editing studio and begin the long hard work of turning microscopically small light-sensitive silver halide crystals into images able to touch hearts and minds. Though his scenes are near the film's end, I find the reel with Dad's performance, his blow-out scene with Jill, my words but his voice, and I spool the film into the viewer. His image holds the screen, neither Brian Edwards nor George Gringo, not even his character from *Exit 23*, but simply my father.

Henry jumps onto my lap, and together we watch the monitor, Dad's face in close-up bringing the dark screen to life.

– 17 –

PART FOUR: JULY 2000

-I-

"What am I supposed to do with this?" her editor asked. "Seriously, Veronica, we've got four hours before deadline. Do you expect me to go to print with this?"

She imagined the scene: a middle-aged white guy pacing his office in an untucked blue dress shirt, the armpits dark with sweat, a cigarette smoldering in the ashtray despite his vow to quit. The harried editor, a stock character in any film involving newspapers, but knowing it was real, Veronica felt sorry for him, and guilty too, for being the cause of his stress. Mark Tompkins had always been an ally, hiring her to write film reviews before she'd even left high school; more than any professor, he had taught her about the need to be succinct. From the start he'd trained her to write with clarity and honesty, so wasn't what she'd written partly his fault? After all his lectures on journalistic integrity, what else could she do but stand behind her review? He might hate what she'd submitted, but she'd written the truth.

"I told you I didn't want to review it."

"It's the most popular film in the country. Our readers expect you to write about it."

"And I did. Do you remember when you hired me, you said I'd always be free to express my opinions? I submitted the review eight hours before deadline, as always. I've lived up to my end, Mark. I'm paid for my opinion on films, and that's what you got. I don't see the problem. It's an honest review."

Even over the phone she could hear the fizz of the Alka-Seltzer dropping into water.

"'I hate this fucking movie' is not a review," he said. "It's a joke, right? The real review is on its way, 450 words of your typical sparkling prose and astute critical eye. It's already in the fax machine ready to go. Right? Please tell me it's ready to go."

On the couch Derek snored peacefully, his bare feet on the coffee table perilously close to knocking over the bucket of KFC wings that she'd asked him not to bring. Naked except for his boxers, he'd fallen asleep playing Madden 98, his Game Boy tumbling to his lap, where it now lay elevated atop his erection. Veronica watched, wondering how long his sleep boner would last and if the Game Boy would fall once Derek's tumescence began to fade. Impressed by the height, she fought the urge to add additional weight to see how much his hard-on could lift. A Chapstick tube, the TV remote, a Yankee Candle; she imagined a tower of household objects held aloft by the strong pilings of his wood. It was more fun that picturing Mark in his office freaking out. When upset, her editor's voice climbed an octave; he sounded like a flute sucking helium.

"First of all, you know we can't print the word 'fucking' in a family newspaper. The publisher would fire me so fast..."

"Change it to 'I hate this *freaking* movie'."

"...and what do I do with the rest of the page? We can't print a newspaper with blank space. We *need* those words."

"I've got an essay on the new Thomas Vinterberg film you could excerpt."

"We're a suburban community newspaper. The only person who sees foreign films in a 100-mile radius is you."

"My priest enjoys them."

"Why are you doing this to me?" His voice rose to the stratospheres of pitch. "This paper's been good to you. I know you don't need us anymore, now that you're a hot shot movie producer, but at least stick around until we find your replacement. Is that too much to ask?"

Since the news had gone public that Miramax had purchased the rights to *Exit 23* for an undisclosed sum (not as much as people thought, but still a big number), everyone assumed Veronica was rich. It was the reason Derek had come into her life again. He'd had a bit part in the film and had shown up at her apartment looking for his cut, unaware that his contract had paid him by the day and his share of any profits was non-existent, a hard message to deliver but one he'd accepted gracefully after asking for gas money for the drive back to his parents' house, where he still lived. The innocent way he'd reacted to the news ("Bummer. I already told my Dad I was gonna be rich.") had endeared him to her, as she'd been cursed out so many times by various cast and crew members it now surprised her when someone *didn't* call her a money-grubbing bitch or a money-grubbing cunt or her personal favorite, a money-grubbing cunty bitch. Two people had even accused her of murdering Kevin for control of the film. Only Dave had remained loyal (she was pretty sure he knew more than he let on) and Derek too, once they'd started sleeping together, but what no one seemed to get was that the money from Miramax wasn't hers. It was sitting in an account waiting for the film's rightful owner to appear. That Kevin had been missing for ten months kept everyone in limbo, and though the New York premier of *Exit 23* was only three days away, Veronica was essentially broke, living in the same studio apartment and scraping by on her film review pay from the newspaper and her paltry adjunct instructor's salary from two community colleges. She was collaborating on a screenplay with Father Blank, but its commercial potential might buy her a postage stamp at best.

Mark's voice continued chirping through the phone, like two blue jays arguing over a seed.

"...and do you know how much ballet lessons cost for *two* pre-school girls? How do I tell my kids that Daddy lost his job because his critic had a hissy fit over the most popular film in the country?"

"It's not a hissy fit," she said, though she knew that it was.

The film, *Diapers 3*, was the latest in the popular series that had grossed over two hundred million in domestic box office, *gross* being the key word. The inane tale of two obnoxious toddlers, their obnoxious parents, and the dim-witted burglars trying to steal the diamonds they think are hidden in the toddlers' Pampers (product plugs, galore!), the film epitomized the brain-dead output of Hollywood, the triumph of crass commercial idiocy over artistic vision. That week after week people flocked to see it left Veronica irritated and depressed. (Trying to explain why he liked it, Derek had cited the scene where two dirty diapers wound up on the bad guy's bald head. "That's funny!" he told her, and had he not been a fantastic lover she would have kicked him out of her life that instant.) But it wasn't just its dumb awfulness that had triggered her 5-word review. She'd seen plenty of Hollywood junk and usually had fun crafting the hostile response. But *Diapers 3* featured a scene so repugnant that the act of reviewing it at all seemed a betrayal of her new beliefs.

In the first act, the idiot family makes friends with a local farmer and his prized pig. Many poop jokes follow, but the pig is a lovable character, and the audience sees him responding to the farmer's call, interacting with other pigs, romping through the grass chasing a butterfly, and finally winning first prize at the county fair. The film's one redeeming moment might be the genuine affection between the pig and the farmer as the town's idiot mayor hangs the blue ribbon around the pig's neck. Yet ten minutes later, when the family again visits the farmer, we see the prized pig roasting over a spit, basted in honey as he rotates over the fire, the idiot father looking shocked for only a moment before saying how much he sure does like bacon, hah-hah. Cut to a close-up of the pig, whose startled face makes it clear he's being roasted alive. Naturally, he farts, (big laughs ensue) and his flatulence fans the flames to a sudden explosion. Cut to everyone seated at the table chowing down on bacon, sausage, and ham, the farmer saying how it sure is easier when a pig blows up and he doesn't have to do any gosh-darn carving. More poop jokes follow until the bad guys arrive and mistakenly shoot a cow instead of the farmer. While the credits featured the usual disclaimer about no animals having been harmed during the production, the jokey way the director treated the pig's fate infuriated her, and when she heard the audience laugh at the farting, exploding pig, her 5-word review was born. *I hate this fucking movie.* The pig, presented as an intelligent animal with friendly relationships with the other farm animals (and even with the idiot farmer), is blown to bits and served on a plate as if becoming a ham sandwich and two slices of bacon were a happy ending. The idea that an animal being roasted alive was considered acceptable comic fodder was outrageous, but the audience's laughter struck her as worse. *The fear and pain and suffering of another sentient being means nothing to these people.* It was all just a laugh.

"Don't take it so seriously," Derek said when she left the theater ready to tear the film apart. "It's funny. The pig realizes he's being cooked, and then he farts...come on, it's always funny when pigs fart."

For a moment she wavered. Had her new concerns for animal welfare left her a humorless scold? She hadn't eaten meat in nearly four months, but wasn't it self-righteous to condemn others for eating the same things she had eaten contentedly for most of her life? Maybe Father Blank was right to keep badgering her with his Prayer.

God grant me the serenity to accept the things I cannot change, the courage to change the things I can, and the wisdom to know the difference. She'd always found it an annoying bit of spiritual cheerleading, a Hallmark card for the soul, but maybe Blank knew what he was doing. Just because she had changed, it was ludicrous and immature to expect the world to change, too. People liked meat and dumb movies with exploding pigs, and nothing she could do would change them overnight into vegan aficionados of smart foreign films. Did she really want to make a decent guy like Mark Tompkins suffer so she could ride her high horse?

The wisdom to know the difference.

"I'll plead guilty to a fit," she said, "but can we strike the word 'hissy'?"

His voice dropped back to normal. "Thank you. Is the real review already on its way?"

"I still have four hours," she said. "I might take it in a different direction. If I send you 450 words, you'll run it, right?"

"As long as the language is G-rated and it's about *Diapers 3*, I won't change a word."

She hung up and turned on her computer, the ideas starting to percolate. No one liked a lecture, and if you told someone that they shouldn't eat meat, most people would bite into a bacon double cheeseburger and flip you the bird. How many times had she heard people resisting benign, helpful rules about seatbelts or motorcycle helmets? *You can have my chicken wings when you pry them from my cold, dead hands.* But if she worked her ideas about the treatment of farm animals into a funny takedown of a popular movie, she might inspire a few readers to reconsider their views. Far from a revolution, but better than empty space under her name on the front page of the Leisure section.

Derek stirred on the couch, rolling his head and opening his eyes, his penis still at full mast.

"I fell asleep," he said.

Veronica ignored him, her argument coming into focus, the sentences already forming as she waited for the computer to boot up. Derek, seeing his erection, moved the Game Boy and plucked another wing from the bucket of KFC.

"Hey babe," he said, nodding at his boner, "check it out. I was dreaming about you." In truth he'd been dreaming about Jill from *Exit 23* but even half asleep, he knew not to say it. "How about we...you know...do it?"

Veronica weighed her options: the half-naked pretty boy with a bulging hard-on chomping on a chicken wing on her couch or the chance to trash a terrible film while suggesting that maybe exploding farting pigs deserve a different fate.

An easy choice. The clock was ticking, and she had 450 words to try to change the world.

· · · · ·

Though almost a year had passed, being in Kevin's house without Kevin still felt strange, her perception of the physical spaces tied to her memories of the two of them together. Against the wall wasn't just a couch—it was the couch where she'd fallen asleep with her head on his lap after their first viewing of *Wild Strawberries*. It was the kitchen where they'd share a pizza and a cheap bottle of wine on Friday nights arguing over who was better, Coppola vs. Scorsese, Godard vs. Truffaut. How could she ever use the bathroom without recalling the morning they recreated the shower scene from *Psycho*, Kevin pulling back the curtain and jabbing her with a cucumber before joining her under the water as they clumsily made love? And with so many of *Exit 23*'s interior scenes shot within the house, it felt too much like being within the movie itself, minus Kevin, of course, and the lights, camera, and crew.

I miss him, she thought, though if he'd walked into the room, she might have slapped him for going underground and leaving her alone to deal with the mess. Yet after the slap they would talk for hours, debate movies, trade ideas for new films, maybe even discuss their moral responsibility to other sentient beings. He'd been her go-to person for so long sometimes she talked to him in absentia. Who else in her life knew her so well?

"What do you think, my dear?" Brian said, walking down the stairs with a careful gait. "If you didn't know I lived here, would you have the slightest idea who I am?"

"Lon Chaney Jr. from *The Wolfman*?" Veronica said.

"Didn't I tell you, honey bear, that you look flat-out ridiculous?" Gloria said, watching from the couch as Brian let go of the bannister, picked up his cane, and ambled into the room.

"Ridiculous perhaps...I'm comfortable doing low comedy, but the question is whether I'm recognizable?"

A dark brown wig covered his head, complemented by a matching fake beard, mustache, and horn-rimmed glasses. Since his heart attack in the Michigan supermarket he'd lost twenty pounds, leaving him gaunt and bony; the extra girth provided by the plastic strap-on tummy hid his frailness but messed with his balance. Unlike some older men who refused the aid of a cane, Brian had adopted it like a favored prop, more stylish walking stick than any admission that his body was failing him.

"Please tell him it's a bad idea," Gloria said. "He won't listen to his wife or his son, but maybe the producer can get through to him."

"I'm not missing the New York premier of my finest performance," Brian said. "Let them throw me back in jail. I dare them."

"It's too big a risk," Gloria pleaded.

"I'm an actor. I was born to take risks!"

In a fit of coughing he wobbled toward the couch and plopped next to his wife, his voice theatrically weak.

"It might be my last film," he said, rubbing his chest. It was mostly performance, but the pathos was real. "Please, dear, I have to be there."

Husband and wife linked palms, Gloria resting her head on his shoulder.

As part of his plea deal, Brian had been sentenced to 90 days in prison, the time served in a minimum-security hospital ward, along with four-months home confinement, two years of probation, and a $25,000 fine, which remained unpaid, the assumption being that Kevin, or whomever controlled the *Exit 23* money in his absence, would eventually pay it. The home confinement would end in three weeks, but not in time for Brian to attend the Manhattan premier.

"If they can't recognize me, and they won't, how am I in jeopardy? The courts have better things to do than check to see if an old man went to the movies."

Because of his pacemaker, he'd been saved the indignity of an ankle bracelet. The odds that anyone would be looking for him were slim, he insisted, and even if they were, the beard and the wig were all the disguise he needed.

"It's perfect," he said, to which Gloria crossed her arms and put on her pouty face, a more effective line of argument than anything she might have said.

Though Veronica hated getting involved in family squabbles, they both looked to her for a decision, watching her like teenagers asking to break curfew.

"Have you tried petitioning the court for an exception? They let people go to funerals. Why not movie premiers?"

"My attorney is working on it," Brian said, "but these past few weeks he's been utterly distracted."

As if on cue, the door opened and Mike and Melanie entered, along with their newborn daughter Cheyenne, Melanie carrying the baby, Mike lugging the diaper bag and the portable seat and the plastic cooler with two bottles of breast milk, the paraphernalia of parenthood that made him feel like a roadie for a tiny rock star.

"Whatever he said about me, don't believe it," Mike told Veronica, who smiled and waved at the baby and said all the right things as expected. It felt forced, but she did it anyway—social niceties existed for a reason—but her real feelings were ambiguous on the topic of children. She liked kids well enough, and Cheyenne was a cutie—something about her eyes reminded her of Kevin—but the arrival of a baby failed to trigger the giddiness and frenzied cooing she'd witnessed in so many women over the years. With thousands of babies born every second, was giving birth really that great an achievement? She couldn't help thinking about Henry and the forced isolation of his infancy. If anyone had grabbed Cheyenne from her mother and locked her in a dark cage for a year, it would be considered the most heinous of crimes, and rightfully so. But replace her with a capuchin monkey or a rabbit and suddenly "heinous" is called "science." It was the scourge of speciesism, the belief that humans were inherently superior to other sentient beings and thus granted license to inflict on them whatever one pleased. If she went through the house, how many bottles of soap and deodorant and cleanser would she find that had been tested on animals in the most brutal way?

If one bothered to think, the refrigerator was partly a coffin, all that dead flesh stripped from the bones of animals slaughtered in gruesome conditions. The decapitated body of a roasted chicken wrapped in a plastic tray, a supermarket staple, everyone eager for a bite, ignoring the reality of the chicken's murder. Veronica could think of no other word for it. She'd learned so much about them, perhaps in penance for all the chicken sandwiches she'd eaten herself. There was evidence of a chicken's ability to form mental concepts and do basic arithmetic; they could demonstrate self-control and self-assessment and communicate in complex ways. Chickens had unique personalities and exhibited evidence of empathy, could make inferences, a capability that humans didn't develop until age seven. Their social interactions with other chickens were sophisticated and complex; there was even evidence that chickens could perceive time intervals and anticipate future events. Yet nine billion were slaughtered every year, scalded alive, strapped to a conveyor belt and slung toward a circular saw that sliced open their necks and bled them to death. Why couldn't people see—

Stop it, she thought. It was all true, all gruesome, but she couldn't let it consume her. *God grant me the serenity to accept the things I cannot change.*

"Is it really so bad if you miss the premier?" Mike asked his father. "You can see it at the mall in a few weeks."

"Why won't they grant a temporary release? It's like they're punishing me."

"They *are* punishing you," Mike said. "You committed a crime. But it's not personal. It's a staffing issue. Do you know how many requests they get every week?"

"Don't they appreciate the glory of a film premier?"

"It's more of an opening than a premier," Veronica said. "It's a small film. There won't be any limos or red carpets and forget about paparazzi. There might be some journalists and a few mid-level execs but the rest will be the public. If I didn't have to go, I wouldn't."

"Oh, no!" Brian said, her attitude wounding. "My dear, a film premier is one of life's great wonders!"

"Brian honey," Gloria said. "You're not going, and that's it."

"Don't worry, Pop, you can stay with us," Melanie said, bringing Cheyenne over to her grandpa for a kiss. "Isn't she better than some dumb old movie premier?"

"Of course, of course, such a beautiful girl!" He pecked her cheek. "Perhaps if I brought her as my date...no one would suspect I'd be accompanied by a newborn..."

"It's not happening, Dad," Mike said.

While Melanie and Gloria chatted about the baby, Brian feigning interest as he stewed over the premier, Veronica and Mike met on the patio to talk business, Mike stopping along the way to grab a cold chicken leg from the fridge. Veronica assumed it was a provocation—he knew she'd gone vegan—but mostly it was appetite. He'd put on more pregnancy weight than his wife, and since Cheyenne's birth, he had the permanent look of a man running on animal fat and fumes.

"We can't let the money sit there forever," Mike said. "Bob and Monica are entitled to their cut and so is the other investor."

"Meaning you."

"It was never a gift. I have a family to consider. With Melanie being out of work for a few months, it hasn't been easy."

"You don't need to justify it," she said. "You're entitled to your money. He also made promises to the cast and crew." She didn't add "everyone but me." Though she'd helped Kevin with all aspects of the production, they'd never put anything in writing regarding her role or potential compensation. "I don't blame them for being pissed, but I'm sick of taking the brunt of it. Everyone thinks I'm hording the money, cackling over a pile of cash like Cruella de Vil. Does he have any idea what a mess he's left us?"

"It takes seven years before he's declared legally dead."

"Kevin's not *dead*," she said, surprised by the force of her reaction. "How can you even think that?"

"*Legally* dead, not *dead* dead. Look, I want him back, too. He should meet his niece, spend time with his father before the old man's gone." He finished the chicken and snapped the bone in two. "All this nonsense over a goddamn monkey."

"It's more than Henry," she said.

"Right. You're part of the ALF now, too."

"I'm not part of anything. I'm just trying to make peace with a very fucked-up world."

"Amen to that," he said.

"The detective couldn't pick up any traces?"

"A few hits. He's probably in Canada, but there's nothing definite."

Inside the house Cheyenne started wailing, her hungry baby cries permeating the sliding glass door.

"I should help Mel," he said, but didn't move, the serenity of the patio tough to surrender. "When Kevin and I were kids, we'd play hide and go seek with our Mom. She always found me in minutes, but Kevin would just vanish. She'd give up looking for him and start cooking and he wouldn't come out until dinner hit the table. He'd have this sheepish look on his face, but he was so pleased with himself that neither of us could find him. It was in this house...who knows...maybe he's been hiding here the whole time."

"Come out, come out, wherever you are!" Veronica called, and for a moment they stood silent, as if Kevin might suddenly appear, proud of his victory.

"The stupid kid hasn't even been charged with anything," Mike said. "He's hiding for no damn reason."

"There's always a reason. Maybe he likes his new life better."

"Bullshit. He's got a film about to premier and two million bucks in an account in his name. What could be better than that?"

"A clear conscience?"

"He's been looking for that since our mother died. But no matter what you tell him, he won't accept that it wasn't his fault. If she hadn't been drinnking, she would have seen the other car coming and stopped in time. Kevin refuses to accept it."

"During shooting we never did a fourth take. He wanted everything done in three, and if we absolutely had to do it again, he'd call 'Take 5'."

Cheyenne's crying grew louder. Mike rubbed his eyes and grimaced as if he might cry, too. "He needs to come home."

The patio door slid halfway, Brian leaning through the opening, the fake disguise replaced by a wide-eyed grin.

"My dear Veronica," he said in his best stage voice, half British monarch, half late-night pitchman. "Your concern for our friend Henry has gifted me an inspired idea of which I'm sure you'll approve."

"Dad, enough already. You're not going."

You had to admire his persistence, Veronica thought. "What is it, Brian?"

When he told them his plan, Mike scoffed, but Veronica, imagining the scene as Brian described it, showed her first real smile in days.

·   ·   ·   ·   ·

The first surprise of the night: Jill Willoughby arriving with an entourage and a new nose.

If Kevin, in a burst of ego-massaging malarkey, had once suggested that his lead actress had the same nose as Gwyneth Paltrow, the well-trained scalpel of Dr. Elizabeth Borowski had made it true.

After *Exit 23*'s surprise Festival win and the accompanying accolades for her performance, Jill had signed with a high-profile agent, quit college and her part-time job at Sears, and arrived at Dr. Borowski's office with a headshot of Paltrow and a request for perfection. Three surgeries later, her nose was a duplicate of its more famous counterpart. Rumor had it that she'd had a breast job, but Veronica had never paid enough attention to note the difference. But whatever Jill had done, it was working. She'd already appeared on episodes of *E.R.* and *Law & Order* and had been cast in a small role in a feature starring Brad Pitt scheduled to begin shooting next month. Perhaps an entourage was premature, but who could fault her for enjoying her moment? Veronica envied her enthusiasm, a sharp contrast to her own lingering malaise about *Exit 23.*

As entourages went, Jill's was small: her mother and her aunt, her best friend from high school, her personal trainer, and a fey, long-haired Frenchman in a pinstriped suit who held Jill's hand as if he were carrying a dead eel.

Inside the theater, Veronica waited alone by the candy counter chomping crushed ice from a supersized soda cup, wondering if any of the cast or crew would acknowledge her existence. During production they'd been a team, but by now nearly everyone involved was bitter over the money and assumed her culpable. She'd become the evil bitch, and no one listened or believed her when she explained that the money was in limbo. John Spindle, who'd played Marty, the male lead, hadn't even responded when she'd said hello outside the theater, walking past her as if she were a homeless person begging for spare change. The closest she'd come to a conversation was with Beth Boswell, who'd played Allison's dying mother, their exchange limited to Veronica's friendly "Hi, Beth," and Beth's curt reply, "I've got nothing to say to you," as she stormed toward her seat.

Damn it, Kevin, Veronica thought. *It's been too long. You need to be here.*

When Jill broke from her entourage and approached, Veronica felt relieved, as if she'd been sitting alone in the high school cafeteria and a popular girl had come to eat lunch with her. Among the cast, only Jill had stayed on good terms; because her career had taken off, the *Exit 23* payday seemed small change and not worth the grudge.

"Can you believe this?" Jill said, touching Veronica's shoulder. "It's like a dream. I used to hold movie premiers in my bedroom with all my Barbies cheering me on. I *so* wanted to bring them tonight. Too weird, right?"

"It's your night," Veronica said, avoiding "our" night despite all she'd done to make it happen. "You can bring whomever you want."

"I know. It's crazy." She leaned in and whispered. "Malibu Barbie is in my aunt's purse, for good luck. Oh my God, isn't that Quentin Tarantino?"

The Miramax team had invited a strange mix of celebrities: the actor Victor Garber; a retired basketball player Veronica had never heard of; the munchkin sex therapist Dr. Ruth; the actress who played Chandler's annoying girlfriend on *Friends*. Unsure of her role, or if she even had one, Veronica had avoided introducing herself as "the producer" or "friend of the missing director." What would she possibly say to Dr. Ruth or a basketball player? Let the Miramax execs manage the hoopla.

"That's not Tarantino," she said. "I think he's one of the ushers."

"How cool is that?" Jill said. "A theater with ushers!" It was a big step up from the mall multiplexes where they usually saw films. "I heard you'd shaved your head and joined a cult."

"No, I just stopped eating meat."

"Me too. I only eat chicken and turkey and lean beef. On Tuesday I had a veggie burger, and when Mom offered me some bacon the other day, I flat out refused."

Why did everyone feel compelled to tell her that they themselves rarely ate meat? How they cut out red meat completely, how their doctor told them they *had* to eat meat for the protein and the iron, how they only ate organic free-range meat bought directly from a loving farmer who sang lullabies to his animals and killed his chickens with sleeping pills and soft music instead of an ax. Veronica rarely proselytized, but people still needed to justify their diets, as if her vegetarianism stood as an accusation. When honest with herself, she hoped that it did.

"I'm glad you didn't shave your head. Your hair is gorgeous," Jill said in that pretty girl way in which *but not as gorgeous as mine* remained unsaid. "When you talk with Kevin, tell him I said, 'Thank you'. I was a pain in the butt sometimes, but he did a wonderful job directing me. *So* much better than those TV directors. They don't care about you at all, it's like you're a talking mannequin. Gerard says I should move to France, where film is a respected art form, but I don't know...aren't French people rude?"

"I haven't seen Kevin since we wrapped," Veronica said for the thousandth time, though no one ever believed her. "I have no idea where he is."

"Crazy, isn't it? I heard he's living in Africa with a colony of chimpanzees. How could he miss a night like this for a stupid monkey? Hey, isn't that Tim Robbins?"

It wasn't, but Veronica let her think otherwise, Jill waving to her aunt to bring hairspray and a comb as she rushed off to chat up the fake movie star. Instead of signaling a thaw, her interaction with Jill seemed to piss off the assembled cast and crew even more. Colleen Herbst, Allison's sister in the movie, flipped her the bird. *How childish!* Veronica thought, but it still hurt. Moving through the room of evil eyes, she stepped outside for some air.

The theater was in the Village, beyond the rush of mid-town, and she leaned against the building, enjoying the casual way people strolled the city streets, how New Yorkers looked different, more comfortable in their surroundings, smarter and more sophisticated, as if they followed a rhythm all their own.

Look at those two, she thought. *Now there's an interesting New York couple.*

An African man in a black suit walked toward her, his arm around a small woman who seemed to be wearing footie pajamas under a long coat, the woman holding a pet carrier. The second surprise of the night: Father Blank and Melissa had arrived for the premier.

"Now this is wrong," the priest said, looking at the marquee over the entrance. "It shouldn't be the title alone. It should read, 'Veronica Merrin Presents...*Exit 23*.'"

"You have to wait for the end credits," she said. "I show up four times, but you'll need to squint."

Blank clasped her hand in both palms and squeezed, his smile warm and genuine. Behind him Melissa stayed close, the carrier against her hip as she looked up, down, everywhere, an indoor cat overwhelmed by the city.

"He made me come," she said, nodding at the priest. "I don't go out much. At all. But I like movies. Oscar does, too."

Inside the carrier the orange cat rubbed his face against the gate, Veronica offering her hand for a sniff.

"It's been years since our friend left the house, and it was quite the row, believe me, to get her out the door, but she wanted to be here, for your premier," Blank said.

"Can we go inside? I like it better inside," Melissa said. Oscar meowed at a fat city pigeon that had caught his attention; his paw reached through the gate.

"Melissa, doesn't Veronica look beautiful?" Blank said,

"Like a movie star, but can we go inside?"

"Of course," Veronica said, wondering what the priest had been thinking. Coaxing a shut-in out of her house might be admirable, but to bring her to Manhattan for a film premier seemed mad. For months Veronica had been visiting the cat woman twice a week, but instead of Melissa being influenced by Veronica to step outside her lair and experience life, the opposite had occurred: Veronica's time with the young cat woman had awoken her own desire to nest.

"The next premier will be *our* film," Blank said, meaning the screenplay he and Veronica were writing, a comedy about Jesus showing up uninvited at a 30th birthday party. The final scenes in which the party guests team up to crucify the quiet Savior seemed unfilmable but Blank was insistent that its meaning was transcendent. Veronica didn't argue; she knew the script was destined for the back of the priest's sock drawer.

"You should be proud," Blank said as Veronica led them into the theater. "Your friend made a fine film, but without you, no one would ever have seen it. I hope you've been compensated."

"The money is still in the bank," she said. "It might go to court."

"I don't think so. I've prayed on this issue. A resolution is coming soon, I'm nearly certain."

"At this point, I just want it done. Making the film was fun. Hard work, but almost communal. Now it's just business, and I'm the villain. They should be pissed at Kevin, not me. He's the one who ran out on them."

"It's frustrating when people don't act as they should," Blank said.

"Don't give me that..." She stopped. It was Kevin she wanted to yell at, not the priest. "Sorry. I'm in a sucky mood."

Dario and Andrea, who'd created the film's music, walked around them without a word, Dario spitting on the sidewalk the moment he passed.

"Perhaps a coincidence, simply too much saliva," Blank said.

"That happens a lot when I'm around."

"Can we go inside *now*?" Melissa said. Oscar's paw jutted through an opening in the gate, batting the air as the pigeon hopped after a pretzel crumb.

Once inside the theater, the usher (*not* Tarantino, but a passable likeness) informed them that cats were not allowed, to which Melissa lowered her head and hissed, Blank ready to intercede, a priest's collar often difficult to refuse, but Veronica, touched that the cat woman had braved the outside world, decided it was time. If the Harvey Weinsteins of the world wanted a rhinoceros in the theater, sure enough, the rhino would be seated and given all the free popcorn it could eat. Getting a cat through the door wasn't too much to ask.

"I'm Veronica Merrin, one of the producers," she said, ready to bite. "They're with me, and they're coming inside. If there's a problem, check with Paul from Miramax. It's our theater tonight, not yours."

Across the foyer, Paul from Miramax—a true Hollywood asshole, but a friendly one—nodded at Veronica, the usher stepping aside and waving them through.

"My apologies, Ms. Merrin," the usher said. "The film will be starting shortly."

At the auditorium entrance, Blank peeked through the curtain and flashed a thumbs up.

"The middle row is for family and friends," Veronica said. "Tell the usher you're with me."

"Wonderful," the priest said. "I look forward to meeting your family."

"You *are* my family," she said. Her mother had declined to attend, and she had little contact with her extended relatives, most of whom had no idea she had helped produce a film. Someday she'd have to tell Blank everything, but not tonight.

"Thank you for letting me come," Melissa said, nervously grooming herself, licking her free hand and rubbing her cheek. "Maybe you'll visit tomorrow, and we can climb the tree."

The priest led Melissa and Oscar into the auditorium, Veronica promising to join them soon.

From outside the theater she heard a burst of excitement, people cheering, car horns beeping, and she hurried past the ticket window to see who it was. Maybe the rumors that Woody Allen was attending were true. Instead, the night's third surprise: the actor Brian Edwards, who sometimes worked under the name George Gringo, had arrived in a full-body monkey suit.

"Hey, it's Curious George!" someone shouted from a passing taxi, and Brian held up his sign: a 3' by 3' poster board he had created that morning: a blown-up photo of a capuchin monkey behind the steel bars of a cage, the words *Free the Animals* printed in block letters.

Though his wife and son had flat-out refused to help, he'd called an old friend in the costume business and rented the monkey suit, then taken the train into the city and a cab to the theater. By the entrance a small group surrounded him, a young couple huddling close for a photograph, an enthusiastic German tourist shaking his paw. *He must be thrilled*, Veronica thought. His life's dream of being surrounded by fans at a film premier finally realized, the costume a complication he'd never anticipated but, considering the circumstances, an acceptable compromise.

"It's him, isn't it?"

The face was familiar, but not until she identified herself did Veronica recognize Special Agent Mahoney without her FBI black pantsuit. Mahoney, dressed in jeans and a casual silk blouse, watched Brian waving the sign as the crowd cheered.

"I knew the old man wouldn't miss this. Kudos for the creativity. I expected him to come as Zorro or in a Jason hockey mask."

"He's not hurting anyone," Veronica said. "Can't you leave him alone?"

"Sure," Mahoney said. "I didn't come to bust him. We're just here to see the film."

A chubby man in Bermuda shorts and a Knicks T-shirt approached with a large popcorn and two soft drinks, handing one of the drinks to Mahoney and smiling at Veronica.

"Is she part of the cast?" the man asked.

"No, behind the scenes, like The Wizard of Oz," Mahoney told her husband.

"Nice to meet you."

"We thought for sure that Kevin might be here, but our sources say he's still in Canada."

"It's not fair...you persecute someone for a courageous action and let butchers and torturers go free. He should be allowed to come home."

"Who says he's not?" Mahoney said. "We can still nail him on possession of stolen property and resisting arrest, but he's never been charged. I hear he likes it up there and doesn't want to come home."

The house lights dimmed, and the lobby emptied fast, the crowd heading inside the auditorium, ready for the film to begin. Mahoney's husband elbowed his wife to follow.

"Good luck. I hope it's a hit," the Special Agent said. "Just curious: are you sleeping with the priest?"

"Come *on,* honey," her husband said.

"Don't worry, we're discreet. It's all part of keeping America safe."

Mahoney winked as she unwrapped a straw and jabbed it into her cup.

Was it true that Kevin didn't want to come home or was Mahoney only messing with her? Everyone assumed he was in hiding, afraid to surface and face the consequences, but what if there *were* no legal consequences? How could he have abandoned his film, his family and friends, and most of all her? Hadn't he proposed to her in his kitchen, sort of? *He's met someone else*, she thought, an instinct she hated, the pitiful woman pining for a man. Though a role she refused to play, she'd seen too many films with that trope for it not to be part of her mental DNA. She saw the film poster displayed on opposing walls, WRITTEN AND DIRECTED BY KEVIN STACEY in bold print below the film's title, and she wanted to grab a black sharpie and cross out every letter. The fourth surprise of the night: she could finally admit that she was furious at him.

"Hey Merrin, let's go," said Paul from Miramax, the house lights dimming for the final time. "They're running the preview for the new Aronofsky film. You'll want to see it."

"Yeah, I'll be right there," she said, though she didn't move.

What was the point of watching the film again? She'd seen it fifty times during post-production, had seen it at the Festival, in screening rooms with the Miramax and Castle Rock people during the negotiations for the rights. She'd been there before *Exit 23* had even existed, when it was just Kevin and a camera and some friends filming scenes in his living room, everyone trying their hardest but doubting it was anything but play. She'd even been there years ago when they'd walked out halfway through the dreadful *Lawnmower Man 2* and Kevin had told her, "I started a new script last night."

She watched the lobby empty as everyone hurried toward their seats, married couples holding hands, families with kids begging for another box of Goobers, groups of friends, from the trio of giggling teenagers to the two old women yelling back and forth checking their hearing aids, everyone had paired off, except for her. As the last customer left the candy counter and the cashiers retreated from the registers, Veronica felt utterly alone, until a furry paw touched her shoulder and a six-foot monkey asked her to buy him a soda.

"I've done costume work before," Brian said, his voice difficult to hear through the suit's tiny opening, "but this is most unpleasant."

Inside the suit he'd duct-taped cold wet washcloths to his forehead and under both armpits, a trick he'd learned on the set of a Christopher Lee horror film, but the heat was punishing for a man of his age.

"I should have brought the cane," he admitted.

The *Free the Animals* sign had been left outside the door, and Brian leaned against the counter as Veronica ordered his Diet Coke. She handed him the cup and the straw, but his line of vision was limited, and two near-drops and one spill later, Veronica held the cup for him, Brian sipping hard and fast, the soda gurgling through the straw.

"Most grateful," he said. "And I'm sorry."

"It's nothing."

"Not about the soda, about my son," he said. "The premier of his first film, such a wonderful achievement, and he's missing it, because of me. I appreciate that you've had difficulties acting in his stead. If I hadn't brought Henry back home..."

So true, Veronica thought. Had there been no Henry, she and Kevin would have celebrated at the best restaurant in Manhattan with a $110 dish of chicken cordon bleu, thinking nothing about the life and death of the chicken. But ignorance wasn't bliss, it was merely ignorance, and while she felt no joy in contemplating the abundant speciesism baked into her world, she preferred to be on the side of compassion.

"I was a dreadful father, always absent, and to his mother a complete rogue."

"Helping Henry was the right thing to do," she said, "and you can't blame yourself for Kevin's choices."

The house lights flashed, the few remaining patrons rushing toward their seats.

"On screen, I was good, wasn't I?" he said. "I brought the character alive, found the man behind the words in the script..."

As he continued rattling about his performance, how only he and perhaps Brando and Olivier could have played the part of the estranged grandfather with the perfect blend of pride and self-pity, Veronica grabbed his costumed paw and led him toward the auditorium, her three simple words enough to quiet him.

"Brian, it's showtime."

• • • •

The new Aronofsky film *did* look great. Veronica was glad that she hadn't missed the clip, though the next three looked like stinkers. As the requisite dancing soda cups and candy boxes boogied across the screen, a final reminder that even at its highest ambition film was a vehicle to sell buttery and salty snacks, Veronica scanned the theater, which was 90% full. *A good sign*, she thought. A bad opening weekend could kill a modest film like *Exit 23*, and though nearly all of the profits would belong to Miramax, as she watched the beams of colored light streaming from the projection booth to the white celluloid screen, she felt that familiar jolt of excitement that always struck the moment a film began.

Though she'd saved a seat for Brian, the oversized head of the monkey suit would have killed the view of anyone sitting behind him, forcing him to watch from an aisle seat on the last row. Too bad—she would have loved to observe his face during his powerhouse scene. In real life he was a blowhard and a ham, but when given a chance, he'd delivered a nuanced performance.

The hell with childhood resentments. Kevin should be writing him into his next script, Veronica thought. If Kevin was even working on scripts anymore.

He walked away, she thought. *He could be here, with me. He chose otherwise.*

With the candy commercial over, it was time for *Exit 23* to begin, but the screen remained blank, and after a few seconds the audience began to stir, a gradual rising of voices, mumbles of discontent. The Tarantino-lookalike appeared in the aisle, shining a flashlight in Veronica's face.

"Ms. Merrin, you're needed in the projection booth."

Two aisles ahead Jill was offering to autograph anything and everything, the unexpected break a chance to curry new fans. Soon the rest of the cast was doing the same.

"If something's wrong, find Paul," she said. "Did the film break?"

"Please, I can't find anyone from Miramax."

He looked dismal, as if worried he might be fired, and she followed him to the exit. When she passed Brian, he nearly tore off the monkey head in panic, his first speaking role about to be squashed by a busted reel. "It's nothing," she whispered, and he settled back, but Brian was no dummy. Films required movement without pause, and any break between the last preview and the start of the film meant trouble.

The usher led her through a door in an alcove behind the restrooms and they climbed a short flight of stairs. Had Mahoney been playing with her? She imagined the worst: the FBI seizing the film as a bargaining chip with the fugitive director.

"What's going on?" she asked, the usher three steps ahead. "If there's a technical problem, I'm the wrong person."

"They just told me you were needed," the usher said.

She turned the corner and saw the projector aligned with its opening in the wall, the 35mm print secure in its spool. The projectionist, a gaunt, grey-haired man who looked like he'd been there since the days of Chaplin, flicked a switch and the film began to roll. From below she heard the crowd respond, sarcastic whistles and scattered applause.

She faced the usher. "What's the problem? Why am I here?"

Kevin stepped from behind the projector as his name flashed on the screen with the opening credits.

"Because there's no one else I'd rather watch a movie with," he said.

Forever the critic, all Veronica could say was, "Too melodramatic."

And then she hugged him, Allison Pinckney appearing on the screen below, twenty-three candles lighted on her birthday cake, twenty-three incandescent wicks.

PART FIVE -APRIL 2003

-I-

It's been almost three years since I left A Better Heart, the sanctuary where I brought Henry after leaving the Redford ranch, and where I stayed for nine months, feeding and caring for the animals, maintaining the grounds, and becoming (I hope) a better person. Getting there was a fraught journey and many angels helped along the way, including Paul Belden, who I knew then only by the name Wally. We crossed the border to Canada but soon crossed back, arriving at A Better Heart, one hundred miles south of Seattle, on a rainy night, the hidden road that led to the sanctuary a mile-long dirt path cut through a stand of evergreens, the only light the circular glow from an old-fashioned gas lantern hanging from the barn. They knew we were coming but not the date or time, and when we arrived past midnight, Laura and Jack were sleeping. For the final two days I'd been driving nearly non-stop, Henry banging twigs against a popcorn tin while I prayed and waited for the flashing red lights that would signal our doom. But they never came.

• • • • •

Two weeks after my return for the New York premier of *Exit 23*, I was arrested and charged on seven counts. For six months I braced for the worst, my lawyer advising that two years was the most likely outcome, and most days I contemplated running. My father, having served his time, only made it worse, describing his 90 days as a mix between *Midnight Express* and *Bridge on the River Kwai*. Some of it was his usual grandiosity, but I could tell he'd been diminished by his sentence, walking with a cane, struggling to catch his breath. I readied myself for Hell, drawing strength from Henry's experience and the tragic lives of the millions of animals consigned to a lab. It helped, but not much.

The prosecution team, expecting me to take a plea deal on the eve of the trial, was sloppy in presenting its case, and my lawyer was half pit bull, half wizard, the jury voting for acquittal on six of the seven charges, the only one that stuck being a misdemeanor resulting in a $500 fine. After the trial I spoke with one of the jurors, who told me they all thought I was guilty as hell, but that eight of the twelve thought I'd done the right thing, and the four who disagreed just wanted the trial over so they could get back to their jobs.

I was lucky. There are people in prison for acts of animal liberation, including Susan Zander and Richard Carlos, the "Bonnie and Clyde" my father and I had almost helped nab in a sting. The FBI found someone else to set them up, and now they're both serving 7 years in a Federal penitentiary. I've met them twice and wrote a screenplay about their lives and what compelled them to act. There's zero interest in Hollywood, and if I ever want to make it, I'll have to produce it myself with independent financing. *Exit 23* did okay at the box office—neither a hit nor a flop; lately it's been on heavy rotation on HBO. My second film is a comedy scheduled to start shooting in two weeks, a studio production with a $20 million budget and a well-known cast. I should be nervous but compared to the trial and my days on the run with Henry, directing a film is a cakewalk. There's still a ton of preparation, but for now I've come to visit the animals, and Laura and Jack, who run A Better Heart, and most of all, I've come to see Henry.

•　　•　　•　　•　　•

"I can't picture you shoveling hay," Veronica says. "You're not a pitchfork type of guy."

"You'd be surprised. Every day I was up at 6:00 AM working in the barn. Chickens don't sleep in."

Three years ago, when I arrived at A Better Heart, I was exhausted, frightened, depressed, paranoid, hyper-caffeinated, a total mess. Henry too was beginning to lose it. One night, as we slept in the car, he bit my nose, tearing my left nostril. Another night he discovered the car horn, pounding it repeatedly, *meek-meek*-ing with every blast, and though I'd been up for 19 hours and my eyelids couldn't stay open one minute more, he refused to let me sleep. I tried strapping him in with the seatbelt but each time he'd wiggle free and lunge for the horn. The same thought looped endlessly: why did I throw my life away for this pain in the ass monkey? One more day on the road and I might have driven straight to the lab and thrown Henry back in the cage myself, but as we approached A Better Heart, knowing I could soon hand Henry over and make him someone else's responsibility, I found enough strength to keep going, my impulsive, half-assed mission almost complete.

It was Jack who greeted me, exiting the main house with a flashlight and an umbrella, shining the light through the window to see who'd disturbed his sleep. Henry sat on the dashboard banging the windshield with a stick, the wipers wicking away the rain, my head on the steering wheel, ready to collapse.

"Welcome," Jack said. He was sixty, nearly bald, a short man with sturdy shoulders from years of heavy work maintaining the sanctuary. "We heard you were coming but didn't know when. And now here you are."

It wasn't the dingy compound I'd expected—no barbed wire, no Keep Out signs with skull and crossbones, just a ranch with a barn and a fenced-in pasture, like Redford's place on a lower-budget scale. But it was dark and my first glimpses were incomplete. Over time I'd know every inch of the place.

Jack opened the car door and patted my arm.

"You must be tired. Come inside and we'll set you up in the guest room."

He reached for Henry, who brandished his stick, his teeth bared.

"Sorry. Sometimes he's friendly, but other times..."

"No worries. He's not the first monkey who wanted to bash me, and he won't be the last. We know what to do." He held out a full palm of pumpkin seeds. "What do you say, my friend? Hungry?"

Henry jumped off the dashboard, grabbed some seeds, and hopped to the back, burrowing under a blanket, his flickering tail thumping the seat.

"A good sign," Jack said. "Sometimes the capuchins take days before they'll eat. Can you carry him in? Does he trust you?"

He stepped away as I exited the car, opened the back door, and scooped the blanket, and Henry, into my arms. Huddled beneath the umbrella under a cold, steady rain, we trekked across the yard into the house, where Laura stood in a blue fuzzy robe, a golden retriever at her feet.

Jack and Laura—for the next nine months, they were the parents I'd needed but never had.

•   •   •   •

"Those wildflowers are beautiful," Veronica says, admiring the jewelweed, the mountain bells, and the wild primrose along the entrance road. When I identify each type she's flabbergasted, like I've just turned a donut into a mourning dove.

"I can name the trees too, if you want to quiz me."

It was her idea that we should visit A Better Heart, to see Henry, to see where I'd spent so many months. A trip that should have been the two of us grew into a family vacation when Dad, despite his failing health, insisted on joining us, Gloria too, and when Mike and Melanie learned the details, they decided to tag along, Cheyenne deemed old enough for her first airplane flight.

"Do you think Henry will remember you?"

"He lives with the other capuchins now. Sometimes it's better if he doesn't remember."

When he and I first arrived, Henry was kept separate from the other capuchins. Non-human primate social relations are as complicated as human ones, and the introduction of a new member is a slow and careful transition. There were four other monkeys then, all retired from a vivisection lab, each adopted by Jack and Laura after negotiations with the owners. I had expected an underground operation, but they were a 503(c) approved organization, respected members of the community, and if some of the animals, like Henry, arrived without paperwork or a clear chain of ownership, Laura, a retired attorney, knew how to handle it. I'd expected an outlaw compound run by the likes of a vegan Baader-Meinhof gang; instead I found a simple farm with 37 dogs rescued from abusive breeders, 34 cats, 112 rabbits, three donkeys, a black bear saved from a roadside zoo, 4 capuchin monkeys, and assorted alpacas, goats, sheep, chickens, and briefly, a Bengal tiger. Over time I'd help care for all of them, except the tiger.

In an open patch between the trees, a family of mule deer graze on dandelion shoots. Veronica rolls down the window, breathing the cool Pacific air.

"I understand why you stayed so long."

She's right, it's beautiful here, peaceful and nurturing, but it wasn't the reason I stayed.

· · · · ·

During our first week at A Better Heart, Henry and I spent several hours a day outside the monkey pen, a fenced-in enclosure on a half-acre plot behind the barn. Capuchins are hierarchical in their social structure, and the small group at the sanctuary was led by Brady, the 10-year-old male who'd been living there for five years after being found half-dead inside a Home Depot dumpster. Upon first seeing Henry, he climbed down from his favorite tree, rushed the fence, and started screaming, his fists balled, teeth bared, arms raised to his tallest height. Henry hid behind my leg, grabbing my knee, but soon started screaming back, and he picked up a rock and threw it on the ground. Brady climbed the fence and looked down, spitting and barking as the other three capuchins joined him, all four monkeys flush against the fence, and I picked up Henry and ran inside the house.

When I described what had happened, Jack smiled and said, "Great. It went well!" On the second visit it was more of the same, except that Brady climbed one less rung on the fence, and Henry, while still hiding behind my leg, let go with one hand, the other one squeezing my pants hard enough to tear the fabric.

"He's never known another capuchin," Laura said. "At the labs, sometimes they see each other being pulled in and out of a cage, but they never touch. Can you imagine never being touched by another member of your species? Henry knows people, not other monkeys."

So we kept returning, ten times a day, approaching the fence closer each time, until after a week, the other capuchins ceased their posturing and vocalizations. Instead they observed us closely, going about their business of climbing and grooming and playing with their toys (balls, mostly, but sticks and rocks, too, along with a stuffed teddy bear and two

Rubik's cubes,) keeping close tabs on Henry the whole time, Brady evaluating whether Henry was a threat to his dominance. Poor Henry. Raised in isolation, how could he know what to do? He avoided eye contact with the others, but they never left his attention. One day I sat against the fence and let the monkeys touch me while Henry watched, their paws patting my hair and tugging my shirt, their fingers petting the bare skin of my neck, until Henry, perhaps jealous, sat on my ankles and pressed his palms against my knees, all five of them trading *meek-meeks.*

The next day we brought Henry into the small holding pen within the enclosure. Again, there was posturing and screaming, but it seemed merely for show, and right before Jack took Henry back to the house, Brady reached through the gate and touched Henry's head. It was the slightest touch, Brady's fingers tapping the scars on Henry's scalp. Henry turned, but didn't scream, didn't grab his stick or his rock. He faced Brady with his arms down, shoulders dropped in a submissive display, and Brady strutted back toward the other capuchins and began self-grooming. It seemed only a matter of time before Henry would be part of the family.

Later, at the dinner table, Laura inquired about my plans, a polite way of asking when I intended to leave. She knew a lawyer in Philadelphia who'd be happy to take my case, someone experienced with the issues surrounding animal liberation.

"He won't make any promises, but you'll get a smart, passionate defense."

Ten years earlier she'd stepped away from a Wall Street job to open A Better Heart, and she'd just celebrated her 50th birthday. She was one of those high achievers whose idea of relaxation was training to run a marathon. The sanctuary was her baby; there was nothing she wouldn't do to save it. "Full disclosure," she added. "He's good at protecting our interests, too."

That night I couldn't sleep. My fate seemed either prison or Mexico, where I'd live out my days as George Gringo, Jr. I was furious at my father, furious at myself, even resentful of Henry. Why did his freedom matter more than mine? During the day, when working to integrate him with the other capuchins, I felt useful, confident I'd done the right thing, but at night, in those endless hours when one stares at the ceiling ruminating over every mistake, grievance, and fear, I was a total basket case. While

Henry slept peacefully in his bed on the floor—we still shared the guest room—I paced in circles, mumbling curses, throwing wayward fists into the air, everything short of barking at the moon.

The room felt too much like a cell. I went to the window, pushed up the screen, and jumped out, a prickly shrub breaking the six-foot fall. I needed the illusion of escape and the front door just wouldn't cut it. My arms took a few scratches, but I stood and started running, no direction in mind beside movement, the moon painting streaks of light across the grounds, the crickets providing a constant soundtrack, Brady and the other capuchins rushing to the fence as I sprinted past. There was a nearby river, but I wasn't sure of the direction. I followed an open path until it narrowed into a stand of old growth trees, a landscape as foreign to me as Mars. My brain whispered warnings about snakes, mountain lions, or my old nemesis, the Blair Witch, yet a storehouse of nervous energy kept my body moving, my lungs wheezing but my legs a perpetual motion machine bringing me deeper into nowhere. Five minutes or five hours? It didn't matter—if I ran long enough, maybe I could disappear.

Eventually the forest began to thin, and the steady gurgle of water over rocks beckoned me toward the river. The ground softened, my feet sinking into the damp earth, until suddenly I came to a clearing, where a double-wide trailer stood in front of the river, the moonlight reflecting off its roof like a halo. The left side had wheels, but the right side was jacked up on cinderblocks and both windows had torn screens, the trailer's half-open door hanging from a single hinge, the wooden steps leading to the door cracked and sagging. A broken lawn chair lay overturned inside a rock circle filled with scattered ash and empty beer cans.

I stopped running, stood with hands on knees waiting for my breath to calm. In the movies nothing good ever happens in a deserted trailer in the woods, but I approached anyway, calling "hello" with each tentative step. Its proximity to the river made it likely an overnight shelter for fishermen, but my mind leaned toward darker places: human trafficking, drug running, or maybe a fugitive animal liberationist hiding from the police. Nine out of ten times I would have turned and ran, but that night I kept walking, and step by cautious step, I climbed the sorry stairs and entered the trailer.

Instinctively I groped for a switch, and suddenly the inside filled with light, the generator in back kicking in. The interior wasn't much better than the outside. There were cobwebs everywhere, curled leaves on the floor, what looked like a wasps' nest stuck to the wall. On one end was a toilet and a shower without a door; in the middle a sink and a table, a 13-inch TV with rabbit ears propped on a carboard box, and on the far end, a murphy bed covered in rumbled blankets, two pillows at the top of the bed. I scanned for dead bodies or a stash of cocaine, but there was nothing illicit, not even a well-thumbed Penthouse or spent shotgun shells.

My dash through the woods suddenly extracted its toll, exhaustion rocking through me like a wave. I walked to the bed to sit down, my legs aching, and that's when I saw it.

I shut my eyes, convinced it was an illusion, my overheated brain playing a practical joke, but when I looked again it was still there, right in the middle of the pillow: a four-leaf clover pressed in a square of wax paper, an exact replica of the one my mother had left beside me every night, the same one that she'd had around her neck when she died. I hadn't seen it for years—the wreckers never found the pendant when they towed away the car—and yet here it was again in a busted trailer in the middle of a Washington forest.

I blinked again, touched it with both hands, kept waiting for the leaves to fall from the clover one-by-one, to dissolve into dust and float away.

"Mom?"

I hadn't seen her ghost since the Michigan supermarket, but I expected her to be there, framed in the moonlight outside the trailer door. But the only presence was a racoon pawing through the fire circle, and though I kept shouting "Mom!" until my voice cracked, she never appeared, and for the first time in my life, I felt certain I'd never see her again. Yet the four-leaf clover remained on the pillow, the talisman my mother promised would always keep me safe. I picked it up and held it against my heart like I'd done as a child, when it would calm and lull me to sleep.

The next thing I knew my father was shaking me awake.

"Kevin, let's go," he said. "Time to get out of bed."

"We were worried about you. How on earth did you find this place?" Mom said.

They stood at the edge of the bed, smiling, holding hands. Only it wasn't my parents, strangely reunited. It was Jack and Laura. I'd been asleep for fourteen hours.

The four-leaf clover was still in my hands.

"We've been thinking," Laura said, "that if you wanted to stay awhile, we can always use some extra hands with the animals."

"When you return to the world, you'll need to be ready," Jack said. "We don't think you're there yet."

"This is more than a sanctuary for animals. Sometimes people need to heal."

With the four-leaf clover tucked in my pocket we walked back to the house, where I stayed for nine months, until I saw the ad in *Variety* for the premier of *Exit 23* and knew it was time to go home.

• • • • •

As the main house of A Better Heart comes into view, we drive past one of the enclosures and Veronica tells me to stop.

"Is that a *bear* in a hot tub?"

A young black bear floats on his back in a 4-foot-high swimming pool, his feet hanging over the edge as his paws slap the water. I shift into Neutral and we watch the bear rub his belly as water sloshes over the rim.

"Sometimes Jack and Laura take in an injured bear or an abandoned cub. While I was here, I worked with a few of them. We once had two cubs who were found starving under somebody's deck. The mother had been killed by a hunter at a bait station. They put out jelly donuts in the woods to habituate the bears to the location, and when hunting season begins, the hunters stake out the donut pile and shoot the bear when it shows up to eat."

The bear dunks his head under the surface, then stands to check us out, his big snout throwing off water with a vigorous shake. It's been two years since I left, and though I've become what I always wanted to be—a "hot" filmmaker with a project ready to shoot and two more in development—it's my time at A Better Heart that means the most. Only last week I was in a meeting with an Oscar-winning producer and an actress who's known around the world, and as they were recounting their impressive string of achievements, I thought not of *Exit 23* or any of my new scripts, but that I'd once bottle fed two black bear cubs, had once rocked a baby pig to sleep, and had been welcomed as family by five capuchin monkeys.

Satisfied that we mean no harm, the bear drops back into the water and floats in the sun. When we reach the main house, my brother's rental car is already parked beside the barn, and Jack and Laura, along with Mike, Melanie, and my father wait by the paddock watching two palomino horses trot in circles inside the fence. Gloria and Cheyenne, who's now almost three, sit in the grass on the other side of the house hand-feeding a trio of baby chickens.

"She'll leave me soon, and I can't fault her for it," my father confessed at the hotel bar the night before. "Gloria wants a child, and I'm too old to be a father. One could argue I was never fit for the part."

He waited for me to object, for reassurance that for all his parental faults he had been a good dad, but despite his declining health and my awareness that someday, perhaps soon, he won't be there as a scapegoat for my every failing, I wasn't ready yet to give him what he needed.

When I exit the car, Jack and Laura greet me with the warmest of hugs. For a moment it feels like I never left, that soon they'll hand me a list of the day's chores and prompt me to get started.

"Is this the famous Veronica Merrin?" Laura says, grabbing Veronica's hand. "He talked so much about you while he was here, we expected you to show up for breakfast every morning."

"Kevin wrote us about your book," Jack says. "How's it coming along?"

"Almost finished," Veronica says. "The last chapter is the hardest."

Though I'd hoped she'd be my partner in a production company, her heart wasn't in it, and Veronica took her cut of the *Exit 23* proceeds and quit her teaching jobs to focus on a book examining the ingrained speciesism in the history of American film. As for a partner, she suggested I team up with her new friend, the priest. It didn't work out, though he calls me weekly with script ideas, the most recent about an African priest in love with a film critic. It makes me wonder.

Some guy I don't recognize approaches with an outstretched hand, eager to greet me. He's bearded, about 30, in overalls, with that barn scent I remember never quite leaves no matter how long you shower.

"This is Deke," Jack says. "He's helping out."

It's the same thing Jack said about me whenever visitors arrived, and I understand that Deke, like me, has come to A Better Heart to heal.

While Jack and Laura fuss over Cheyenne, who adores the chickens and seems fascinated by the long orange leash hanging from Deke's pocket, Mike pulls me aside, waiting until Dad is out of range before making his pitch.

"I'm not in charge of casting," I say, for the hundredth time. "I gave his resume and headshot to Lynn, but we don't really need a man of his age."

"He doesn't believe you, and on this one, I agree with him," Mike says. "He thinks you're punishing him."

"It's not always about him."

"That's not what he thinks. Come on, what's the big deal? Can't you give him one last shot? You owe me one."

It's a recurrent theme between us, my debt to him, though the terms of the debt are never explained. My dalliance with Melanie is long past, and since I've returned, we've never spoken of it. Mike is Cheyenne's father, and whatever the genetic possibility to the contrary, the origins of a particular sperm cell have nothing to do with parenthood.

"Come on guys!" Melanie calls, Jack and Laura leading the group toward the dog pens. "We're heading over to see the puppies. Cheyenne wants her Daddy with her."

"It will be a miracle if we make it home without adopting something," Mike says. "And please, think about using Dad in your film. Just one scene—that's all he's asking."

We reach the group as Deke describes a typical day of caring for the dogs. It's a routine I know well, and I promise to join them in a few minutes. Laura smiles, knowing where I'm headed, and I'm almost there when I notice my father hobbling after me, a slight limp in one leg, his black cane in his right hand, his balance precarious but his determination clear, and I wait until he joins me, knowing the moment belongs to him as much as to me, and together we walk to the enclosure, where six capuchin monkeys, Henry among them, live in community with each other, their habitat, if not the natural environment they deserve, a compromise based on compassion and the higher angels of the heart, a patch of earth where pain, suffering, and cruelty disguised as science can no longer claim them.

"My God: look at them," Dad says. "It reminds me of the scene in *Out of Africa*."

"It's nothing at all like that scene," I say, though truthfully, it's a film I've never watched. But I need him to be quiet.

We stand by the fence, the capuchins at the far end, all of them seated on a downed tree trunk eating oranges, the peels scattered by their feet. I spot Brady immediately—he's older now but still the boss, perched at the raised end of the trunk. Since I left, one capuchin died and two new ones joined the crew, Laura describing the introduction in a wonderful 6-page letter I read whenever I need to feel hopeful.

Dad's hand finds my shoulder. Is it a moment between us or is he tired and needs my support?

"I thought all I was doing back then was making an easy buck," he says, "and it wound up changing our lives. I've met so many legends...Mr. Hitchcock, Peter Fonda, Bob Redford..."

"Dad..."

"Who would have thought the most memorable would turn out to be a monkey?"

Growing up my strongest memories of him were always images on a screen, the body in the background. That strong, handsome mysterious figure Mom always referred to as "Daddy" is long gone, replaced by a stoop-shoulder grey-haired man who starts each day swallowing a dozen pills to keep himself alive. Hanging from the fence is a wooden plaque, A Better Heart printed in red letters, a plaque I painted myself during my first month in residence, the name of the sanctuary, but also a challenge about how to live one's life. Taped in the corner of the plaque is the four-leaf-clover.

"After we leave, I have to fly to L.A.," I tell him. "Maybe you want to come? There's a scene we're shooting on the first day. You'd be perfect for it."

His shoulders raise, his posture straightening.

"A part in your film? Hm, I'll have to read the script, but my calendar does appear open. I remember our first day on the set of *Jeremiah Johnson*..."

He stops, and at that moment we finally see him, the other capuchins remaining on the log as Henry jumps down and scurries toward the fence, an orange in his hand the same way he once carried his cherished tangerine, and maybe he's drawn by our voices or our faces or something about us that only capuchins can sense, but it's clearly him, the scars on his scalp covered with new hair, the indentations, where steel bolts had once been drilled, still visible on his temples, his tail swishing as he hops over a rock, his *meek-meek* growing louder as he nears.

"He remembers us!" Dad says. "Kevin, he knows who we are!"

Henry climbs the fence until his face is even with ours, his one good eye moving between us, his hand reaching through the chain-links to touch my hair.

"Henry old pal, you look marvelous!" Dad says, Henry's right hand on my father's palm, his left one stroking my cheek.

"Wonderful, simply wonderful," my father says, and Henry stays with us, *meek-meek*, his small hands over mine, Dad's hands over both of us, the three of us connected until the other capuchins call him back to the group, and we watch from behind the fence as Henry walks toward his adopted family, safe, happy, and free.

Acknowledgements

This is a work of fiction, not a primer on the topic of animal rights. Anyone interested in learning more should read Peter Singer's *Animal Liberation, Free The Animals* by Ingrid Newkirk, and *A Plea for the Animals* by Matthieu Ricard. There are many other fine books exploring this topic. Henry's ordeal as a laboratory subject is based on real experiments performed on non-human primates. Additionally, while the characters in this novel face limited legal consequences for their actions, over the years many individuals have served significant prison sentences for acts of animal liberation.

The character "Robert Redford" is a fictional creation and is not meant to imply that the real actor Robert Redford shares any particular belief or view related to animals and the environment.

A Better Heart is set in the years 1999-2003. Since that time many advances have been made on the issue of animal testing, including legislation in several states banning the sale of cosmetics that have been tested on animals. While progress has been made, there is a long way to go before animals like Henry will be spared the horrors of vivisection. Readers are encouraged to visit the websites of People for the Ethical Treatment of Animals (PETA), the American Anti-Vivisection Society, White Coast Waste Project, and the Humane Society USA for more. In New Jersey, the Animal Protection League of New Jersey (www.aplnj.org) has for decades been a tireless advocate for animals and is worthy of reader support.

The passage in Part Four in which Veronica considers the plight of chickens is based on the article "The World According to Intelligent and Emotional Chickens" by Marc Bekoff, PhD, published on the *Psychology Today* website on January 3, 2017. As of this writing, it is still available online.

Thanks to Fred Leebron and members of the Tinker Mountain Writers Workshop for their input on an early draft of this novel. Thanks also to my wife Sheri Burkat, our dog Bella, and our cats Smokey and Gracie, who walked across the keyboard hundreds of times as I wrote this. If you spot any typos in this book, blame them. A special mention to Miles Stanley Burkat, a "quality cat" who was with us when I started *A Better Heart* but did not live to its completion.

Finally, thanks to Reagan Rothe and the Black Rose Writing team for bringing this book into the world.

About the Author

Chuck Augello is the author of the novel *The Revolving Heart*, a Best Books of 2020 selection by *Kirkus Reviews*, and the story collection *The Inexplicable Grey Space We Call Love*. His work has appeared in *One Story, Literary Hub, Juked, Fiction Writers Review, Smokelong Quarterly, The Coachella Review*, and other fine journals. He publishes *The Daily Vonnegut*, a website exploring the life and art of Kurt Vonnegut. He lives in New Jersey with his wife Sheri, his dog Bella, his cats Gracie and Smokey, and a menagerie of unnamed birds and squirrels that inhabit the backyard.

Note from the Author

Word-of-mouth is crucial for any author to succeed. If you enjoyed *A Better Heart*, please leave a review online—anywhere you are able. Even if it's just a sentence or two. It would make all the difference and would be very much appreciated.

Thanks!
Chuck Augello

We hope you enjoyed reading this title from:

BLACK ROSE
writing™

www.blackrosewriting.com

Subscribe to our mailing list – *The Rosevine* – and receive
FREE books, daily deals, and stay current with news about
upcoming releases and our hottest authors.
Scan the QR code below to sign up.

Already a subscriber? Please accept a sincere thank you for
being a fan of Black Rose Writing authors.

View other Black Rose Writing titles at
www.blackrosewriting.com/books and use promo code
PRINT to receive a **20% discount** when purchasing.

CPSIA information can be obtained
at www.ICGtesting.com
Printed in the USA
BVHW080829221021
619363BV00005BA/187

9 781684 338269